NEW ORLEANS NIGHT

By Stephen Leather

New Orleans. They call it the Big Easy, but there's nothing easy about Jack Nightingale's latest case.

Dead usually means dead, but corpses are coming back to life and carrying out targeted killings.

The supernatural detective is called in to investigate, and he soon discovers that Voodoo is behind the spate of murders.

Whoever is making the dead rise obviously has a plan - a plan so heinous that even the Devils of Hell are concerned.

But there are darker forces at work. And they have Nightingale in their sights. His life - and his soul - are on the line.

CHAPTER 1

The clock on the mantelpiece chimed twelve times to mark the start of a new day and the end of Paloma's life.

She was sitting in her favourite armchair in the sitting room of *Casa del ruiseñor* reading a detective novel in Spanish, when she felt the sudden pain in her jaw. She turned her head and opened her mouth, but the pain intensified, and spread rapidly down her left side. She never had a chance to know what was happening or cry for help, before her heart shut down, and she slumped back in the chair, her long, chestnut hair in disarray, her eyes wide open and staring unseeing at the big window which overlooked the back garden.

It was an hour later that Sooty pushed through the bars outside the open kitchen window, padded across to her chair and rubbed against her ankles. Instantly he sensed something badly wrong, looked up at her face and mewed in fear, his back arching and his tail vibrating. Bemused at her lack of response, he wandered over to his half-empty food bowl and ate a few mouthfuls. Paloma had always filled it up before going to bed, but now there was nobody to feed him.

It was Sooty who managed to raise the alarm two days later, when Esperanza, the next-door neighbour found him outside her back door, mewing furiously. She knew the little black cat well enough, but Sooty had never shown any signs of wanting to come in before. She picked him up, walked through her house and out of the front door, turned left, walked down to Paloma's front door and rang the bell.

Getting no response puzzled her. The little English woman was generally at home at this time of day and the hatch in the old-fashioned wooden door was propped open with a large wooden mouse. Esperanza took a look at the house and saw that the blinds were down on the ground floor windows, which was very unusual. She was starting to get a bad feeling about this. She went back to her own house, opened a tin of tuna for Sooty, left him eating and went back outside.

1

She tried the door knocker again, to no response, then walked down the street and turned right into Calle Real, the single street which constituted the centre of Don Miguel. Her first stop was the village's only small hotel, where Raquel, the owner, smiled a welcome at her from behind the bar. 'Hola, Esperanza. ¿Qué tal?'

'Bien, ¿has visto a la inglesa hoy?'

'Hoy no. Ayer tampoco. Normalmente toma su café aqui todas las mañanas.'

'No contesta a su puerta, y su gatito tiene mucho hambre.'

'¿Vale la pena hablar con la Guardia Civil?'

'No sé. Voy a hablar con José-Luis en Bar 21.'

She walked down another fifty metres, but José-Luis hadn't seen the little English woman for two days either. She often popped in in the evenings where she sat quietly at a table, drank a couple of gin and tonics, made polite conversation in her improving Spanish and wandered home after an hour or so.

Esperanza tried the fruit shop, the butcher and the little local supermarket, with no success, and finally headed into the main square where the Guardia Civil had their barracks, an impressive term for what was really just a couple of rooms next to the hairdressers. She pushed open the door and walked in. Sargento Francisco Rincon Alvarez looked up and smiled at her. He was a tall, fit man of thirty, with the same brown hair and eyes as almost all the people of Don Miguel. He had known Esperanza all his life and had married her second cousin's daughter. He waved her to a seat, picked up a pen and began to make notes.

He listened attentively to Esperanza's concerns, but was puzzled by how little she knew about the young English woman. No surname, no mobile phone number, not even any information as to exactly when she'd arrived in the village other than 'a couple of years ago'. The officer himself had seen the woman around the village, and exchanged the odd greeting, but no more than that. She had mostly kept to her house, and hadn't socialised very much in the village, though that may well not have been helped by the language barrier. Very few people in Don Miguel knew much English, and Paloma's Spanish had been very limited at first, though she'd made great efforts to improve.

Normally Francisco would have dismissed Esperanza's fears, suggesting that the English woman had gone away for the New Year, but the cat worried him. The English were famously sentimental about their animals, and he couldn't see her leaving Sooty to fend for itself. He sent a quick WhatsApp message to his Uncle Pedro, then pulled on his hat, collected his colleague Guardia Laura Mendez Rincon from her office and all three of them walked out to the Guardia car parked outside.

By the time they'd driven the few streets to Paloma's house, Uncle Pedro had arrived. He was a short, fat man in his early sixties, his face flushed from too many nights in the local bars. He ran the hardware shop at the top of the village, and was quite skilful at opening locked doors. He stood to one side as Francisco knocked on the door and rang the bell. When there was no response, the officer stepped back and looked at the house. The name *Casa del ruiseñor* had been stencilled just above the door, in black letters against the traditional whitewashed wall. He wondered briefly to himself why a woman named after a dove had chosen to call her home *Nightingale House.* He sincerely hoped he'd be able to ask her soon.

The policeman nodded, and his uncle picked up his bag of tools and went to work. The lock was fairly basic, and inside a minute the hatch was open, and he put his hand inside to lift up the latches on the door itself, then pushed it open. Francisco gestured to the two older people to stay where they were, then he and Laura walked in, clicking the hall light on.

They were out again inside three minutes, their faces pale and set. They had both seen death many times before, Don Miguel was a small village with an ageing population, and far more funerals than baptisms, but neither of them had seen such a young victim. Esperanza and Pedro shot them an enquiring glance.

'Esta muerta,' said Laura. 'Me parece un infarto de corazon.'

Of course, it was no part of the police's duties to diagnose a heart attack, and Francisco was already back in the car, making the calls to set the routine in motion for dealing with an unexpected death. A local doctor, then transport of the body to a mortuary, while next-of-kin were contacted and a decision made on the need for a post-mortem.

More officers to search the premises for any evidence of a crime, and locate ID and names and addresses of next-of-kin.

The first part went remarkably smoothly. There had been no crime, she had locked herself in the house alone, and the local doctor and police surgeon agreed that the signs of a heart attack were unmistakeable. In accordance with Spanish law, the body was embalmed within 48 hours, pending someone claiming it for burial or cremation.

That was where the problems started.

A careful search of the house turned up not one item of identification. No passport, driving licence, resident's card, credit cards, bank-books, not even any item of correspondence addressed to the woman. She had no mobile phone, land-line or computer. The police were unable even to discover her surname, and nobody in the village had ever thought to ask her. At first they thought they might discover something useful from the utility companies, but it soon emerged that all the bills were sent to a post office box in Madrid, and paid in cash at various banks up there. The police did find large amounts of money in 50 euro notes, stored in envelopes in a drawer, a thousand euros per envelope, but none of the envelopes had ever passed through the post.

As a last resort, a judge gave permission for fingerprints and DNA samples to be taken and run through the Spanish system which produced nothing, and then through Europol specifically aimed at the UK. The British system went into overdrive as soon as the information was received, with the woman speedily identified, and a request made for the body to be repatriated to London. .

In a small town like Don Miguel, it took far less than a day for the news to leak out and spread round every household. A deputation of villagers demanded a meeting with the mayor and the priest, insisting they guarantee that the English woman should never be buried in their cemetery. They were relieved to be told that the body would be removed the next morning. Many of the women were in tears to think that such a monster had walked amongst them, been treated as a welcome guest, and, worst of all, had been near their children.

Back in London, the dead woman was officially identified, and her death made headline news in all the major papers. Her real name was

Robyn Reynolds, and she had escaped from Rampton secure psychiatric hospital two years before, where she had been serving a life sentence for the ritual murders of five young children.

None of the papers mentioned that she was also Jack Nightingale's half-sister.

CHAPTER 2

At midnight, Jack Nightingale had been slightly drunk and standing across the street from the First United Methodist Church of Cheyenne, Wyoming, talking to God, who, as ever, didn't seem to be answering. The huge, sprawling, biscuit-coloured old building was a strange mixture of flat roofs, sharp-pointed triangular eaves supporting vast amounts of grey slate, arched windows in the side walls, narrow rectangular windows at the front and a giant round stained-glass window over the main entrance. To the left a square three-storey tower clung to the side, looking like an architect's afterthought. Europe had given up on Gothic architecture in the 16th Century, but Cheyenne's Methodists had been happy to use it over three hundred years later.

Nightingale was talking to God, but the few people who passed him probably thought he was talking on a hands-free phone. Whatever they thought, nobody paid him much attention. He was wearing his shabby raincoat and a fairly recently-acquired pair of Hush Puppies, and smoking the first Marlboro of the New Year. He wondered, briefly, if it might be sacrilege to smoke while talking to God, but he seriously doubted whether God was listening. He shivered. Cheyenne in winter was well below freezing, and his thick sweater and thin, woollen gloves weren't helping much.

'So, it was her birthday, God. Thirty-three. Which means she's dead. Or she would be if she was here. Or does it happen at midnight tonight? Or some time in between. But then I don't have any idea what time-zone she's in, she could have died twelve hours ago. And how does she die? An accident? Suicide? Natural causes? Or does Lucifuge Rofocale send a thunderbolt, or an Elemental? What are the rules?'

He took a deep drag on his cigarette, while he waited for some answers. He looked up at the stained-glass window, focused on the figure of Christ and shrugged. 'Not available tonight then?' said Nightingale. 'What a surprise. A bit of chalk, some candles, a herb or two and a few magic words, and I can summon up any number of

6

devils. I've done it, far more often than is healthy, and got away with it so far. But summoning up a saint, an angel...there are no instructions for that are there? You know, I don't even think you're around any more. Look at all the gruesome stuff I've seen, enough to drive anyone mad, but you never intervene. Maybe I am mad now, nobody could go through all that and stay sane. Maybe that's why I'm here, trying to get some sense from a myth. Maybe there are only bad guys, and you were never here, or gave up on us all long ago.'

Nightingale decided it was time for him to give up too. He dropped the remains of his cigarette on the pavement and walked away briskly, in search of the first drink of the day. The *Keg'n'Cork* was the first place he came across, and he went inside, enjoying the sudden blast of warmth.

The place looked as if it had modelled for *Cheers*. A long wooden bar, with a row of leather-cushioned bar stools in front of it, tables and chairs dotted around the room, and a few hardy souls who had braved the Wyoming cold to see in the New Year. Most of them looked like strangers to salad, and regular drinkers. Nightingale took a seat at the far end of the bar, away from other customers.

A plump brunette barmaid in her late thirties walked over and flashed him a smile. 'Good evening, stranger. What'll it be?'

Nightingale thought for a moment.

'A bottle of champagne, please,' he said.

'Sure, what are you celebrating?'

Nightingale thought that telling the truth might take the woman well outside her comfort zone, so settled for something simple. 'A birthday.'

She smiled again, put a flute glass in front of him, followed by the bottle, which she'd managed to open without fuss or spillage. It wasn't actually champagne, of course, but Cook's Californian Champagne, an American sparkling wine, still managing to use the name, much to the disgust of French producers, and despite years of lawsuits and negotiations. Nightingale thought it would probably get the job done. He raised his glass to the mirror behind the bar, and started talking to someone who wasn't there. If the barmaid or the other patrons noticed or cared they gave no sign of it.

'Here's to you, Robyn, my last and best flesh and blood. Anyone who believes in a merciful God should read your life story. Fathered by a satanist to some woman we never found, your soul traded away at birth to boost his power. Given away to some childless couple, the father a bastard who raped you on your 16th birthday. Hypnotised by another swine of a satanist who convinced you you'd murdered five kids, then found guilty and locked up in Rampton for life. And just when it looked as if I'd found you a get-out-of-jail card, they told me they'd only let you live two more years. Well, I hope to God they were two good years, you bloody deserved them. But did any of it ever really happen, or was it all just an echo from another life? I wish I understood any of this stuff. I dunno. I did the best I could. I'm so sorry.' Nightingale stood up, raised his glass again, then drained it. 'Here's looking at you, kid,' he said to his reflection.

He smiled at the barmaid and said, 'Finish the bottle for me, love, I've celebrated enough.'

She smiled back. 'Happy Birthday.'

He dropped some bills on the bar, pulled on his gloves, buttoned up his raincoat and headed out into the cold of the Cheyenne night.

CHAPTER 3

Fourteen hundred miles away from Nightingale and an hour ahead, the weather was a little more bearable, hovering around forty degrees, with a light rain falling. In the more popular parts of the city, the New Year celebrations were still in full swing, bars and restaurants packed with revellers, enjoying their last few hours of excess, before their resolutions kicked in, and they stopped drinking, smoking and eating fast-food, embarked on diets and fitness campaigns and posted 'New Year, New Me' on every social media account they possessed. In most cases, they wouldn't last till the end of January.

But there was no revelry here, in pretty much the last place anyone would choose to welcome in a New Year. There was nobody to see the three figures who left the dark sedan, forced their way through a hole in the fence that had been made two hours earlier, and made for their target. All three wore long black coats over hooded sweaters, the hoods pulled up and tied tight. Two were tall and heavily built, one was carrying a soft holdall. The third, who led the way, was shorter and slimmer. None of them spoke as they covered the few hundred yards across the grass.

They stopped in front of a small stone building, the size of a garden shed, but with two slender mock-Greek columns holding up a miniature pediment above the door. The leader nodded. The two larger figures produced crowbars from inside their coats and it was the work of seconds to pry the stone door open. The leader nodded again.

'Follow.'

The voice was soft, but commanding, and the two taller figures followed the leader into the tiny space. An oak casket stood on a plinth inside, the brass handles shining in the beams of the flash-lights that the two taller figures were now holding.

'Open it.'

One of them held his flashlight steady, while the other gave three strong jerks with his crowbar, lifted the lid, and placed it on the floor. The two stepped back, and their leader approached the casket.

'It is good, she has not been here long, and the weather has been cold. Had we not come for her, she would have passed through the Seven Gates of Guinée soon, probably on Twelfth Night, when the passage is easier. Then no power could call her back.' He gestured at the door. 'Leave the bag, return to the car. I shall join you directly. These are things that only people of elevated rank may witness.'

The two underlings shuffled out, and the leader approached the casket again. The woman inside was black, her face beautiful and unmarked by life or death. She wore a long, white gown, trimmed with lace at the hem, wrists and neck. The figure in black bent over her, and muttered some unintelligible words in a language that no living person still used for communication. The woman in the casket gave no sign of hearing anything.

The figure in black bent low over her, and breathed gently three times into each nostril, then held her mouth open and breathed into it another three times. The long, delicate, black-gloved fingers traced intricate patterns on the woman's head, heart and womb. Finally three more words were spoken, much louder this time, and a red powder was blown into the woman's face.

The eyes sprang open, then widened in terror, as the mouth opened to scream. A gloved hand stifled it.

'Hush, my child, there is no cause for alarm, no need to fear. You have slept a while, and now you are awake. I know you saw me in your dreams, is that not so?'

The hand was withdrawn, and the woman made as if to speak, but no sound came. Instead she nodded fearfully.

'Good. And you know that now you live only to serve me, to do my bidding, in your second life?'

Again the nod.

'Then arise, my child, and come with me.'

The black woman climbed clumsily from the casket, sat on the plinth and then stood on the floor, each movement slow and deliberate, as if she were re-learning how to use a body. The figure in black took another hooded sweater from the bag at her feet, and another long dark coat. The black woman gazed at them, without seeming to understand their purpose.

'I know you do not feel the cold, my child, but it is necessary that you do not arouse attention before we take you to your new home. Put them on, and come with me. Soon you shall sleep again for a while, and then there will be work for you. Important work, to serve our cause. Come Bethany.'

The figure in black led the way back to the car, the black woman walking stiffly behind. The two got into the back of the sedan. At a nod from the leader, the two taller figures returned to the tomb, to prop the door back in place, so that the damage would not be apparent to a casual glance.

Three minutes later, the car drove off into the night.

CHAPTER 4

The young man lay back on the long leather couch and tried to
relax, as the soothing voice of the Doctor kept encouraging him. The
young man was six-foot three, weighed two hundred and ten pounds
and was magnificently built. He was naked, and his skin was like
ebony, flawless, except for two white scars in the region of his right
shoulder.

The Doctor kept on talking.

'Just empty your mind of all negative thoughts now, my friend. I
want you to feel a healing blue aura around you, feel it surround you,
feel it take away your pain.'

The Doctor touched a button on the desk behind them, and the
rhythmic sound of drums started up, so quietly that it could barely be
heard, sending the young man deeper into the hypnotic trance that the
Doctor was creating for him. His chest rose and fell more slowly now,
his eyelids drooped, and his breath came slowly.

'And now, my friend, you can feel no pain, no pain at all. And you
will feel no pain, until I awaken you.'

The doctor opened a small wooden box on the desk, took out a
hypodermic, and fitted a fresh needle. He pinched the skin on the
young man's forearm. There was no reaction. Gently he tapped a vein
to bring it to prominence, then skilfully inserted the needle and drew
off the blood he required, He removed the needle carefully, then
dabbed the tiny wound with a small amount of green ointment from a
bottle on the desk. He rubbed the ointment off, and there was no trace
of blood or bruising. The doctor walked into the back room, emptied
the contents of the syringe into a small bottle and corked it tightly.

He returned to the young man, took some leaves from a vase and
rubbed them gently over the scarred shoulder. He raised the volume of
the drums, and started to chant in an ancient language, all the while
rubbing the leaves over the young man's skin. At last, he stopped, took
the used leaves, placed them in a long copper dish, then lit a long black

taper from a burning black candle on a low table, and set fire to the leaves. He waited till the flames had consumed the leaves entirely, then took the ashes and rubbed them on the shoulder.

Finally, he turned off the music of the drums, blew into the young man's nostrils, and spoke gently to him.

'It is done, my friend. You will feel no more pain. Wake now, and be healed.'

The young man's eyelids flickered open, he took a moment or two to gather his senses, then looked up at the Doctor and smiled. He worked his shoulder round, gently at first, then with growing confidence.

'Wow. You know it feels better already. Hasn't felt this strong since I took the hit.'

The Doctor smiled at him. 'Your pain has been banished. I am pleased to have been able to help you, Cameron.'

'You know, it feels like it really has. I can't believe it. What do I owe you?'

The Doctor shook his head. 'I don't have a scale of charges, I am happy to help those who need it. Some of those I help choose to make a donation, that is a matter for them, but I make no demands.'

Cameron's donation arrived the following day, and the Doctor smiled greedily at the size of it.

CHAPTER 5

The three tall black girls looked equally stunning, their breasts bursting out of their crop tops, their long legs showing to maximum advantage in two tiny skirts and a pair of shorts that looked almost painfully tight. Spike was mightily impressed and took the door off its heavy chain straight away. He let out a long low whistle. 'Well hello now ladies, to what do we owe this pleasure, and believe me it *is* a pleasure,' he said.

None of the girls spoke, but the two on either side looked at the one with the long blonde wig who stood in the middle and was holding a large pink envelope. She held it out to Spike. He scratched his shaven head in puzzlement, before carefully taking a pencil from the top pocket of his super-large Armani jacket and slitting the envelope open. He pulled out the card, gazed at the large blue rabbit on the front for a moment, opened it and read the message aloud. 'Happy Birthday, Delroy. Enjoy the little present. Best regards, Harold Jefferson.'

Spike pushed out a pudgy bottom lip and wrinkled his forehead in thought. 'Shit,' he said finally. 'I thought Delroy's birthday was in June. Guess I was wrong.'

The girls still waited silently outside the door and Spike decided to open it fully and beckoned them in.

'Delroy gonna love you ladies,' he said, a wide grin on his face. 'He likes his pussy plural. Just one little thing 'fore I introduce you. Can't be too careful.'

None of the girls was wearing enough clothes to conceal a weapon, but Spike still ran his hands over them, lingering far longer than necessary around their breasts and buttocks, and pressing his three hundred pounds firmly against them. He then carefully searched their bags, none of which contained anything except make-up, purse, cigarettes and lighter. No condoms. That would suit Delroy, he always preferred to feel the flesh. Finally Spike looked them all up and down one more time. Prime black flesh, not too young, but plenty of good mileage left in them. They all seemed to shop at the same jewellery store, all with the same thin necklaces, silver wire, two big wooden beads in the middle. Funny them wearing silver and wood, most of the hookers preferred to flash as much gold as possible. Still, these three didn't need no enhancements. 'Follow me ladies,' he said and led the way down the corridor and opened the door into a huge opulently furnished lounge.

Delroy was lying full length on the bigger of the white leather sofas, wearing a dark suit and matching fedora, but with his gleaming white high-top Nikes kicked off onto the floor. He was smoking a large joint and focusing his attention on *Tattoo Wars* on the giant-screen TV opposite. He looked up and sniffed as Spike walked in, the girls behind him.

'The fuck's this?' he asked the huge bodyguard. 'Don't remember phoning for company.'

'Present from Mr Jefferson,' said Spike, handing him the card. 'Happy Birthday, boss.'

'T'ain't my birthday till May,' said Delroy. 'I guess the boss just extra pleased with me after that last deal. It *was* sweet. Maybe not as sweet as these three fine bitches though.'

He spent a while looking the girls over, and a huge grin spread over his face.

'Spike, you be so kind as to bring in some champagne fo' me and the little ladies. Get yourself a beer while you at it.'

Spike headed for the kitchen, and returned inside half a minute with a laden tray. He placed it on the coffee table in front of Delroy. The girls still stood near the door, slight smiles on all their faces as they stared at the flickering pictures on the TV.

'Why thank you, Spike,' said Delroy. 'I do believe that will be all for a while. Perhaps you wouldn't mind giving me and my new friends a little privacy here? You be real good, maybe I let you have some seconds, if they still have the stamina. Though I do hear you prefer them a little younger, and not quite so female.'

Spike forced a weak grin and left the room, shutting the door silently behind him.

Delroy's smile widened even further, as he poured out the champagne into four glasses and turned to look at the girls. 'Well now,' he said. 'Let's not be so shy, why don't y'all come and sit over here while we get acquainted.'

The three girls obeyed instantly, arranging themselves on the sofa around Delroy. The one in the yellow top flashed a gold tooth at him, put her hand on his thigh and started to stroke and squeeze her way upwards. The blonde started unbuttoning his shirt, while the girl with the bobbed red hair sat on the arm of the sofa and watched.

Inside three minutes, Delroy was completely naked, the blonde running her long black leather boot up and down his erection while the girl who'd formerly worn the yellow top rubbed her breasts against his face. Still the third girl looked on. Delroy looked over at her.

'Hey, baby. What's the problem? Join the party,' he said. 'Ain't there something you'd care to be doing to old Delroy?'

The girl nodded and stood up. At the same time, her friend slid further up his chest and sat on his face, blinding him and almost stopping his breathing. He pushed her aside angrily.

'Hey, bitch, stop that. Delroy don't chew no pussy. The fuck....'

The sharp pain stopped him and dragged his gaze downwards. His eyes widened in disbelief and fear.

'My God,' he whispered.

The third girl had unfastened her necklace and held one of the giant wooden toggles in each hand. Her hands were crossed over each other. The razor-sharp cheesewire in between the toggles was wrapped around the base of Delroy's penis and his scrotum. Blood was already beginning to seep onto the sofa. Delroy's erection had vanished, and tears were running down his cheeks. His lips trembled, and he babbled in terror.

'Ohmygodohmygod...no...please...don't...'

The other two girls got up, put their tops back on and stood by the door. Neither Delroy nor the girl holding the weapon had moved for well over two minutes. Finally the blonde nodded.

The girl with the short hair pulled her hands apart at lightning speed and with almost superhuman strength, the wire slicing straight through the soft flesh. She moved swiftly aside as a fountain of blood drenched the room, Delroy gave one agonised scream as his body spasmed in agony and his heart stopped with the unendurable shock. The door burst open and Spike ran into the room. 'The fuck...'

16

That was all he managed, as the blonde swung her own necklace around his huge bullish neck, caught the flying toggle in her other hand, shoved her knee into his back and pulled back with all her strength.

Spike was a huge man, but the sharp wire was pulled straight through the rolls of fat, his jugular veins and his larynx before he could use his immense strength for anything. The blonde pushed him forward before any blood could spurt onto her skimpy outfit and gazed blankly at the TV for a while as the bodyguard died gurgling on the carpet. Once she was certain that both men were dead, she nodded at her companions, who picked up their bags and walked back out of the apartment, into the elevator, down to the lobby and out into the waiting car.

CHAPTER 6

Tyrell Biggs never referred to himself as a pimp, though that was surely his line of work. He always felt the word lacked class, though he had no problem with the profession itself. After a few tries, he'd finally found a description that he liked the sound of, so his business cards bore the phrase '*Entertainment Procurement Consultant*' under his name, with a cellphone number in the bottom right corner. He'd never seen the need for an office.

Whatever his job description, it couldn't be denied that Tyrell had done well in his chosen career. He had a five-room penthouse apartment on one of the more fashionable streets in the French Quarter, two custom-made cars in the parking lot under the building and a wardrobe full of handmade clothes in the more lurid colours available to his tailor. Women were no problem, he could keep his hand in, or any other part of him he chose, with a selection of his less used-up girls, and his thick bill-fold ensured no shortage of escorts for more sophisticated encounters. Life was pretty good, and he wore a big smile as he barrelled down the highway towards Baton Rouge in the long white Cadillac, with the gold roof and wheels, that some fool had once called 'That pussy Tyrell's Fagmobile', just before his premature death. Whoever said that crime didn't pay had clearly had no aptitude for the work.

Stan Dembowski, by contrast, was an honest, hard working, God-fearing man and so had never amounted to anything much, though he'd always managed to keep a roof over his family's head. Stan weighed somewhere over three hundred pounds, not that he ever bothered stepping on the scales, smoked three packs a day and his only exercise was popping the ring pulls on his Buds and shouting abuse at the TV from his sofa during Saints' games. His vehicle had none of the Cadillac's class, speed or babe-magnetism, though it did weigh around forty times more, being an eighteen wheeler, trucking a full load of timber from Baton Rouge up to the Big Easy. Stan lit another cigarette and flexed his left arm which seemed to be cramping up a little. He took another bite out of the cheeseburger he'd picked up at the last stop as an after-lunch snack.

Tyrell had long ago given up cigarettes, and now favoured foot-long Havana cigars which a cousin of his with a Florida connection let him have at family prices. He pulled out the lighter from the dash and lit one now, puffed out a smoke ring or two and glanced over at his younger brother, asleep in the passenger seat.

Tyrone was eighteen months younger than Tyrell, but hadn't aged nearly as well. Maybe he'd felt inferior from birth, due to their mother's insistence on giving him almost the same name as his brother. She'd died of an overdose at seventeen before her originality could be pushed any further. Tyrone inherited nothing from her, except her predilection for addiction. If he'd shared his elder brother's taste for euphemism, he'd have handed out cards with '*Recreational Pharmaceutical Distributor*' printed on them, but he just thought of himself as a lightweight street pusher, on the increasingly rare occasions that his sampling of the merchandise allowed him to think at all. His outfit of black jeans, plain white T-shirt with added soiling and aged brown leather jacket was in complete contrast to his brother's immaculate pink suit, wide-brimmed pink fedora and floor-length fur coat. Central Casting couldn't have done better if asked to supply a pimp and a pusher for a Hollywood movie.

Stan Dembowski had outgrown his last suit around a hundred pounds and ten years back, and only remembered it now from his wedding photos. Judy had gained quite a few pounds since then too. These days he favoured the largest T-shirts in the store, worn under plaid shirts which he could rarely find large enough to button. His outfit was completed by elastic-waisted jogging bottoms, and knock-off running shoes. The outfit was designed for comfort, not speed. Just like Stan.

Tyrell rolled his left shoulder. Damned cramp. In the passenger seat of the Cadillac, Tyrone stirred, opened his reddened eyes, lit a cigarette, inhaled deeply, gave a long sniff and looked out the windscreen onto the dark highway and at the lights coming towards them.

'We nearly there yet?' he asked.

'Bout thirty minutes now,' replied his brother. 'Turn-off coming up in about twenty.'

Tyrone shuffled round in his seat to look over his shoulder.

'Them bitches sure don't say much,' he said.

Tyrell glanced in his mirror. The three young black girls in the back stared straight ahead, their only sign of life being the constant chain smoking since they got in the car. Their outfits came in a variety of styles and colours, but were all designed to show maximum leg and breast to potential clients. In the dark, Tyrell hadn't noticed the spatters of blood dotted around their clothing when they'd got back into his car.

'Not a word,' said Tyrell. 'These girls never open they mouths it seems, 'less they mean to use them for business.'

'Shame most other women don't see things that way,' said Tyrone.

'Damn straight,' said his brother. 'Whore's mouth only good for one thing. Dunno what they're on, but it sure do make them docile and ...er... biddable.'

'How 'bout we pull over for a half-hour, take us some free samples?' said Tyrone.

'Shit,' said Tyrell. 'You remember who you dealing with? You mess with them, that be the last thing you do with yo' dick in this world. That guy curse it right off for you. We just deliver them as arranged.'

'So why we the errand boys on this?' asked Tyrone. 'Don't the Doc own a car?'

'Maybe he's busy,' said Tyrell. 'It seems he likes to sub-contract things. Not too keen on the personal appearances, they say. Plus, easy money is generally to be accepted readily.'

'Man, the way you talk. Sure gets him some tasty ass, though. That tall one with the blonde wig do me nicely.'

'Not hardly,' said Tyrell. 'Only reason they headed out to the bayou now is cause they pretty much all used up. They very assiduous in managing the shelf life of the merchandise. Jesus Fuck...'

Stan Dembowski's heart attack had been massive and instantly fatal. He slumped over the wheel and eighty thousand pounds of speeding death lurched to the left, charged across the centreline and smashed into the oncoming traffic with the force of high explosive.

Tyrell Biggs's Cadillac was the fourth car it hit, but it still had momentum enough to total five more before it lurched up onto the verge and rolled over. There were twelve fatalities. At least twenty people were lucky to escape with their lives, none of the Biggs party was amongst them.

CHAPTER 7

The private ambulance drove down the rutted track that led to the old farm, passed unchallenged through two gates manned by heavily armed, crop-headed white men in camouflage clothing, circled the main ranch building and parked in front of a huge wooden barn, which looked to have been refurbished and painted recently. The two tall black men got out from either side of the passenger cab and walked round to the rear. They opened the tailgate and manoeuvred the gurney out and onto the ground. The old man's body lay quietly on it, blankets up to his chin, an IV tube running into his left arm from the bottle on the stand. He coughed loudly, then looked up at the attendants. 'Hurry it up,' he said.

The voice was weak, but clearly used to being obeyed. Neither of the attendants spoke as they wheeled the gurney towards the barn doors, which opened as they approached.

A tall slim Creole man appeared, dressed in an immaculate black suit, matching fedora with black band, blue shirt and a black tie. The two black men bowed their heads before him, but still said nothing.

'You are a little late,' said the man in the cream suit.

'We are sorry, Docteur,' replied the nearer of the black men, but offered no explanation.

'No matter, bring him in and place him on the altar.'

They pushed the gurney through the doors and into the cavernous barn. The inside of the building was covered with sound deadening insulation, and the floor was carpeted in black. A large wooden altar was set up at the far end, the crucifix mounted upside-down and bound in grasses. A marble slab stood in front of it, with a smaller wooden table by the side. The barn held just six people, all men, all white, dressed in loose white pants and cotton shirts. Along the left hand side of the barn stood a row of four large drums.

Everyone stood in silence as the two ambulance attendants wheeled the gurney to the altar and lifted the old man onto it. He cursed them for their clumsiness, as his knee scraped against the side of the altar. The attendants removed the blanket and sheet from round him, took out the IV tube and left him on the altar, clad only in a hospital gown. They returned with the gurney to the door, went back outside and closed the door behind themselves.

Still the barn was silent.

The Creole Docteur emerged from a side door, his suit now replaced by a sarong of snakeskins, hanging down from an alligator-hide waistband. Around his ankles he wore knotted grass, but his feet were bare. His only other garment was a hollowed out black goat's head which covered his face down to the base of his nose. The two huge horns curled upwards, giving him the illusion of extra height. His body was striped with white paint, as was the visible part of his face beneath the goat's head. He carried a long black staff in his right hand, a plume of feathers at the top. He tapped it three times against the altar.

In response to his signal, one of the men pressed a switch behind the altar, and the sound of drums began to fill the barn, a rhythm born in Africa and steeped in hundreds of years of tradition. Smoke started to rise from incense burners around the room, as the rhythm increased in tempo.

Docteur Amede took a small bottle from the table, uncorked it, and used a hypodermic syringe to suck up the contents. He laid it back on the table, then removed a white cloth from a small cage, where a small white mouse scurried helplessly. He removed the mouse with his left hand, holding it firmly by the neck, inserted the needle with his other hand, and pressed the plunger down with his thumb. The creature squeaked in pain, but could not escape.

'Come now,' shouted the Docteur, a side door opened, and a figure clad from neck to foot in a white robe emerged. The head was covered by a similar goat mask to Docteur Amede's. The new arrival held out both hands, and took the mouse in a firm grip. Docteur Amede held up a small bottle of water and dripped it over the mouse.

'*Avec l'eau beni, che te baptise, avec le nom Cameron Lattimore. V'zete donc lui, qu'il souffre comme toi.*'

The mouse squealed at the touch of the holy water, but gave no other reaction to its new name.

The Docteur held up his staff and the music stopped. He shouted to the room.

'*Qu'il souffre.*'

The others echoed the words back to him.

'*Qu'il souffre.*'

The drums began again, at a still faster pace. The Docteur picked up a small woven straw coffin, no more than six inches long, and removed the lid, From inside, he took out a cloth doll, crudely put together and with no attempt made to depict facial features. He held the doll up to the room, and again the drumming died instantly.

'*Qu'il souffre,*' he shouted.

'*Qu'il souffre.*' came back the response, and again the drumming resumed.

The Docteur set down his staff, and picked up the last two objects from the table, a short copper knife and a small glass flask. Moving back to the old man, he made an inch-long cut in his left breast, over the heart, then another at the base of his penis, just over the pubic bone. put the knife down and squeezed blood from both into the flask. He dripped two drops of blood from the flask onto the doll, just where a human's heart would be, then just where the penis would be. The other figure in the goat mask handed him the mouse, and Docteur Amede cut off its head, and rubbed its blood all over the doll. He picked up the staff again in his left hand, and held it, and the doll, up to the room. Silence fell.

'*Qu'il renaisse,*' was his shout this time.

'*Qu'il renaisse,*' the others responded.

He knelt before the altar, and the drums were silent. Everyone else knelt too, their gaze on the floor, most of them trembling, as they knew what was to come.

Docteur Amede spoke in a whisper this time, though it carried to every ear.

'*Vienne, Mere, vienne. Acceptez li conjure, acceptez li Conjure de Dhahibu, Vienne.*'

As he spoke the final word, he felt the staff move in his hand, as if struggling to escape his grasp. He looked at it, and shuddered at the huge yellow and black snake that now writhed in his fist, but his grip never slackened. The room was silent, save for the gentle tread of approaching bare feet.

They stood in front of the altar now, but none of them dare raise their eyes to see. The Loa had been summoned, and had arrived.

The voice that spoke was gentle, almost kind, but everyone there trembled at it. The old man on the altar had his eyes pressed shut, and his lips were twitching.

'I accept your sacrifice. I shall not lead this one to the Seven Gates. He shall be healed. A long life awaits him. Another shall go in his place. The sacrifice has been made, the sacrifice has been accepted.'

The drums started yet again, the Docteur placed the doll back in its straw coffin and replaced the lid. He laid it down on the table, then bent over the old man's face. He blew sharply into his nostrils, and took his right hand, pulling gently. The old man slid his legs sideways, put them over the side of the altar, then slowly raised his upper body until he was sitting on the edge of the altar, then almost immediately, responding to Docteur Amede's steady pull on his arm, jumped down onto the floor, where he stood, before the room, which fell silent for the final time.

Ten minutes later, the old man now dressed in a dark-grey suit, walked unaided to the waiting black sedan, which drove him away in the direction of the city.

CHAPTER 8

Across the city, Cameron Lattimore felt the first twinge of pain in his lower stomach.

Jamella lay in bed, shivering and sweating simultaneously. Her coffee-coloured skin had grown paler over the last two days and her lips were cracked and blue, despite the water that Claudine kept moistening them with. Claudine had no money to call a doctor, and no idea what was wrong with her older sister. She'd come home to the small apartment in the French quarter the night before to find her sister passed out on the sofa, her breath coming in sporadic rasps. She'd managed to manoeuvre Jamella into her bedroom and under the blankets, but the older girl had shown no sign of improvement.

Occasionally Jamella had opened her eyes and babbled incoherently for a few moments. Claudine had been unable to make sense of what she'd said, something to do with shoes and steak, but her sister rarely ate meat. There was no shortage of shoes in Jamella's room, most of what little spare money she made went on clothes and footwear. She always made sure to dress the part. Claudine had no idea which shoes her sister might want, and she was surely in no state to eat steak.

At nearly seventeen, Claudine didn't know what to do in this kind of situation. She'd come to live with Jamella when her mother died the year before, and Jamella had always been the strong one, the one who earned the money to keep the rent paid, the two of them fed and Claudine in school. It was coming up to the end of Claudine's final semester and already Jamella had hinted that her younger sister might have to go to work, rather than worry about graduating High School. Claudine had no real idea what work her big sister might have in mind for her, but she was happy with the idea that she'd be contributing to the household income.

But that was all in the future, for the moment her problem was to get some help for her big sister. Jamella might have money for a doctor, but Claudine had no idea where she would keep it. Maybe it might be best to call one of Jamella's friends, but Claudine had only ever met one of them, a guy called Lewis, who came round every couple of days to spend time with her sister. Usually Claudine was told to go out for a few hours when he came around. She wasn't at all sure she liked Lewis. He always wore sharp suits and had shiny white teeth, some of them with gold edging. Jamella always seemed a little scared of him, and once or twice her face had been a little puffy after he called. Still, it was the only name Claudine knew, so that was her one hope. She looked in her sister's bag for her phone, scrolled down to contacts and pressed the phone symbol next to Lewis's name. The call was answered quickly.

'Hey baby, what's happening. You got some money for me?'

'Hello, is this Lewis? This is Claudine, Jamella's sister. Jamella's real sick, I need to get her some help.'

'Call a doctor, baby. Or take her to the emergency room.'

'I don't know any doctor, and I can't drive. And I don't have any money.'

'That's too bad. Probably ain't nothing, she be better in a few days. Nuttin' I can do.'

He hung up, and Claudine burst into tears.

She went back into her sister's room, moistened her lips again with water. 'Jamella, what can I do?'

Her sister's eyes fluttered open, and her lips moved. 'Call Amede. Call Docteur Amede.'

'Who?'

'His card is in my bag.'

Jamella's eyes closed again.

Claudine searched through the bag she'd seen her sister using last, and finally found the card in a side pocket. It was black, bore the name *Docteur Amede* embossed in gold. There was a phone number written on the back. Claudine called the number.

'Oui?'

The voice was soft and comforting. Claudine felt reassured.

'My name is Claudine. My sister is Jamella, she's real sick. She had your card in her handbag, said to call you.'

'I see. Give me your address.'

Claudine told him.

'I will be there in half an hour. *Courage, ma soeur.*'

Twenty-seven minutes later, Claudine answered the door to a tall, slim Creole man, dressed in an immaculate black suit, matching fedora with black band, blue shirt and a black tie. She shuddered at the scars on his face He removed the fedora, to reveal a shiny, shaven head.

'*Ma soeur*, I am *le Docteur Amede.* Take me to your sister.'

Claudine showed him into the bedroom. He bent over Jamella, took her hand, then felt her forehead.

'Leave us now, *ma soeur.*'

Claudine obediently left the room, shutting the door behind her. Amede took a syringe from his bag, filled it with green liquid from a small bottle, then injected it into Jamella's neck, behind her ear, under the hairline, where the needle mark would never be noticed. The girl in the bed gave a gasp, exhaled deeply, then lay completely still. Docteur Amede nodded to himself, capped the needle on the syringe and returned it, with the bottle, to his bag. He opened the door.

'*Ma soeur*,' he called. 'I regret, I am too late. The *pneumonie* it was too far advanced. I am sorry, but your sister is dead.'

Claudine dissolved into tears, babbling questions at the man. He put his hand on her shoulder.

'Try to calm yourself, *ma soeur*. We must make arrangements for your poor sister. We cannot leave her here like this. Here, drink this, it will help you to relax.'

Docteur Amede took a powder from his bag, dissolved it in a glass of water and gave it to the girl, who drank it obediently. She didn't sleep, but the next hour or so passed in a dream. She remembered nothing of the call Docteur Amede made on his phone, and barely noticed the two burly men with the stretcher who arrived twenty minutes later, and loaded the motionless form of her sister into an unmarked ambulance. Docteur Amede stayed another ten minutes after them, staring into the girl's eyes, and speaking very gently.

'Now, *ma soeur*, you will grieve for your sister. You will remember her always. But you will forget le Docteur Amede. I was never here, you have never seen me. You will forget.'

Docteur Amede made sure he didn't forget the little black card as he left.

CHAPTER 9

January is the coolest month of the year in New Orleans, but Jack Nightingale had no complaints, especially after experiencing winter in Wyoming. Temperatures in the mid-sixties suited him fine, and the trusty raincoat kept the chillier night air at bay. So far he'd been in the city twenty-four hours, landing at Louis Armstrong International after three hours in the air and an hour on the ground in Dallas. Valerie's first message to Nightingale's pay-as-you-go mobile phone in Wyoming had been to ask him for his location, followed ten minutes later by boarding passes sent to the phone. Typically she hadn't bothered asking him whether he'd finished with whatever had taken him to Cheyenne, but Nightingale was done and happy to leave. Joshua Wainwright's secretary was highly efficient, but this time it appeared she had forgotten to book Nightingale into his usual seat between the fat couple, and in front of the crying baby, so he'd enjoyed a restful flight. He'd picked up yet another Ford Escape at the airport, which was now valet parked, at extortionate cost, at the Crowne Plaza Astor Hotel on Bourbon Street.

There was no sign of Wainwright yet, if indeed he planned to be here at all. Nightingale hadn't seen or heard from the Texan billionaire since the mess in Memphis, which had robbed the man of his entire family, and nearly his life. Nightingale had begun to wonder if he'd ever hear from him again, though all his credit cards seemed to keep functioning without any problem. Nightingale had enjoyed the freedom, but always known it could only be temporary.

Meanwhile, he was coming to the conclusion that New Orleans agreed with him. He had been brought up on Trad jazz music, with both his adoptive parents and his Uncle Tommy as big fans. Uncle Tommy could swing a mean trumpet himself on occasions, and Jack had often thought about learning in his childhood. Discovering smoking had probably put paid to that, but he still enjoyed the music, and where better to listen to it than its spiritual home? A few dollars to the concierge at the hotel had produced a recommendation for *Vaughan's Lounge* in the Bywater district, along with advice to travel there and back by cab.

From the outside, the place looked far more like an old wooden shack than any kind of a lounge, but it had a great atmosphere inside. Kermit Ruffins and his trumpet were authentic New Orleans legends, the band was tearing up the place, the joint was jumping and the dance-floor was full. Nightingale was tapping his right foot on his bar stool, but not planning to do any dancing. White men in their forties were best advised to keep their dancing for family weddings, in his opinion. Or, better still never. He was nursing his second Corona, and decided he was probably feeling happier than he had in years. He wondered how long that would last.

As ever, the only little problem was his smoking habit. The Crowne Plaza receptionist had smiled pityingly when he'd asked about the possibility of a smoking room, but he'd been optimistic about the possibility of a cigarette with his beer in a Louisiana bar, until the bartender had advised him that New Orleans had stronger prohibitions than the rest of the state. No smoking inside anywhere, not even bars or casinos. Cheyenne had been a nightmare, also with a complete ban, and Nightingale had cut down considerably, rather than endure the freezing temperatures outside. The New Orleans climate was much friendlier, so he put a beer mat over his bottle, nodded to the blonde barmaid and held up his pack to show he planned to return, and headed for the door.

He sat down outside on an unoccupied bench and lit up. He pulled the smoke deep into his lungs, held it and exhaled upwards.

'You got a spare one of those?' asked a quiet voice behind him.

Nightingale turned his head, saw a middle-aged black man in a dark suit standing a few feet away and passed his pack and lighter over. 'Sure, help yourself,' he said.

'Thanks, Jack,' said the man.

Nightingale twisted round again and took a proper look this time. It was pretty much the last person he'd have expected to see at a New Orleans dive bar.

'Joshua?'

Wainwright was looking a little less like the carefree smiling billionaire that Nightingale remembered. His hair was longer, and streaked with grey, his face had acquired lines by the eyes and mouth, and deeper ones on the forehead. He was wearing a black suit, white shirt and a loosened black tie and his trademark lizard-skin cowboy boots. 'Jack, been a while, eh?' he said, offering his hand.

Nightingale took it. It felt clammy to the touch, and the grip was not as strong as he remembered. 'Joshua, how you been?'

'I'm getting by,' he said. 'How was Wyoming?'

'Bloody cold.'

'What were you doing up there?'

'You know what a Wendigo is?' asked Nightingale.

'I do. Yes. Of course.'

'Well that's what I was doing. Joshua, Why am I here?'

Wainwright sat down on the bench and took a long drag on his cigarette. He gestured with his head at the shack.

'Pretty good band, eh?' said Wainwright. 'Didn't have you figured as a jazz fan. 'From way back,' said Nightingale. 'How did you find me?'

Wainwright looked at the glowing tip of his cigarette, then down at the floor. He nodded, as if making a decision. 'I can always find you, Jack,' he said.

Nightingale shivered. He knew Wainwright was an experienced and powerful Satanist, though mostly just by reputation, and it was disconcerting to be reminded occasionally of the man's abilities. Though, then again, maybe Wainwright could just trace him via the GPS in his mobile phone. He'd given it to Nightingale, after all.

Wainwright called a waiter over, ordered a large single malt and looked expectantly at Nightingale. 'Corona,' said Nightingale.

The two man sat in silence, as if by some unspoken agreement, until the waiter returned with the drinks.

'What brings you here, Joshua?' asked Nightingale. 'Not sure I'd have had you figured as a jazz fan either.'

'I can take it or leave it,' said Wainwright with a shrug. 'I'll need to owe you for another cigarette.'

Nightingale gave him a cigarette and lit it for him. Nightingale waited for Wainwright to get to the point. His training as a police negotiator in another life had taught him always to let the other guy speak first, however long it took.

'You know the history of jazz, Jack?' asked Wainwright. 'Born right here in New Orleans.'

Nightingale nodded, but said nothing. Whatever was on Wainwright's mind probably wasn't to do with the history of jazz, but he'd get to it in his own time.

'That's right,' said Wainwright. 'Born right here, grew out of the Voodoo drums and rhythms. Louis Armstrong used to try to get into places like this. Maybe a hundred years ago, when he was just thirteen or so, back when they had a whole red-light district called Storyville. Course, there was no way they'd let kids in while liquor was being served. So he used to show up with two bricks and a bucket.'

Nightingale raised a quizzical eyebrow, this was a new one on him.

'He'd smash the bricks together till they was nothing but dust, then sell the dust to the patrons. That way they'd let him stay in.'

'And why would anyone want to buy brick dust?' asked Nightingale.

'Protection. Lots of Voodoo curses are passed through the feet. Foot-root magic. You spread brick dust on your door step every morning, nobody can curse you.' Wainwright took a sip of his fresh Glenlivet, reached into his suit pocket, took out a sheet of paper, unfolded it and passed it across to Nightingale.

Nightingale looked at it. It was a newspaper cutting. An obituary. A man named Cameron Lattimore. There was a photograph of him in a football uniform. Nightingale looked at Wainwright expectantly.

'I'm guessing you never heard of Cameron?' said Wainwright.

'You guess right, though I deduce he was a football player.'

'You'd be the only guy in the Continental United States who never heard of him. The all-time best quarterback the Saints ever had. That's why the suit. I knew the guy from way back, liked him. I was at his funeral this afternoon. He died a week ago.'

Nightingale nodded, but stayed silent. Wainwright would get to it in his own time.

'He died of cancer, Jack.'

'Young,' said Nightingale. 'Says here he was twenty-seven.'

'Yeah. I saw the medical report. He died of advanced prostate cancer.'

Nightingale frowned in surprise. 'At twenty-seven? Surely that's an older man's disease?'

'Pretty much. It's not impossible though. Apparently the youngest ever victim was sixteen.'

Nightingale glanced back down at the press cutting, and his brow furrowed again. 'It says here that he played his last game ten days ago. How would that be possible with terminal cancer?'

'Well here's the thing, Jack, the guy didn't have cancer ten days ago.'

Nightingale's jaw dropped. 'What? Cancer doesn't go from nothing to dead in ten days.'

'Cameron had just come back from a long-term injury. He'd had shoulder surgery. These athletes get serviced better than Indy cars. He had a full physical two weeks ago before he came back into the team. I doubt they'd have missed a chipped toenail. They sure as hell wouldn't have missed terminal cancer.'

'Maybe not, but what can I do about it? Surely it's medical negligence?'

'No, I think there's more to it than that.'

'What are you saying?'

'I'm saying we're done listening to jazz for tonight. Call us a cab.'

'You're a cab.'

Wainwright frowned in confusion. 'Say what?'

'British humour,' said Nightingale.

CHAPTER 10

The private ambulance that had collected Jamella arrived at the old abandoned church, though the ambulance markings on the side of the van had been removed. Two big men got out from either side of the passenger cab and walked round to the rear. They opened the tailgate and manoeuvred the stretcher out and onto the ground. The young girl lay motionless, a white sheet covering her up to the neck. Neither of the men spoke as they carried the stretcher towards the main door of the church, which opened as they approached.

A figure in a long hooded cape nodded at them, and ushered them into the church and along the nave. They deposited the girl's body on the ruined old altar. The figure pulled a wad of notes from a coat pocket, peeled off a few bills and handed them over. The two men turned and left without speaking.

'A wooden crucifix was mounted upside-down and bound in grasses above the altar. A marble slab stood in front of it, with a smaller wooden table by the side. A long wooden handle protruded from a coal barbecue to the left of the table. The church was empty, except for the figure in the cape and the body of the young black girl.

The cowled figure took a large terracotta flask from the table, uncorked it and poured a green liquid onto the soles of the girl's feet. Three breaths were given into each of her nostrils, then her mouth was held open and three more breaths given. The long fingers traced patterns on her head, heart and womb. Finally three more words were spoken, much louder this time, and a red powder was blown into the woman's face.

'Qu'elle renaisse!'

The empty church echoed the words.

'Qu'elle renaisse.'

'Qu'elle vive encaire.'

'Qu'elle vive encaire,' came back the response from the walls.

'Qu'elle fasse mi volonté,' was the shout this time.

'Qu'elle fasse ti volonté,' echoed the walls.

The long fingers took her hand, pulling gently. The girl slid her legs sideways, put them over the side of the altar, then slowly raised her upper body until she was sitting on the edge of the altar. Responding to the steady pull on her arm, she jumped down onto the floor, where she stood, naked and blank-eyed.

The figure in black took the wooden-handled branding iron from the burner where it lay heating, spat on the end, and heard the sizzle. He held the girl by her left shoulder and pressed the hot iron hard into her right shoulder blade. The smell of burning flesh filled the church. The girl didn't flinch or utter a sound, The figure replaced the branding iron, and rubbed her shoulder with ointment from a small bottle.

'Venez, ma soeur, z'avez du travail à faire,' said the figure, leading her away from the altar and into the remains of the side room. Jamella followed, her eyes fixed straight ahead, her legs stiff and unbending, oblivious to her surroundings and the cold in the church, following only the one commanding voice in front of her.

CHAPTER 11

A cab ride later, Nightingale was in Wainwright's suite at the Four Points Hotel, overlooking Bourbon Street. Wainwright opened the French doors onto the balcony. 'So, we're allowed to smoke here?' asked Nightingale hopefully.

'Nope. No smoking hotel rooms in the whole city, and no smoking on the balcony either, we're a persecuted minority,' said Wainwright, flicking his lighter and applying it to one of his favourite foot-long Cuban cigars.

Nightingale lit a Marlboro and took a deep drag. 'So we'll end up in prison together?'

'I'll soothe their injured feelings with a little cash,' said Wainwright. 'I still have some left.'

'Times are hard?' asked Nightingale.

'A little harder than they were. I seem to be a target these days. Lot of deals going bad, lot of stocks that should be going up are going down when I get into them, lot of people not wanting to do business with me.'

'Any idea who's behind it?'

'They don't advertise. But they don't wish me well. Here I am in a cheap suite with fake ID, when I used to take a whole floor in the best hotel in town. I get the feeling the fewer people who know where I am and what I'm doing, the safer I'm likely to be. I put my head above the parapet a little too often. Made myself a whole bunch of enemies.'

'But you don't know who?'

'We both know who, even if we have no names. But, if I had to guess, I'd say the American branch of those guys who drove you out of England. Your father's old friends.'

Nightingale shuddered. He didn't much care to be reminded that he was the natural son of one of the most powerful Satanists England had ever known. 'The Order of the Nine Angles? They're that powerful over here?'

'Powerful everywhere. Just like in Memphis, They go all the way to the top it seems. And I mean the very top.'

Nightingale took a long drag on his cigarette, and closed his eyes briefly. 'So I'm here to help you fight the Order Of The Nine Angles?'

Wainwright shook his head. 'Nah, they'll keep. Or maybe they'll get me. Nothing you can do about it anyway, we'd be needing a hell of a lot of help to go up against them, and not just from this world. You're here to find out what happened to Cameron Lattimore.'

'We know what happened to him. He died of cancer. Now he was very young, and very unlucky, and the Saints medical team should have spotted it, but that's a medical negligence issue. What can I do?'

'Come on, Jack. You know me better than that. "Once is happenstance, twice is coincidence, three times is enemy action" - you ever hear that saying?'

'Sure,' said Nightingale. 'James Bond wasn't it? Dr No?'

'Goldfinger,' said Wainwright. 'Well, I can show you three. In fact I got four.'

He waved Nightingale to an armchair, then pulled an attaché case from under the bed, clicked it open, took out a blue cardboard file and handed it to Nightingale. He sat by the desk and smoked in silence while Nightingale opened the file and looked through the contents.

There were three more obituaries, two from the *New York Times* and one from the local *New Orleans Advocate.* Also copies of three autopsy reports, which Nightingale found more difficult to process, though in the end the findings seemed very clear. It took him fifteen minutes to read through the six documents, then he lit a fresh cigarette, and looked up at Wainwright. 'So?'

'So tell me what you read,' said Wainwright.

'OK. Tiffany Davies, from New Orleans. America's sixth ranked tennis player. Dead at twenty-four. The medical report says advanced Alzheimer's disease. Trevon Clark, guard for the New Orleans Pelicans, basketball team. Dead at twenty-five and they say it was Parkinson's disease. And from the local paper, Sandy Gonzalez, second baseman for the New Orleans Baby Cakes minor league baseball team. Is that really their name? Baby Cakes?'

'It really is.'

'The autopsy says advanced lung cancer, and he was twenty-two. Wow. That's bad luck.'

'So what do they have in common?'

'Okay, four young people, top level athletes, all of them dead of diseases you'd normally associate with old people.'

'Yeah. And the word is Sandy Gonzalez never smoked a cigarette in his life.'

'Non-smokers get lung cancer too,' said Nightingale.

'Yeah, it can happen. But not often, especially at twenty-two. Anything else?'

'As far as I know, these are all long-term degenerative illnesses, but all of these guys were playing top-level sports until just before they were diagnosed, which was days before they died. And the national level sports players would have been regularly monitored. One could be negligence, but four, all in Louisiana and all in the last two months?'

'Yeah,' said Wainwright. 'Enemy action. I don't believe in this number of coincidences in one place in a short time.'

'It looks strange,' said Nightingale, 'but I'm no medical expert. You sure that we might not find similar patterns if we took a look at deaths in any big city over a few months? Coincidences happen, all the time.'

'I'm pretty sure it's not a common pattern. I asked some people who are medical experts.'

Nightingale nodded. It seemed that whatever current problems Wainwright had, he was still well connected.

'And there's another thing, Jack. Something maybe nobody else would believe. Maybe not even you.'

'Try me.'

'I told you I'd been to Cameron's funeral. It was an open casket affair and the body was on display at the service.'

'And?'

'You know me and what I am. You know I have some abilities that others don't, I can sense more than the civilians. I touched Cameron's head, maybe just to say goodbye, but I got a feeling from him. Jack, he was murdered.'

'A feeling?'

'Call it ESP, psychic awareness, whatever. I just know Cameron didn't die a natural death.'

'But the doctors disagree. I don't suppose you got chance to run your eye over any of the others?'

'No. But one was enough for me.'

'OK, let's assume someone, or some thing, is making this happen. How could they do it? If it were small pox, or black death, maybe somebody could be injecting them with viruses, but cancer and dementia aren't caused by bugs. It's impossible to pass them on to someone.'

'New Orleans is pretty much a centre for Hoodoo, Voodoo or any other kind of dark stuff you might want to get into. Or stay out of. I got a bad feeling about these deaths, Jack, and my feelings tend to be right. If someone is powerful enough to do this, they could be serious trouble, and very dangerous.'

'Well, at least if it goes pear-shaped, I can get a jazz funeral.'

'I'll see what I can do,' said Wainwright.

'One more question,' said Nightingale.

'As many as you like.'

'Why do you even care what happens here? I know you fed me that line about the Occult needing to stay in the shadows so that civilians never learned about it, but there's a lot more to it than that, isn't there?'

Wainwright's cigar had lain unattended in the ashtray for ten minutes, but now he picked it up and took his time relighting it. He blew a neat smoke ring, then looked back at Nightingale. 'Maybe we're at war here, Jack. Maybe there are too many people trying to break the rules. They tried to raise Bimoleth up in San Francisco, summoned Lilith and her friends in New York, then unleashed Dudák and that fool Tyrone up in Tennessee. Now this.'

'But those weren't the same people.'

'How would you know who was behind them? Maybe it's all connected. We know how powerful and widespread the Order Of The Nine Angles is. Maybe they're beginning to use that power.'

'That's quite a leap.'

'Well, maybe you should ask your girlfriend.'

'Who?'

'Who do the Order swear allegiance to? Proserpine, and you seem to have her number on speed-dial.'

'Allegedly,' said Nightingale.

'You know, I never understood that. You faked your own death, and beat it out of England to escape the Order, and so they wouldn't murder the few people close to you they hadn't already killed.'

'Allegedly,' repeated Nightingale.

'But the Princess of Hell who they swear allegiance to, knows you're alive and knows where to find you any time. Yet she doesn't sic them on to you. How come?'

'You know, Joshua, I really have no idea.'

'Maybe she's playing both sides.'

'Well, she is one of the Fallen. You can't expect them to play by the rules.' He sighed. 'So, where do I start? Who do I talk to about young people dying of diseases they shouldn't have?'

'Maybe you're looking at this the wrong way round.'

'What do you mean?'

'Maybe you should be looking at some old people *not* dying of diseases they *should* have.'

Nightingale frowned in confusion. 'I don't see how that gets me any further forward.'

Wainwright looked at his watch. 'Time's up for me, Jack, I need to be a long way from here pretty soon. Anything you need, you know how to find me. Give it your best shot, Jack. Cameron was a friend, and I don't like the idea of him being taken before his time.'

CHAPTER 13

'Jack Nightingale. Jack Nightingale. Save me. You must save me. Only you can save me.'

Nightingale opened his eyes, though he knew he was still sleeping and stared into the mist that surrounded him. Was he on the astral plane again? This time there had been no sensation of flying upwards. He only knew one person who could have summoned him there, and the voice wasn't Alice Steadman's. Much stronger, and far younger. He looked around him, but there was only mist.

'Jack Nightingale. Jack Nightingale. Save me. You must save me. Come when I call you. You must save me.'

This time, as Nightingale stared into the mist, his eyes caught a flash of green, and he moved towards it. Again the voice called to him, unmistakably female now. And young.

'Oh, Jack Nightingale, you must come when I call you. You must save me, only you can save me.'

Nightingale stepped ever closer, and could now make out a dark green dress, billowing in a wind that he couldn't feel. It reached from chest to mid thigh, and, as he stared at it, the woman's body came into focus. She seemed nearly as tall as him her figure the very definition of the hourglass cliché, the dress cut tight from bust to waist, but then looser further down and playing in the wind.

'Save me, Jack Nightingale. Come to me when I call.'

'Who are you?'' called Nightingale, as he took another step forward.

Now he could see her face. A young woman, maybe late twenties, a mane of red and copper hair hanging loosely over her shoulders. Bright green eyes that stared firmly into his, but couldn't hide the fear behind them. Her skin was pale, with two patches of red at her cheeks, the lips full and crimson, though she seemed to wear no make-up.

Nightingale had rarely seen a woman he had thought more beautiful, the gaze of her emerald eyes, and the soft lilt of her voice held him motionless, as she called out once again.

'Say you will come for me when I call, Jack Nightingale. Say you will save me.'

Nightingale shook his head, and blinked, trying to clear his thoughts. He must be asleep, this could be no more than a dream. But still, he spoke. 'Save you from what? Who are you? How can I find you? What danger are you in.'

The woman lifted a hand, held out the palm to stop him, then put a finger to her lips.

'Now is not the time for questions, just promise you will come when I call, Promise you will save me. Promise.'

The green eyes widened and seemed to pull him downwards into their depths. He heard a voice speaking in the distance, and recognised it as his own, though he wasn't conscious of choosing the words.

'I promise. I will come when you call me. I will save you.'

The full, red lips parted in a smile. Was it relief or triumph?

"I knew you would. I knew. Go now, Jack Nightingale. The time will be soon when I shall call you.'

She was gone. The mist was gone. Nightingale was awake in his hotel bed.

CHAPTER 14

Jack Nightingale woke the next morning in his hotel room at 8.17am. The dream was still vivid, but he told himself it was just a dream. Probably. He thought about lighting a cigarette, remembered he was in New Orleans, and decided to assess the situation without the help of nicotine. He really couldn't see a way into this one. On the plus side, he wouldn't be having to deal with the police this time. There was no way he'd ever be able to convince the NOPD that four people dying of natural causes might be connected to some Satanic conspiracy. There was no crime here, no detective assigned to any case, and the best Nightingale could hope for was a little time in an asylum if he pursued it with the boys in blue. He did spend ten minutes wondering whether some time in the peace and quiet of an asylum might actually be preferable. Could the last few years really have happened?

Finding out his parents had actually adopted him, his soul had been sold to a demon, he had a serial-killer sister, he was pursued by a Satanic order, a variety of demons from Hell were on his trail, he'd seen and caused so many deaths, he was a pawn in some kind of game between the Fallen and the Angels...

It was too much. He couldn't rationalise any of it. All he could do, as ever, was try to play detective, talk to people, ask questions, pull strings and see where it got him. And then hope to whatever God might exist that dumb luck might bail him out. But this one was different. There was so little to go on.

Nightingale headed for the bathroom, where he shaved and showered.

An hour afterwards, the young black maid opened the door of his room, took the disposable razor from the waste basket, placed it in a self-seal plastic bag, and dropped it into the pocket of her overall. Then she got on with changing the towels, making the bed and some cleaning.

CHAPTER 15

Nightingale's first call was at the Lattimore mansion over in the Lakewood area of New Orleans. Nightingale's guide book informed him that this was pretty much the richest area of the city, and it certainly looked it. The New Orleans traffic was pretty heavy, as the GPS voice guided him to his destination.

A concrete-slab wall ran round the property, making sure that all guests had to present themselves for scrutiny at the electric gates. Nightingale would never have stood a chance of getting past the security guard in his office just inside the gate, if Wainwright hadn't called ahead to speak to the wife of his old friend. Widow of his old friend, Nightingale corrected himself, as the side gate opened, and a large black man in a blue uniform walked out and stood beside Nightingale's car door, one hand on the butt of the pistol on his right hip.

'Can I help you, sir?' he said, once Nightingale had slid the window down. Nightingale gave his name, and the man nodded. 'Mrs Lattimore is expecting you. Straight up the drive, follow it round to the left and you'll come to the main entrance.'

'Thank you…'

'My name's Charles Winston sir. Nice to meet you. I'm just about to go off shift, so it'll probably be my brother Emmot who lets you out.'

'Brothers?'

'Yes sir, we're cousins of the Lattimore family. Cameron tried to help his family once he moved up in the world. We sure miss him.'

Winston walked back through the side-gate and into his office. Nightingale pressed the switch to close the window, and waited until the electric gates ahead of him had swung fully open, before setting off up the drive.

Cameron Lattimore had surely moved up a long way in the world, if his house was any indication. Nightingale had no idea how much an

NFL quarterback got paid, but it appeared he hadn't been short of a few million. The house reminded Nightingale of a French chateau he'd once seen on television. It had two wings at right angles to each other, separated by a squat tower, The walls were painted some shade of yellowy-cream, which probably had a special name, but only in a paint catalogue. The roofs were steep, made of dark-grey slate, and punctuated by regular dormer windows. The lawns, flower-beds, trees and hedges all looked as if they had been trimmed to perfection that morning, and the gravel drive was freshly raked. A hundred yards of tree-lined drive took Nightingale past tennis courts, a swimming pool and extensive gardens, up to a large turning area in front of the main house.

As Nightingale braked to a halt, the door opened, and a silver-haired man in a grey lounge suit came down the steps. As he drew closer, Nightingale guessed his age at around sixty, though he evidently kept himself in good shape physically, and his hair was immaculately cut. He got to the car door just as Nightingale shut it behind him.

'Mr Nightingale? My name is Roberts, I'm the Lattimore family Major Domo. Welcome, sir. If you will follow me, Mrs Lattimore is waiting in the west drawing-room.'

'Major Domo?'

'I run the household, Sir. The titled derives from Major Domus, Latin for principal of the house, though it probably came into English via the Spanish mayordomo.'

Nightingale followed him up the steps. He did briefly wonder if Roberts had been included in the package when the Lattimores had built the house, but he kept the thought to himself. Roberts didn't look as if he'd appreciate English humour at this early stage.

He followed Roberts down a corridor to the right. The walls were painted in what looked to be the same shade as the outside, most of the artwork on the walls being very modern paintings or photos of football players, along with some glamour shots of a stunning blonde woman.

Roberts knocked on a door, opened it without waiting for a reply, then stood back to allow Nightingale to enter. 'Mr Nightingale, Mrs Lattimore,' he said, then closed the door behind him, and Nightingale heard his footsteps echo back down the hall.

'Please come in, Mr Nightingale,' said Mrs Lattimore. 'Make yourself comfortable on the sofa.' Nightingale sat on a white leather sofa, as instructed, then took a good look at the lady. She was the original of the model shots in the hall. Mid-twenties, long blonde hair, tallish, as far as he could judge with her sitting, with a very good figure, her complexion was tanned, but fading, showing the pallor of stress beneath. She hadn't risen to greet him, and he wondered if the large glass of colourless liquid on the table next to her had anything to do with that. She looked at him, as if appraising what she saw, then gave a small nod.

'Charmaine Lattimore,' she said. 'But you know that.'

'Can I offer my con…'

She raised a hand to stop him.

'I know. Everyone does, even if they never knew Cameron. I'm a little tired of hearing them, but thank you anyway.'

Was it Nightingale's imagination, or was there a slight slur in her voice? Tears didn't seem far away. She clenched her hands into fists, but not before Nightingale had noticed that her fingernails were bitten down to the quick.

'Sorry,' she said. 'That was probably a little graceless of me. I'm very new to widowhood, I loved my husband very much, and I'm not coping as well as I should.'

'There are no rules,' said Nightingale. 'You feel how you feel, don't set yourself targets. One day at a time.'

She smiled. 'I bet you say that to all the widows. With me it's an hour at a time. But let's not wallow. Joshua Wainwright asked me to see you. He'd known my husband a long time, I didn't know him well, but I think he had Cameron's interests at heart. You know him well?'

Nightingale paused while he tried to think how well he really did know Wainwright. 'I've known him for a few years now, and helped him with several things. Do you see him often?'

'I met Joshua maybe three or four times during the four years I knew Cameron. Usually at very expensive parties. A man of great personal charm, I thought, though I was never sure how deep it ran. Very confident, very attractive to women, and knew it.'

'And how did you meet your husband?'

'I met Cameron at College,' she said. 'UCLA. I was studying psychology, he was on a football scholarship of course. We met at a dance. You've heard the saying, opposites attract? Well, we did, and never unattracted. We moved here after he was drafted by the Saints, four great years, until his injury. As you may have noticed, my psychology studies gave way to modelling. Of course I was Charmaine Hayes before.'

Nightingale nodded, though the name meant nothing to him, women's fashion wasn't one of his specialist subjects. 'You mentioned his injury. That was the most recent one?'

'Pretty much the only one, he was always very lucky with injuries, never anything serious. He used to tell me he had a Guardian Angel on his shoulder, to steer him out of harm's way.'

'He was religious?'

'Not so much, though I think he probably believed a little more than I did. I think it was just a saying. Ironic thing is, that it was his shoulder that caused all the trouble. Do you follow football, Mr Nightingale?'

'Not the American kind, I'm afraid.'

'You English prefer soccer, I hear.'

Nightingale nodded.

'Well, about eighteen months ago, he took what they call a big hit from some guy playing for Miami. Knocked him flying, and he landed on his right shoulder, Broken and dislocated. An easy fix, they thought at first, but after two operations, it still didn't seem to be a hundred percent, and it was really getting him down.'

'What was the problem?'

'For most people, there wouldn't have been a problem. The surgeons did a great job. If it had been my shoulder, or yours, we'd have been perfectly happy with the results.'

'But your husband wasn't?'

'No. Cameron was a top level athlete, his job was to use that shoulder to throw a football fast, far and accurately. His shoulder was about ninety-five percent, but it's that five percent that separates a good quarterback from a great one. And Cameron needed to be great.'

'So what did he do about it?'

'Pretty much everything. He saw specialists, physios, tried all kinds of special exercises, cryotherapy, those pressure chambers they put divers in, the whole works. He even joked about going to a faith healer, or getting someone to light some candles for him. I told him not to be so silly, and he forgot the idea.'

'But he wasn't religious?'

'Not really, but he was desperate, and people clutch at all kinds of straws. Anyway, something must have worked, it finally started to improve a few weeks ago, to the point where he'd got back what he'd lost and the club doctors passed him as fit to get back to playing. He played just one more game, then the next day he woke up in agony, couldn't...couldn't pee, blood coming out. I guess you know the rest. He was dead ten days later, and it was just awful. So much pain.' The tears had started halfway through the story, and were now pouring down her cheeks. She took a handkerchief out of her handbag, tried to dab them away, then took a large gulp of her drink. 'I'm sorry about that, it's all so fresh I'm still so angry, it just wasn't fair.'

Nightingale nodded, but there was nothing he could say.

'So why are you here? Cameron's dead, nobody's to blame. What's Joshua's interest, and yours? You don't think there's some reason for it all? Are you a lawyer? There's nobody to sue, he had the best care possible, and there's nothing to suggest he was exposed to anything cancerous. The shoulder treatments were all pretty standard.'

'No, I'm not a lawyer. Far from it. I think Joshua was just concerned about his friend dying so young, so unexpectedly, and of a disease that usually affects much older men. Maybe he's hurting too, and is trying to make sense of something that makes no sense.'

'Well, for sure it makes no sense. It's a disease that almost never strikes young men, and it's pretty much unheard of for it to come on so quickly. Or so they told me, I've learned a lot more about prostate cancer than I ever wanted to. But then, I guess...I guess shit happens. It surely did to us.'

Nightingale figured he wasn't going to get anything useful from Mrs Lattimore so he thanked her for her time and stood up. 'I'm sure Joshua Wainwright would add his thanks. As I said, maybe he's trying to find answers that aren't there. Maybe it's a natural reaction when things happen that shouldn't.'

48

There was an intercom on her table, and she pressed the green button.

'Thank you for coming,' she said to Nightingale. 'And thanks to Joshua too, but there's nothing we can do or say. Roberts will show you out.'

She made no attempt to get up from her chair, and by the time Nightingale arrived at the drawing-room door, Roberts was holding it open.

The front door had barely shut behind Nightingale, before Charmaine Lattimore was punching one of the speed-dial buttons on her phone.

CHAPTER 16

Nightingale was also making a call, reporting in to Wainwright. 'So, the lady had nothing helpful to say?' asked Wainwright.

'What were you expecting, Joshua? Some kind of confession? She's hurting badly, struggling to make sense of a senseless death. Though she did speak quite highly of you.'

'Good to know. Jack. Look, I have something else for you to look at.'

'Instead of this?'

'As well as. Something just tells me there might even be a connection. I got a call this morning. Guy I don't know, but he's heard of me. Elijah Cole. His wife is Deborah. Maybe I owe him one. Can you see him this afternoon? I'll send the location to your cell. Two o'clock will be fine.'

'Another impossible case?'

'I'll let him tell you about it personally.'

'Excellent, what's better than two impossible cases?'

'Maybe this one won't be so hard. Cole was a friend of my late brother-in-law.'

Nightingale flinched at the memory of the Reverend Matthew Fisher, and the death of his whole family in Memphis. 'In connection with people dying early?'

'Well, it is and it isn't. I'll let him tell you in his own words But, you know. I got a feeling…'

'Yeah, I know. OK, I'll be there.'

'I never doubted it.'

Nightingale left his hotel at one thirty and caught a cab. The drive took them along the Mississippi towards the Garden District, along tree-lined residential avenues, the houses built in New Orleans unique colonial style. The driver pulled up opposite a long, low, white church and gestured at the house on the left. Nightingale reached for his wallet, paid the meter fare and added a generous tip. The driver nodded his thanks, then pulled away. Nightingale looked up at the house. It was nowhere near the size and standard of the Lattimore mansion, a basic detached home, but it looked well-maintained, with a neatly-cut lawn in front. Nightingale walked up the steps to the verandah and rang the bell.

The woman who answered was small, a little over her ideal weight, with long copper-coloured hair and a complexion that Nightingale had heard described as *café au lait.* At first glance, he put her at mid forties, but as he moved nearer, he decided that she was probably ten years older than that. Her dark brown eyes were surrounded by sunken black circles, and he thought she'd been doing more crying than sleeping recently.

Nightingale gave his name, and held out a hand, but the woman didn't seem to notice. She sighed, and shook her head quickly, as if to clear her thoughts. 'Please come in, my husband is in his study, and expecting you.'

Mrs Cole led him down the hall. The wood panelling looked old, but cared for, and the walls were lined with framed pictures of what Nightingale assumed were family members, present and past, interspersed with some photos of old American churches. Mrs Cole knocked on a heavy wooden door, and pushed it open.

Mrs Cole opened the study door, and stood aside to let him enter. Elijah Cole was wearing a light grey suit that looked as if it had been tailored for him, over a light blue shirt with a clerical collar. Nightingale hadn't been expecting a Satanist to send him to a churchman's house. But then maybe after meeting Wainwright's family in Memphis, it might make some sense. His own sister had married a Christian pastor.

Elijah Cole was darker than his wife, a tall, powerfully built black man. He offered his hand to Nightingale. His grip was firm, though Nightingale would have bet that it could have been a whole lot more powerful if he'd wished. 'Thank you for coming, sir, please sit down.' He gestured at a brown leather Chesterfield sofa at the opposite end of the room from a large mahogany desk, and sank into a matching armchair facing them. He put a hand on each arm of the chair, looked from his shoes to the ceiling, then at Nightingale's face, then back again at his shoes. He cleared his throat, and finally began. 'This is very difficult for me, Mr Nightingale. I've never met either of you before, and still only ever spoken to Mr Wainwright, on the phone. I contacted Joshua Wainwright because his name was mentioned to me on occasions by a former colleague of mine, Reverend Matthew Fisher. His brother-in-law. Matthew told me Wainwright had...he had...certain...connections, in areas of which he himself knew little, but disapproved. I...er...understand my friend is deceased now?'

Nightingale nodded. 'He is, I'm afraid. His family, Joshua's family too. Probably something to do with what he disapproved of. Maybe he was right all along. But how did you come to know him? He lived in Memphis.'

'We attended the same seminary. We kept in touch afterwards. We were close enough friends that he felt able to express his...reservations...about his wife's brother.'

'So obviously you maybe know Wainwright chose a different path from his and yours. Why would that recommend him to you?'

The priest took a couple of newspaper cuttings from his inside coat pocket, unfolded them and passed one across to Nightingale, who held it in his left hand. 'Take a look at that,' said Cole.

It was a report of a road traffic accident a week or so before on the 43 Highway between New Orleans and Baton Rouge. A truck driver was thought to have had a fatal heart attack at the wheel, his truck had veered into the path of oncoming traffic, wrecking a dozen cars and killing twelve people. There were photos of various lumps of twisted and burnt metal that had once been cars, and also of emergency vehicles attending the scene. Nightingale read it through, then looked up at the priest. 'Okay,' he said.

Cole passed across a second cutting.

This one dated a few days later, was a list of fatalities in the accident, including the dead truck driver. Nightingale glanced at it without much interest and read through the list of names.

Dembowski, the driver of the truck, Wheeler, James, Ali, Carson, Javed,Tyrone and Tyrell Biggs. Cole...

'A relative?' asked Nightingale when he spotted the name.

'My sister,' said Cole. 'Bethany Maria Cole.'

'I'm sorry,' said Nightingale, and meant it. The man had clearly been suffering. 'But it looks like a complete accident. They say the truck driver had a heart attack, and lost control.'

'No doubt it was an accident,' said Cole. 'No doubt at all.'

'So…'

The priest passed across the third and final cutting. It was an obituary notice, for Bethany Maria Cole, aged thirty, who had been interred at St Francis Cemetery, after a service at St Mark's Baptist Church.

Nightingale looked up, puzzled. 'I don't understand,' he said, 'it says here that she died after a short illness.'

'It does,' said Cole. 'I wasn't informed until several days after. The doctor who signed the certificate said pneumonia. I have my suspicions that her lifestyle may have brought about her death.'

'But…'

'Check the date Mr Nightingale.'

Nightingale did as asked. He frowned. 'This is dated two weeks before the accident,' he said. 'So, it couldn't have been her in the car.'

'Exactly. But it was, she was identified from her fingerprints and DNA.'

'But then the girl who died of pneumonia…'

'Was identified by friends and I saw her myself. It was Bethany.'

Nightingale paused, and his hand reached automatically for his cigarettes, but there was no sign of any ashtrays, and it seemed the wrong time to ask permission to smoke. 'Well, I guess there would be one way to make sure, if the cops have her DNA and fingerprints, then exhuming the first body would settle things for sure.'

'That's what we can't do,' said Cole. 'There is no body. It's disappeared.'

'You mean someone dug it up?'

Cole gave a weak smile and shook his head. 'You're not from around these parts. We don't tend to bury our dead in New Orleans. The water table is very high, dig down a few feet and you hit it. Caskets would float away. We have an old tradition of interring our dead in vaults above ground. They call the collections of vaults *Cities of the Dead*, you can even take tours of some of the more famous ones. Bethany's casket was empty when we checked her vault the day after the police came to us when they made their identification. The second time.'

Nightingale stared at the priest unable to believe what he was hearing. He tried to think of his next question.

'You're a smoker, Mr Nightingale?' asked Cole.

'How did you know?'

'My nose, and you've patted your side pocket five times in the last fifteen minutes, just to reassure yourself that they're still there. I gave up twenty years ago, but I recognise the signs. Go ahead, it won't bother me, I'll get you an ashtray.'

He rose from his chair, walked across to his desk, opened a bottom drawer, took out a heavy glass ashtray and put it on the sofa arm next to Nightingale, who lit up gratefully. Cole sat down again.

'I imagine you'll have thought of some questions now?' he said.

'A little background first, if I may. You said you didn't find out about her death...the first death...until a few days afterwards. Do I take it you weren't in regular contact?'

Cole sighed, laced his fingers together, and directed his gaze over Nightingale's right shoulder, then spoke as if addressing the wall.

'Our paths had diverged quite considerably. She was very intelligent and well-educated. She used to have a job at Brower. But some years ago she threw it up, and, for some unaccountable reason, went into the...entertainment business.'

Nightingale nodded. 'Entertainment' could cover a lot of areas, some of them not so salubrious. He kept silent and the Reverend filled the silence.

'Basically she was a hooker,' said Cole, 'though I suspect she would have used a more sophisticated term. "Escort", maybe. Anyway, she had dates with businessmen in top hotels, made a good living from it.'

'And how did you know this?'

'She told me, back when we were closer. Maybe she wanted to ease her conscience, I don't know. I'm not criticising her, we all do what we do. I found my way in life, I thought she had found hers, but it seems it didn't last. I heard, from various sources, that she'd gone down a few levels lately. The last time I saw her, she seemed rather stressed and twitchy. She was wearing long sleeves, but I've seen junkies before.'

'So you lost contact?'

'Not entirely. She would call, we'd talk for a while. I tried to listen, rather than to judge. After all, she was still my sister. Oddly, she still seemed to maintain a connection to the church. Not my church, but she spoke of meetings and services, though was never specific about where.'

Nightingale nodded again. Not all religions held their meetings and services in churches. And not all ceremonies in churches were Christian.

'Well,' said Nightingale eventually. 'As I see it, there are two possibilities. Either the girl who died of pneumonia or the girl in the crash was misidentified. I suppose there might also be the tiny possibility that the doctor who certified her dead made a mistake, but that seems vanishingly unlikely. Even the most useless quack could find a heartbeat or pulse.'

'That would indeed seem the logical answer. Except I know the girl in the tomb was Bethany, and the police know the girl in the crash was her. Her...activities...had resulted in arrests. Her details were on file.'

'What do the police say?'

'They seem sure that the girl in the accident was her, and tend to doubt the identification of the body in the tomb, since it wasn't based on any scientific evidence, and they can no longer test it. In point of fact, they are extremely interested in Bethany, since they consider her to be a prime suspect in a double homicide committed just before her death.'

Nightingale's jaw dropped in surprise. This just kept getting weirder. 'I'm sorry, what?'

'A woman answering her description, together with two others, who were also identified in the crash, was seen leaving the residence of a Delroy Lane, where his body, and that of his bodyguard, Simon Lisgard, were later found, rather horribly murdered. There was evidence that women had been with them at the time of their deaths.'

'What do you think happened?' asked Nightingale. 'You must have some idea of your own, otherwise you wouldn't have contacted Joshua Wainwright.'

Cole took a long pause, looked longingly at Nightingale's cigarette, then shook his head. 'I scarcely dare to voice it,' he said, his voice a hoarse whisper. 'It will seem impossible to you.'

'Go ahead,' said Nightingale. 'I've seen an awful lot of impossible things in the last few years. Joshua Wainwright has too.'

'I'm a religious man, Mr Nightingale. I believe in God, I believe in Redemption through Christ. But there are other religions, with different beliefs. We're in New Orleans, in Louisiana. It's the home of Voodoo. And you know one of the main stories that believers in Voodoo tell?'

'Oh, come on, not the walking dead. You can't believe that. You might as well go looking for vampires.'

The priest raised his eyebrows and pursed his lips. 'I'm not sure I'd even discount vampires. You know what that countryman of yours said, "More things in heaven and Earth than are dreamed of in your philosophies." Maybe he was talking about vampires. Or Voodoo. Or just the fact that my sister seems to have died twice in two weeks.'

Nightingale stopped arguing. A few years ago, he'd have found the whole idea too stupid for words, but he'd had enough experiences since then to make him far less sceptical in many areas. After a run-in or two with demons from Hell hungry for his soul, the idea of zombies maybe wasn't so ridiculous after all. He looked at Cole, and tried to think of something useful to say. He lit another cigarette to give himself some time. 'That's a pretty big jump, though, from a misidentified body to the idea of her being turned into a zombie. Isn't that supposed to be the result of a virus anyway?'

Cole shook his head. 'Perhaps you've been watching too many movies, or TV shows,' he said. 'This isn't about some fictional plague driven apocalypse, this is a far older tradition. One about which, to be perfectly honest, I am no expert. The Voodoo tradition comes out of Africa, as did my ancestors many hundreds of years ago, though I have moved far away from it. But I know the basics. The witch doctor causes someone to die, or at least take on the appearance of death, and then re-animates the corpse. But the person chosen now has no true will of their own, and is just a slave, completely controlled by whoever reanimated them.'

'And this can go on forever?' asked Nightingale.

'I don't think so,' replied Cole. 'The body eventually starts to decay, but, as I said, I'm not well-informed.'

'I still think it's a pretty big leap,' said Nightingale. 'Surely it's easier just to assume that the police made a mistake identifying the second body. Maybe this girl had somehow gotten hold of your sister's driving licence or credit cards. And anyway, why would anyone go to the trouble of creating a zombie, just to use them as to kill some drug-dealer? Isn't the usual system a drive-by, or a car bomb? In the UK they tend to hack away at each other with machetes.'

'I would have no idea,' said Cole. 'I'm not in the business of murder. I'm still struggling to believe that it is possible. Maybe someone had a grudge against Bethany. Maybe to send some kind of message to the people who employed Delroy Lane. Maybe it is part of their ritual. I am out of my depth.'

'Me too,' said Nightingale.

'Mr Wainwright said that you, and he, would try to find out what happened.'

Nightingale nodded. 'If he said so, then that's what'll happen. But I'll need to start asking some questions, and so far I have no idea who to ask. Can you give me the name of the cop handling the case? And would you have any idea of any friends she might have had? Or whether she found her clients through an agency?'

Cole went back to his desk and took a zip-loc plastic bag from a drawer. 'The police asked me the same things, but I made a decision to plead ignorance. I didn't want Bethany's name dragged through the mud. It seemed impossible to me that she could have murdered anyone. She was a gentle soul. Misguided, maybe even lost. But not a vicious murderer. I was given the contents of her handbag when she died. When she died of pneumonia, I mean. Whatever she may have been carrying in the car crash would have been burnt beyond recognition.'

Nightingale looked through the zip-loc bag. There was an address book, which might or might not prove useful, a set of keys, including a BMW car key, and a few business cards, mostly from men with out of state contact numbers. And several gold visiting cards, with *Dreamgirls International* embossed in black. A phone number, and a website, but no address. 'Can I take these?' asked Nightingale, holding up the book and cards.

'Of course. Nobody knows I have them.'

'What about her car and mobile phone?''

'I have no knowledge of either. I had a phone number for her, but it just comes up unavailable now.'

'Hold on a minute. You said you'd heard about her from friends? Any names?'

'I spoke to several of her friends at her funeral, none of them had seen her for months. It seems she had cut almost all connections, Even Sarah, who had been her closest friend, had lost touch with her. Sarah was the only name the police could find in her address book.'

'Then you have her name, and address?'

'Yes. Sarah Williams. I have a number too, but only a work one. It was Sarah who reported her death, she'd apparently had a call from Bethany asking her to visit at her latest cheap apartment. She went round two days later and found her dead in bed.'

'Was it your doctor who certified her dead?'

'No, apparently Sarah found a card in her bag and called Bethany's own doctor. I don't remember the name, it'll be on the death certificate, I suppose. I can look for it and call you with the name.'

'Could be useful, who knows?'

'Do you think you can help me, Mr Nightingale? I'm not a rich man, but I'd be prepared to pay whatever I can.'

Nightingale shook his head. 'I work for Joshua Wainwright, and I doubt he'd take your money. As for whether I can help. All I can say is that I'll do the best I can.'

'God bless you.'

'See now, that's more your area than mine, but I have to say that I've never noticed Him trying to bless me.'

'It can happen whether you notice it or not. I wonder, would you care to see Bethany's tomb? It might give you an idea as to how her body disappeared.'

'Sure, that might help.'

'I'll drive you.'

CHAPTER 17

Cole drove them to the cemetery in a black Cadillac. 'Normally the cemetery is closed now, except to authorised tour groups,' said Cole. 'It was prey to vandals and muggers who attacked tourists. As a clergyman, and with a family tomb here, I have certain entry privileges.'

Cole parked and unlocked a black metal gate and they walked through a pillared entrance. 'People go on tours to cemeteries?' said Nightingale. 'Bit macabre, isn't it?'

'They're a very famous aspect of our city. Mark Twain called them 'Cities of the Dead', and suggested they were the only interesting architecture to be found in New Orleans.'

Nightingale had never seen anything like the cemetery. There were rows and rows of individual vaults and tombs, most of them old and sun-bleached, some chipped and crumbling. The more elaborate ones looked like miniature houses, even having their own iron railings round them, and were set out like streets. The walls were made up of smaller, individual vaults, stacked on top of each other, like drawers in a morgue.

'People are still buried here?' asked Nightingale.

'Oh yes, but not many. My family has had a vault here for decades. Just around this corner.'

The Cole family vault was a small and simple crypt, in white stone, with the family name carved on the front wall. It seemed far too small to have held more than one or two coffins.

'It's so small,' said Nightingale.

'Yes. By tradition, the body is left entombed for a year and a day, which, in the New Orleans climate, is generally long enough for decomposition to be completed. Then the remains are removed to the *caveau*, the space at the bottom of the tomb. The coffin is destroyed, and the tomb is ready for the next family member.'

'But that didn't happen in Bethany's case?'

'No, the tomb door was prised open, and her body removed. It seems to have happened on the night of the 31st, though it was only noticed on the 1st when a groundsman saw the damaged door.'

'Must have taken some force to move that door.'

'I don't know, I suspect it wasn't constructed to keep thieves out.'

The Reverend Cole bowed his head, and began to recite a prayer. Nightingale bowed his head too, out of respect for the man, rather than his God.

'So where is she now?' asked Nightingale.

'There was little left of her after the crash and fire, but her remains are once again inside the tomb. I could not face another funeral service for her, so she was interred with just some prayers from myself and my wife.'

Nightingale nodded, but couldn't think of anything to say. There were tears in Elijah Cole's eyes, and he wiped them away with his sleeve. 'Has it helped at all?'

'Not in the sense of offering me any clues,' said Nightingale, 'but at least I know how easy it would have been for a determined group of people.'

'Well,' said Cole, 'since you are here, you may as well see the most famous tomb of all.' He led the way down a few rows, then stopped in front of a squat, square grey tomb. 'This is the tomb of the Glapion family, and said to be the last resting place of Marie Laveau, whose husband was a Glapion.'

'The Witch Queen of New Orleans?'

'Exactly. Quite the place of pilgrimage for Voodoo believers. It used to be covered in graffiti crosses, left there by people who thought they could have their wishes granted, but they were cleaned away some years ago, and there are fines in place now for damaging the tomb.'

'People will believe anything if they're desperate, I suppose,' said Nightingale.

'Quite. She is New Orleans's most persistent legend.'

As they walked out, Nightingale's attention was drawn to an incongruous white pyramid, standing some nine feet tall, and obviously a very new addition. He looked at the name plate, but it just had a Latin inscription, *Omnia Ab Uno.* He shot a questioning glance at Elijah Cole, who grinned at him. 'Nicholas Cage's tomb.'

Nightingale frowned. 'He's an actor, isn't he? Or wasn't he?'

'Hah, he's not dead yet, he's just thinking ahead. Though he probably doesn't even remember he still owns it. The local citizens are none too pleased that he was allowed to have a plot here, but I guess money talks.'

'Mostly it shouts.'

'True enough. Now where can I drop you?'

'I'm fine here, I'll walk for a little while and take a taxi. I'll stay in touch and let you know if I find anything.'

As Cole climbed into the Cadillac and drove off, Nightingale lit a cigarette, pulled out his phone and called Wainwright, who listened in silence to the report of the meeting.

''So we now have two mysteries,' said Nightingale. 'Which end do I try pulling first?'

'Beats me, you're the hound dog. Who knows, maybe you'll find they're connected. It all seems to centre round deaths at the wrong time.'

'Same old same old,' said Nightingale. 'I just keep making a nuisance of myself, see who gets annoyed, and hope I duck before they shoot.'

'While you're waiting for the bullets to fly, maybe talk to that friend.'

'I'm on it.'

CHAPTER 18

Nightingale decided to talk to the only other mourner at Bethany's funeral, Sarah Williams. The lady hadn't offered Reverend Cole either her home address or phone number, but had told him she could be contacted through Brower, a leading aerospace design company in New Orleans. Through Google, Nightingale learned that Brower had quite a few important contracts with NASA, so he suspected that their security people wouldn't take too well to him showing up unannounced to try to talk to an employee who'd never heard of him. Instead he left a message with their switchboard, including his mobile phone number and name, and mentioning Reverend Cole.

It was only ten minutes before his phone rang, with an unfamiliar number on the display. 'That would be Jack Nightingale? Sarah Williams, you left a message.'

The voice was low, precise rather than warm, with an edge of suspicion.

'Thanks for getting back to me so quickly, Ms Williams,' said Nightingale. 'I was hoping to be able to talk to you sometime. I understand you were a close friend of Bethany Cole.'

'I *was*, though I'm afraid I hadn't seen her for a couple of months before she died. Why would you be interested?'

Nightingale decided to stick to as much of the truth as he could. 'I'm working for her brother, Elijah. I believe you met at her funeral. He hadn't heard from her in a while, and the circumstances of her death were pretty unusual, so he's asked me to look into it. So far you're the only friend I've managed to turn up.'

'Bethany wasn't the most sociable of people lately, and I don't know anyone who'd seen her in a while. How could I help?'

'Could we meet?'

'Sure. I don't usually tend to take lunch breaks, but I can see you after work. Where are you based?'

Nightingale gave her the name of his hotel.

'I know it. Meet you in the bar at seven. I've got auburn hair, I'm wearing a dark green suit today.'

'I'll have a rose between my teeth and be carrying a copy of Playboy.'

'Playboy has been digital only since 2020.'

'I did not know that. So just the rose, then.'

'See you at seven.'

She hung up before Nightingale had a chance to get any idea of what she might look like, but she clearly had no problem picking him out in the bar when she arrived ninety minutes later and strode right up to his table. The fact that he was the only single man in the bar might have given her a clue. She made no effort to shake hands, but raised a finger to the waiter and ordered a sparkling water before sitting down opposite him. 'Elijah Cole is a good man, and Bethany and I used to be close,' she said. 'So I want to help you in any way I can.'

'He mentioned you as maybe her best friend. What can you tell me about her?'

'You'd been here eight months ago, I would have said a lot. I thought I knew her back then, but it appears I was wrong.' She shrugged.

'How come you hadn't seen her in all that time?'

'She wasn't around to be seen. She quit her job, sub-let her apartment, called me to say she was going away for a while. The whole thing was a complete surprise. She never even dropped round to explain or say goodbye.'

'You were pretty close friends then?'

'A lot more than friends once,' she said, gazing over Nightingale's right shoulder, through the window behind him.

'When did things change?'

'A year or so ago. We'd met at Brower, but she left pretty soon after that, and went into the escort business.'

'She told you that?'

'She did. It was not a decision of which I approved, but it was her life, not my place to lecture her.'

'People have to make their own choices.'

'I'm not so sure it was entirely Bethany's choice after a while. At first she used to get excited about the glamour and the money, but after a while, she stopped talking about it altogether. That was around the time she stopped seeing me.'

'Did she give any reason?'

The waiter returned with her water and she sipped it. 'None directly. I sort of gained the impression she was into some kind of religion, she kept blowing me out because she had meetings, but wouldn't say what. Eventually I gave up the struggle. Next thing I knew, her brother contacted me, told me the date and time of her funeral.'

'And you went?'

'Sure, I went. She'd moved on from me, but you don't forget people, do you?'

'No, you don't. It's always there.' said Nightingale. 'Based on something her brother said, do you think she was using?'

Sarah Williams was silent for a moment, and again looked over Nightingale's shoulder. 'Not when I first knew her, not when she left Brower, but the last time I saw her, I remember thinking she looked strung-out. Or how I imagine that looks, it's not an area in which I'm an expert.'

Nightingale nodded. 'Her brother had the same suspicion.'

'About that, what does her brother want to find out? Bethany's dead, they said pneumonia.'

'Do you think it might have been an overdose?'

'Maybe, but what difference would it make? Either way, she's dead, poor kid.'

'Perhaps he just wants a few answers, wants to know if he could have done something.'

'The shrinks call it closure, don't they? It's a pretty thought that everything in life can be neatly parcelled up, tied with a bow and forgotten about. I don't think life works like that, things that affect you are never really over, are they?'

'Maybe not,' said Nightingale.

She finished her drink and stood up. 'I'm sorry I can't help you, or Elijah Cole. He's looking for answers that only Bethany would have, and they died with her.'

Nightingale watched her leave, wondering if he should have broached the subject of the car crash. It seemed obvious the news of it hadn't reached her. Maybe next time.

Nightingale sighed to himself. The time had come for his least favourite part of any case.

The police.

CHAPTER 19

Detective Matt Johnson was probably in his early thirties, and looked as if he kept himself in pretty good shape. His dark grey suit fitted him well, and the white shirt and blue tie were good quality. His eyes were small and dark, and darted suspicious glances at Nightingale as he sat in the chair on the other side of the desk from him. His desk was bare, apart from the neatly arranged filing baskets on the left, and an open blue folder in front of him. He had given no sign of enthusiasm or interest as Nightingale was shown into his office, certainly not enough to get up or offer a greeting. He ran his hand through his thinning brown hair, and studied his visitor for a minute before speaking. 'Front desk says you want to talk about the Delroy Lane case. What's your interest in him?'

'None at all really,' said Nightingale. 'I'm more interested in Bethany Cole.'

'The hooker?' said Johnson. 'What was she to you?'

'Nothing, but I've been asked to look into her death by her family. Her brother, in fact.'

'So what does her brother want to know? No mystery to it, a truck totalled the car she was riding in. Killed her, four other people in the car with her and another half-dozen or so in other cars. Not counting the truck driver, he was apparently dead before he hit them. Heart attack.'

'That much I know, but I understand she's a suspect in a murder case.'

'If she was still alive, she'd be a person of interest in the murders of Delroy Lane and Morgan Fletcher, known better as Spike.'

'What can you tell me about the murders?' asked Nightingale.

Johnson almost completely closed his eyes, as if he were concentrating on projecting ill-will. 'You have our roles all wrong,' he said. 'I'm a police detective, my job's to gather information, not give it out to anyone who cares to ask. I don't need to tell you anything about the murders. They have nothing to do with her dying, unless you figure Delroy's ghost frightened the truck driver to death.' Johnson smiled at his own weak joke.

'Doesn't seem likely, does it?' said Nightingale. 'Her brother just wants to know how come she got mixed up in this murder thing. He knew she was an escort, but she was no killer.'

'Escort?' repeated Johnson, dragging the word out as long as he could. 'I don't think so, she was with Tyrell Biggs, and he didn't used to deal with escorts. Chicken ranch whores one step away from an overdose and the morgue. And talking of the morgue…'

Nightingale waited to see if Johnson would finish the sentence, but it seemed he was waiting for a prompt.

'What about it,' he said finally.

'Well, there's the thing,' said Johnson. 'Once we start to dig a little deeper into this Cole girl, we find she's already been reported dead once before, few weeks ago.'

'So how could that happen?' asked Nightingale.'

'Pretty obvious that it can't,' said Johnson. 'If she died in that wreck, which she did, she didn't die two weeks before. So either she faked the whole thing, or someone misidentified a body as hers. Trouble is we can't check on that. Since, whoever died, there's no body there now.'

'Someone stole the body?'

'Cemetery vaults don't usually come with security details. Around here, the body is left in its casket for a year and a day inside the tomb. After that, they remove the casket, and leave the body inside. Temperature gets up to two hundred and fifty inside those vaults on a good day, so soon there's not much left but ashes. But somebody saved the sun the trouble. Casket was empty when we looked.'

'So what are you doing about it?' said Nightingale.

Johnson deepened his natural scowl. 'Now there you go again, asking questions you ain't entitled to. I smell cop about you, you used to be one in England?'

'In another life,' said Nightingale.

'But not any more,' said Johnson. 'Remember that. You licensed as a PI by the state of Louisiana? Or any other state?'

'No,' said Nightingale. 'I've just been asked to look into it by the family, as I said.'

'Yeah, well my sympathies to the family on their loss, but it gives them no special rights. You either. In which case we don't have much to talk about, do we? Girl died in a car crash, that's all they need to know.'

'Maybe I could help?' said Nightingale.

'What kind of help you think some English ex-cop going to be round here? Mister, I think you seen too many movies, where the cops call in amateurs to do their job for them. Nobody who knew Delroy is going to be seen with you, let alone open his heart to you. Trust me, we're not going to be buddies on this. Looks like the girl and her friends hit Delroy and Spike, but they won't be telling us who sent them, nor will the Biggs brothers, so we got nobody to ask. Case closed. Close the door on your way out.'

It seemed pointless for Nightingale to try any further, so he got up to leave. With his hand on the door, he tried a long shot. 'Who's in charge of the Cameron Lattimore case?'

Johnson's mouth gaped open.

'What Lattimore case? There isn't one. Guy died of cancer. Sheesh, some detective you are.'

'Seems I was misinformed.'

He left as instructed. Two minutes later, Johnson opened his office door again and walked out through the detectives room.

'I'm going across the way for a decent coffee, boys,' he announced to anyone who cared to listen.

He did indeed buy a coffee, but the phone call he placed was of far more importance.

CHAPTER 20

Nightingale phoned Wainwright as he walked away from the station house. 'Joshua, I'm going to need some help in this town, there's way too much legwork for one guy who doesn't know his way around.'

'I'm not sure who we've got locally, Jack. I'll get Valerie to send you a name when she's looked through the records. Whoever it is won't know anything about my...special interests, and I'd like it to stay that way. You can mention my name though.'

Nightingale chuckled. 'Chances are they'd never believe me anyway.'

Twenty minutes later, Nightingale's phone buzzed with a WhatsApp message, It said simply 'CHRIS DUBOIS' followed by a mobile phone number. Valerie, Wainwright's assistant was supremely efficient, but she never wasted words or friendliness on Nightingale. He called the number. A deep female voice answered. 'Yes?'

'My name's Jack Nightingale. Joshua Wainwright suggested I call and speak to Chris Dubois.'

'That would be me.'

Nightingale wondered if Valerie had deliberately tried to wrong foot him by just using the 'Chris'. 'I need some help with a case, Mr Wainwright said you might be able to provide a little local knowledge and insight.'

'Mr Wainwright's office called before you did, and has retained my services for as long as you need them. What can I do for you, Mr Nightingale?'

'Can I come round?'

'I prefer not to conduct business at my home and I don't maintain an office, so let's combine it with some food, Dave's Grill on Bourbon Street at seven. You know it?'

'I'll find it.'

'Any taxi driver will know Dave's Grill. How will I recognise you?'

'Dark hair, light raincoat and a boyish smile.'

'Leave it at home,' she said. 'You won't be needing it, I'm immune.'

She hung up before Nightingale had a chance to get any idea of what she might look like.

Stunning, as it turned out. She was over six feet tall in her heeled boots, slim and elegantly dressed in black pants and jacket over a high necked red shirt. Her skin was the colour of milk-chocolate with red blusher highlighting her high cheekbones, and matching red eye-shadow. The jet black hair was short and razor-cut. Nightingale was reminded of Grace Jones in an old Bond movie, but there seemed nothing 1980s about this lady. She walked straight over to the table where he sat nursing a Corona, nodded at him and sat opposite. She made no attempt to shake hands or smile, but smiled at a passing waitress and ordered a tomato juice.

'So, you're Jack Nightingale?'

'Guilty as charged.'

'I'm guessing from your accent you're not from around these parts. England?'

'Manchester.'

'I was near there a few years ago for a conference. Mostly it rained.'

'Mostly it does,' said Nightingale.

'I need to eat. If you're new in town, you'll be wanting to try the shrimp Po'Boy.'

Nightingale raised his eyebrows in a question.

'It's a fried shrimp sandwich, basically,' she said.

'Sounds good.'

The waitress returned with the tomato juice, and Dubois ordered two Po'Boys.

'Strange name,' said Nightingale.

'Apparently goes back to a Streetcar strike in the 1920s. The public gave sandwiches to the 'poor boys' who were striking, and the name stuck.'

'You should be a tourist guide.'

'I've had friends visit from other cities who wanted to find out a little of the history of the place, so I've picked things up. I guess it's not your field of interest.'

'Not exactly.'

'So,' she said, 'let's get to it.'

'First why not tell me a little bit about you, all I know about you is your name.'

'That's pretty much all you need to know. Still, for background, I run a detective agency. Inherited from my father, also called Chris, but he was Christophe. He left it to me when he died of cancer three years ago. Well, he left it to the two of us really, but my sister is way too busy modelling to get involved. I handle all the usual dull stuff. Process serving, divorce surveillance, missing persons, industrial security, insurance injury claims, plus the occasional gig for Mr Wainwright.'

'Such as?'

She flashed him a tight smile. 'He said to offer you whatever help you needed, he didn't mention gossiping about his confidential affairs.'

'Sorry, forget the question. How's business?'

'Steady, but I don't need to rely on it. I do a fair amount of work designing and maintaining websites, which brings in a lot more money. Now, what do you need, Mr Nightingale?'

'I need to find out how a young girl managed to die twice inside three weeks.'

He was expecting a reaction, but Chris Dubois just stared straight ahead. Waiting for him to continue.

He gave her the story that Elijah Cole had told him, as near verbatim as he could recall. Then he waited.

A minute passed, before she said anything.

'Okay, people only die once, so there are a couple of obvious possibilities. One, she didn't actually die the first time, which seems pretty unlikely. Two, there were two different girls, and one or other of them was misidentified as Bethany Cole.'

'Logical, but it seems not. The girl was certified dead by a doctor, then placed in a tomb. Her brother identified her, there was no mistake.'

'And the second time?'

'She was identified by fingerprints and DNA at the crash scene.'

'And the cops had them why?'

'She'd been arrested twice for soliciting.'

'Curiouser and curiouser. You have a theory?'

'Not one that makes sense. I'd like to talk to some people who knew her.'

'You talked to her brother already?'

'They'd been out of touch for a while, her career choice took her down a different path from him.'

'Friends?'

'He didn't know any. Well, just one, and she wasn't much help.'

'Pimp?'

'She worked for an agency. He found these in her handbag.'

Nightingale handed over the 'Dreamgirl International' cards. Chris Dubois looked at them and nodded. 'You tried calling this number?'

'Yes. A guy answered and asked for my password. When he realised I didn't have it, he hung up.'

'Not surprising, confidentiality is pretty important in that kind of business. Prostitution is rather illegal in Louisiana.'

'No doubt, but it leaves me at a dead end. Cops can't help, or won't, but I suspect they have nothing to go on.'

'You talked to them?'

'One, a detective named Matt Johnson. I don't think we're going to be friends.'

'You show him these cards?'

'Do you know, I don't think I did.'

'No doubt you had a reason.'

The food arrived, neatly saving Nightingale from thinking of a suitable response, and they ate in silence for a while. New Orleans's trademark spicy shrimp sandwich seemed good enough to Nightingale, who was no gourmet, and frequently forgot to eat at all. Chris Dubois pushed aside the last third of hers and waved away the waitress's offer of dessert. Nightingale shook his head too, but ordered coffee.

'Maybe I can help with *Dreamgirl*. Even though they won't welcome passing trade, they have to get the word out somehow about their services.'

'I tried Google.'

'I doubt they'd advertise that plainly. What do you know about the Dark Web?'

'Sounds like a heavy metal band,' he said. 'Joke.'

'Don't quit your day job,' she sneered. 'I'll take that to mean you know nothing.'

'Not much, it sounds nasty.'

'It can be, it's a place where you find a lot of things that maybe shouldn't be found. Drugs. Weapons. Sex.'

'And you're a tourist guide for that too?'

'Hardly, but on occasions I've needed to find my way down there. Give me some time and I'll see if I can come up with anything on Bethany Cole or *Dreamgirl International*. Shouldn't be that hard. It's not a place I care to spend my time, but I know where to find it. Maybe I could find what's left of Bethany down there.'

Nightingale frowned. 'What do you mean?'

She looked around. Dave's Grill was getting quite busy, and the noise level was making it harder for them to hear each other without raising their voices.

'Let's go somewhere a little quieter,' she said. 'This place fills up early, we could try Jill's Lounge, that fills up late.'

He followed her down a couple of side streets and into a bar where there were only another eight or nine customers. All women, Nightingale noticed. It made no difference to him, and nobody gave him a second look. She waved him to a booth at the back.

'You plan on driving tonight?' she asked.

Nightingale shook his head. 'No, I'll get a cab back to my hotel.'

'Why not try a Sazarac then, the official cocktail of New Orleans.'

'When in Rome…'

The two drinks arrived, She took a sip, nodded approvingly, then watched as Nightingale tried his.

'Strong,' he said. 'Very strong. What's in it?'

'Rye, absinthe, sugar and bitters. I suggest you take it slowly and stop at one.'

'Ah, absinthe makes the heart grow fonder.'

'Say what now?'

'It's a joke.'

'Ah. Okay.'

'So, what do you know about Voodoo, Ms Dubois?'

The question came out of nowhere, but didn't seem to phase her. 'Not so much, probably much the same as the average tourist. My background isn't from Africa. My father's family were French, my mother's Choctaw. It's an interesting blend, but no African magic in there. Why do you ask?'

'I'm told that Voodoo has legends about people living on after they've died. Bethany's brother mentioned it.'

'That's odd for a priest. You don't really think I should be spending my time chasing zombies, do you? Whatever the explanation is, I doubt that will be it. What is it you and her brother expect to find out? And what can you do about it anyway?'

'I really don't know,' said Nightingale. 'I think her brother just wants some kind of explanation, some sort of closure.'

'No such thing. You never close the door on people you love. The wound's always there. Maybe you just learn not to pick at it so often.'

'Maybe. Let's get back to what you said about finding what's left of her on the Dark Web. What did you mean?'

'If she was hooking, she'll have needed Johns, needed them to be able to contact her, either in person, or via this Dreamgirl thing. There'll be traces of that around.'

'What if she wasn't using her real name?'

'You have a photo of her?'

Nightingale handed over the photos that Elijah Cole had given him. Chris Dubois pulled out her phone from her handbag and took shots of each one.

'Now I can search with photo recognition programs. Chances are she wasn't using her real name for professional purposes. And I'll do my best to find *Dreamgirl*.'

'Wouldn't whoever have deleted it all when she was killed?'

'Nothing ever really disappears on the internet. Not if you know how to bring it back. You have a card?'

'A credit card? Sure.'

'A business card. With your phone number.'

'No. Sorry.'

She handed him her phone. 'Tap in your number so that I have it,' she said. 'Once he'd finished she took back her phone and stood up. She put a twenty dollar bill on the table.

'Drinks are on me. I'll be in touch. Soon. Don't walk home from here. It's not the best of areas.'

CHAPTER 21

Nightingale woke up, blinked his eyes open as he felt water drop on his head, then stared around him in disbelief. He was fully dressed, including his raincoat and Hush Puppies, and standing on a windswept cliff, covered in rough grass, with bare white stone at the edge. He looked down at waves crashing against grey rocks, a hundred feet down and instinctively he stepped backwards, to put more distance between himself and the cliff edge. He was dreaming, obviously, but he couldn't help feeling that he'd been here before, though maybe not in this life. He closed his eyes tight, concentrated on being awake and back in his hotel room, but when he opened them again he was still gazing out on the wildness of the sea, while overhead dark storm clouds were gathered, and light rain was falling.

Where was this place? When had he been here before? In this life, or another?

Could he have been summoned to the astral plane? If so, it hadn't looked like this any other time, and there was nobody waiting for him. He tried another system for waking himself, which had worked in the past. He closed his eyes again focused all his attention on the big toe of his right foot, and started to wiggle it. After a minute, he gave up, and opened his eyes again. No change.

There was a loud crack, which seemed to come from all directions at once, and an appalling, screaming roar from behind him sent his heart racing, propelled him several feet forward, and dangerously close to the cliff edge. He spun round, half knowing what he would see, but still terrified.

The creature was impossibly huge, covered in dark scales, larger than any dinosaur Nightingale might ever have imagined. Its narrow, red, reptilian eyes glared hatred at him, as its giant leathery wings flapped furiously. The stench when it roared was so overpowering that Nightingale's head started to swim, and the pointed snout and jagged teeth lost focus in front of him.

Nightingale made a huge effort, shook his head, straightened up and forced himself to smile.

'I know who you are,' he said. 'And now I remember where I am. This is the Nowhen, time and place have no meaning, and you can't hurt me here.'

The creature opened its mouth, screamed in rage, and a sheet of flame shot out, passing so close to Nightingale's head that he felt his hair scorch. A massive, scaled claw shot out, and slashed across his stomach, and he felt the blood start to pump out of the wound.

'Oh shit,' he said, 'looks like I guessed wrong.'

He sank to his knees as blood poured from the gaping wound. Behind him was the cliff edge, and a hundred-foot drop to certain death. He closed his eyes, started a silent prayer, and waited for the inevitable.

There was another deafening crack, the awful roaring and heat were gone, the foul stench disappeared, and there was a moment of silence.

'Get up, you fool,' said a petulant high-pitched voice.

Nightingale stayed where he was, his hands pressed firmly against the gaping wound in his stomach, blood pumping through his fingers. He opened his eyes and looked down at the grass. 'I can't,' he said, I'm too busy dying.'

'Meh. Always the weak humour.'

Nightingale saw the end of a riding crop slash across his stomach, and in a flash the pain, the blood and the wound were gone.

'Now get up, and pay attention to me.'

Nightingale stood up, and raised his gaze from the ground, well aware of what he would see, but still terrified by the thought. There he stood, three feet high, the large head topped by curly black hair, the eyes blood-red, the childlike face twisted into a malevolent sneer. The body was thick, and perched on tiny bow legs. The jacket was sky-blue this time, still with the gold buttons and epaulettes, and he wore the same black jodhpurs and shiny black boots which always put Nightingale in mind of a toy soldier. The dwarf held the riding crop in his tiny right hand, and slapped it impatiently into his left palm.

'Lucifuge Rofocale,' said Nightingale.

The dwarf gave a vicious leer. 'In person. Or one of my many persons. Would you prefer another?'

'No, I'm good with this one. First you almost kill me, then you fix me. Why?'

The dwarf gave a long laugh, which held absolutely no humour. ''Because I can. Think of it as a lesson Nightingale. A lesson to disregard appearances. And there may come a time when it will serve as a useful reminder.'

'But this is the Nowhen. Nothing can happen here. You couldn't hurt me last time.'

Another evil laugh, even longer. 'Fool. This is where I want it to be Nightingale. I chose this backdrop, but you may have another if you wish. Welcome to Hell.'

The cliff and the sea were gone, and Nightingale stood on volcanic rock, inside a twenty-foot high circle of flame. He tried to hide from the appalling heat, but he was already in the middle of the circle. The smell of burning flesh and sulphur was intolerable, but the roaring of the flames was drowned out by the most appalling cacophony of tortured screams and anguished shouting. Nightingale pressed his hands against his ears, but nothing could keep out that awful noise.

The dwarf walked through the flames as if they didn't exist, and his voice was clear above the noise.

'You prefer this setting, Nightingale?

Nightingale looked him squarely in his evil red eyes. 'Why don't we stop with all the special effects, and you can tell me what you want?'

'Maybe I just want you to suffer, Nightingale?'

'Nah, there are rules to this. I would be dead now if that's what you wanted. Let's talk.'

The flames and the awful noise were gone, and the two stood in a wood-panelled office, looking for all the world as if it had been borrowed from a 1950s bank manager who had just popped out to see a customer. Lucifuge Rofocale walked behind the heavy oak desk and climbed up into the high leather chair that stood behind it.

'Sit,' he commanded.

Nightingale sat in the smaller leather chair opposite him and patted his pockets. 'I don't suppose…' he said.

The dwarf gestured with his riding crop, and a lit cigarette appeared between the first and second fingers of Nightingale's right hand. He took a deep drag, and his face twisted in disgust. 'It's menthol,' he said.

The dwarf gave another evil grin. 'Sorry, Nightingale, this is Hell, it's all we have.'

'Did somebody once tell you you were funny?'

'Never once, Nightingale. They are generally too busy screaming and begging for mercy.'

'Let's get to it. What do you want? I have no idea where this is, or how you got me here, but I know it wasn't just to show me your CGI skills and make cheap jokes.'

'My word, Nightingale, you are arrogant, even by the standards of your species. You have no idea of the power I wield, or the danger you put yourself in. Such ignorance and folly.'

Nightingale tried to keep his face a blank. Actually he was well aware that the dwarf could blast him out of existence with a twitch of his finger, and he was terrified, but no good could come of showing that. He forced his breathing into a steady rhythm before trying to speak again. 'We both know you can't have my soul, and if you just wanted me dead, I would be dead. You once swore to make the rest of my life a complete misery, is this the next instalment?'

Lucifuge Rofocale slapped his riding crop on the desktop. 'Happily for you, it is not. You seem to be a uniquely fortunate man, so far, Nightingale. Twice has your soul been pledged, yet still you possess it. Twice was your sister's soul pledged, yet she died with it intact.'

'Bastard,' said Nightingale. 'You killed her.'

'A price was demanded, and she paid it. She is of no importance. It seems you owe four souls, Nightingale. To me, Proserpine, Frimost and Sugart. Four Princes of Hell have cause to revenge themselves on you, yet still you live.'

'So far and not for want of trying by you, in New York and Tennessee.'

'My time will come. Or has come. I forget, for your kind time is linear.'

'Let's not get into that. What do you want, and why should I do it?'

The dwarf opened a small box on his desk, took out a pinch of snuff, and took a sniff up each nostril.

'I'm guessing that's not menthol,' said Nightingale. Lucifuge gave another malevolent grin.

'*Noblesse oblige,*' he said. 'I have a task for you Nightingale, an important task.'

Nightingale shook his head. 'Just had a quick think, and I don't seem to remember owing you any favours. Quite the reverse.'

Lucifuge pursed his bloodless lips. 'Perhaps you will wish to perform it. Perhaps we can come to terms.'

'And exactly why would I trust you?'

'Have you ever known one of my kind to break a pact?'

Nightingale absent-mindedly took another drag on his cigarette, then threw it to the floor, as he took a mouthful of peppermint. 'I've never known one of you actually to welch on a deal, but you're very good at finding loopholes for yourselves.'

'You people never read the small print,' sneered Lucifuge.

'So what are you offering?' asked Nightingale.

'You have seen what I can do, once before.'

'You mean reset time for me?'

'Indeed, I could take you back to a time before the Order Of The Nine Angles were aware of you, where your family and friends still lived, where your so pretty secretary still wanted to…'

'Move on,' snapped Nightingale.

'Where your appearance in London would not have you arrested for murder, where…'

'Okay, I get the picture. Last time it happened, things just started repeating themselves, people ended up dead again, just the same as before. I had to leave the country.'

Lucifuge shrugged his shoulders. 'I can reset time for you, I cannot guarantee the future. But perhaps you will be able to change it this time, make better decisions.'

'It's tempting. But not tempting enough to sell my soul for.'

'Your soul is not required on this occasion.'

Nightingale shuddered at the emphasis laid on the last three words. 'So tell me about it, I'm guessing that whatever you want, it's not going to be easy.'

The dwarf was silent, steepled his chubby, spatulate fingers together and fixed his fiery eyes on Nightingale. No human could have met that gaze, so Nightingale looked away, and looked round the office, trying to affect a casualness he certainly didn't feel.

Lucifuge slapped one hand on the desk to recall Nightingale's attention. 'So Nightingale,' he said, 'what do you think of Hell?'

Nightingale grinned at him. 'You're playing games, aren't you? None of this is real, you've set it all up just for me, all the things I hate most. I'm guessing if I wanted something to eat and drink, it would be liver and warm bitter. I didn't know you guys did party tricks. My guess is you're just trying to keep me off guard.'

Lucifuge gave a cruel smile. 'Of course, a mere illusion, plucked from your own memories. You see what you imagine. A simple parlour trick, but necessary. I cannot ascend to your world unsummoned, so it was necessary to bring you to mine, but if you were to see the reality of Hell, you would be a screaming imbecile by now. Amusing as that might be for me, now is not the time.'

'But I can't really be here physically. It must be like ascending to the astral plane, where my essence leaves my body.'

The dwarf shrugged. 'Rationalise it as you wish, but here you are, and here you stay until I choose to dismiss you.'

'No. I'm pretty sure that's against the rules too. If I'm really in Hell, then it's not a holding cell. My soul is my own, and you can't have it, or me.'

'I should be very careful when telling a Prince of Hell what he can and cannot do, Nightingale. You understand not the millionth part of my world.'

'Allegedly. You really can't stop with the threats, can you? I think you're actually avoiding telling me why I'm here. Not sure of your decision?'

The dwarf's face twisted in fury, and he slapped his riding crop on the desk top. 'How dare…' Lucifuge broke off, and the anger in his face ebbed away. He shrugged. 'Perhaps you are correct. What I propose involves a huge step for one of my kind, but I see no remedy for it. The situation has become most worrying, and steps must be taken. But they must be taken in your world, a world to which I have no access.'

'You're still not getting to it,' said Nightingale. 'Tell me, and how about a real cigarette while you do.'

The dwarf nodded, a lit Marlboro appeared, or seemed to appear, between Nightingale's fingers, and he leaned back to listen to Lucifuge's problem.

'You are aware, of course, of the organisation which calls itself the Order Of The Nine Angles. It is a widespread group, though its origins are not as ancient as some of its members would wish to believe.'

'Of course I know about it, they pretty much chased me out of London. I've often wondered why the American branch has never come after me.'

'A simple answer. The group has no central structure, it exists as a series of cells, which they call nexions. Associates of a cell may know others in the cell, but they have no knowledge at all, and no communication with other associates in other nexions. The only one with such knowledge would be the one to whom they all pledge allegiance.'

'Your friend Proserpine.'

'Indeed, though she is no friend to me. She to whom your soul was first pledged, and who still intends to recover it, and see you damned for all eternity.'

'She's not so bad,' said Nightingale. 'She saved me from you at least twice.'

The dwarf threw back his head and roared with laughter. 'Oh, you poor fool. How little you understand. In New York, her plans ran counter to mine, and I was foolish enough to have put myself in the wrong, so she was able to thwart me. As for that fool in Tennessee, I kept my pact, and gave him the power he craved. Since he was a fool, he had no idea that such power could not long dwell inside a human, Proserpine was merely the instrument sent to complete his destruction. On both occasions, your survival was but a by-product of the situation. You believe she has your best interests at heart? Hilarious.'

'Well, that's not the way I saw it,' said Nightingale, 'and I'd trust her a lot further than you.'

Again came the laughter, this time with a cruel, mocking edge to it. 'Imbecile. You would *trust* one who has done you so much damage? Where is your home, where are your parents, your aunt and uncle, your best friend? All dead at her behest, and many others too, who merely crossed your path. Had you not offered something she wanted more, she would have taken your soul and blasted you to Hell, with no more thought than you would spare a crushed ant beneath your shoe. Trust? Bah.'

'Well, there is that,' said Nightingale. 'So, anyway, what about the Nine Angles?'

The dwarf fixed his red eyes on Nightingale, and continued quietly. 'It seems that a group of them are moving to seek great power. Power which is not to be gained by your kind. And it may be that one of my kind is instrumental in granting them this power.'

'You mean Proserpine?'

Lucifuge nodded. 'She would seem the most likely. But I cannot be sure. I am able to sense things in your world, but I see them through a haze, It may be another who is offering them what must not be offered.'

'I only know of one thing that a demon can't offer in exchange for a soul.'

'That is what is now being offered. Immortality.'

'But if it's against the rules…'

'Rules, Nightingale? Princes of Hell are not renowned for their acceptance of authority, nor their adherence to rules. They are The Fallen, it is why they are here. Yet, usually fear of the consequences keep them in check. This time, it seems, the lust for power is stronger.'

'But what can they gain, by lengthening people's lives?'

'More time for their Earthly influence to grow. More time for plans to mature. More time to bring about what they wish. But be assured, this will represent a serious threat to the correct way of things.'

'To The Balance?'

'Use that term if it helps you towards some faint gleam of comprehension.'

'You know, someone who wants a favour might just be a little more polite.'

Lucifuge narrowed his eyes, and the hatred shone through them. 'I do not ask for favours. I offer a pact. On this occasion you could be useful to me, but do not delude yourself that our account will ever be settled until I have your soul and you are screaming in Hell. Find this demon who is offering immortality, stop them, and I shall reset time for you as you require. What say you, do we have a deal?'

'You make it all sound so simple. But I wouldn't know where to start looking.'

'Of course you do, you are already there.'

'Good to know. And what am I supposed to do if I find this demon? Call Ghostbusters?'

The dwarf gave a sly smile. 'No, you call me. So, now we are moving on to details. We have a deal?'

'Maybe. What happens if I don't manage to track down the demon?'

'You will probably be dead, since the creature and its followers will assuredly become aware of your interest. They probably already are. We have a deal?'

'Why not?' said Nightingale. 'What do I have to lose, I'm already marked down for death.'

The dwarf smiled, and leaned back in his chair. 'Good. Now, listen to me, carefully.'

CHAPTER 22

Nightingale woke up, terrified and shivering, too frightened even to open his eyes. He moved his hands and feet, felt soft, cotton sheets, and the weight of the blankets on his body. He eased one eye open, and saw the sun coming through the thin inner drapes of the hotel bedroom. He opened the other eye, and looked around at the comforting reality of the generic hotel furniture, and its palette of dull, neutral colours. He had never felt so pleased to see such typical anonymity. He needed a cigarette so took one from his pack and flicked his lighter at it. The smoke from the Marlboro felt as good as any he'd ever tasted, another piece of welcome familiarity to anchor him back in reality.

He lifted his legs onto the floor, then stopped dead, wincing at a stab of pain in his stomach. He swore under his breath and looked down at his stomach, dreading what he knew he would see,

There it was, a fine line of slightly paler skin, the width of a knife blade, or maybe a claw, running from one hip to another. He ran his fingers along it, pressing tentatively, but there was no pain now, just the thin mark, which seemed to be fading almost as he watched it.

He reached for his cellphone and pressed the only number in its contacts memory.

Wainwright answered immediately. 'Jack. What can I do for you?'

'Exactly how much do you know about the Order Of The Nine Angles?'

'I know you faked your own death to avoid them and they chased you out of England.'

'But beyond that? Ever heard of them operating over here?'

'Only rumours that they go right to the top, and, of course, the acolytes you came across in Memphis. Why? What have you heard?'

'I got what you might call a tip-off,' said Nightingale. 'Maybe they might have something to do with what we discussed.'

'Tip-off from who?'

Nightingale took a drag on his latest cigarette while he made a decision. He'd learned from harsh experience that demons weren't too keen on having their names mentioned. 'Believe me, you don't want to know,' he said.

'Someone you trust?'

'I really wouldn't go that far. Or anywhere near it. But it might tie in. You know anyone who might be better informed?'

'Not me,' said Wainwright. 'But, I'm guessing that if it's happening in the Big Easy, it'll be tied in with Voodoo. Most things are.'

'And that's an area you do know about?'

'Well, some. I've spent some time in Haiti, but a lot of what happens in New Orleans goes back further than that, all the way to Africa.'

'You have nobody on the ground out here who could give me more information? Ideally I'd like to talk to a coroner?'

CHAPTER 23

Doctor Sheila Townsend looked to be about fifty years old, was slightly overweight and wore thick-rimmed black glasses and had her grey hair tied up in a bun. Not at all like the last pathologist Nightingale had seen on US television, who had been a six-foot tall black woman in her twenties, dressed in mini-skirt, stilettos and a tight black vest top. Dr Townsend seemed more realistic on all fronts, though Hollywood might not be queueing up to use her. Her office was small, her desk covered with folders and two computer screens, the shelves crammed with books. 'Have a seat Mr Nightingale. Mr Wainwright asked me to see you, and to answer any reasonable questions you might have.'

'You know Joshua?'

'I met him once, in Brownsville, Texas, where I was attending the opening of their new hospital, which, I believe he helped to fund. He has, since then, and for no apparent reason, kept in touch via occasional emails, and some substantial donations to my department. My gratitude to him got you this appointment, and also got me to access the files of the other two cases.'

'Other two?'

'I performed the autopsies on Cameron Lattimore and Alejandro Gonzalez myself. The other two deaths occurred outside my jurisdiction. An autopsy finding is a matter of public record, so there will be no problem in answering questions on them, I was not, of course, their physician in life, so I will be unable to answer questions about their medical history.'

Nightingale nodded. 'I understand.'

Dr Townsend patted the pocket of her white coat, and Nightingale wondered if she might be another frustrated smoker. No point pursuing it, since the regulations in a hospital would be draconian. She looked over his shoulder at the clock on the far wall, and he took the hint. She was clearly busy.

'First, is there no possibility of any error in the findings?'

She pursed her lips. 'I'll pass over the slur on my competence, and that of my colleagues, and give you the layman's answer. None at all. Cameron Lattimore's prostate was hugely enlarged, the cancer spread to his bones, liver, pancreas, lungs and brain and killed him. Alejandro Gonzalez had multiple tumours in both lungs, which had also metastasised to other organs, but he died of lung failure. According to the reports from my colleagues, Trevon Clark's brain had all the classic signs of Parkinson's disease, and Tiffany Davies's brain showed every standard symptom of advanced Alzheimer's disease. If I had time, I could go into more detail, but I doubt you would understand the technical language. Long story short, there is no doubt at all about what killed these four young people. Of course…'

She broke off and shrugged, but Nightingale said nothing.

'Of course, maybe the reason you are here, is that these are very unusual things for young people to die of.'

'How unusual?'

'Well, the youngest recorded death from prostate cancer was at seventeen, but it is more usually a disease of men over fifty, and especially later. Your medical practitioner, no doubt, examines yours as a precaution at your routine check-ups.'

Nightingale shuffled uncomfortably in his seat. His last visit to a doctor had been for his annual Metropolitan Police medical, many years before, and he had no desire to repeat the experience. Dr Townsend continued. 'Lung cancer can strike at any age, but in younger people there are usually aggravating factors, heavy smoking, working with dangerous materials, and apparently Senor Gonzalez had neither of those. As for Parkinson's, its likelihood also increases with age, though younger people may suffer from it, you may be aware of Michael J Fox, the actor?'

Nightingale nodded. 'He was only in his thirties when diagnosed?'

'Correct. But Alzheimer's is almost exclusively a disease of the elderly, though, again, the youngest reported death was at twenty-two.'

'So it's very unusual for four people in one city to die of those four diseases within six weeks of each other?'

'I doubt that anyone has ever collated any data on it, since the diseases have no common cause, but I would have said that it is probably unusual.'

'You're very careful in your choice of words, Doctor.'

'I'm a scientist, Mr Nightingale, I deal in facts.'

'Another thing, in your opinion, would all of these diseases have been spotted at a thorough physical exam?'

She took a sip from a bottle of water on her desk.

'Undoubtedly. I doubt any competent physician would have missed the signs of the prostate problem, a simple chest X-ray would have revealed advanced lung cancer, and advanced Parkinson's and Alzheimer's would not have been difficult to diagnose.'

Nightingale nodded again. 'But all four of those people had very thorough physical exams in the two weeks before they died, after coming back from injuries. I don't know about the Baby Cakes minor league team, but wouldn't the Saints, the Pelicans and the LTA have outstanding medical teams?'

'I don't know any of them personally, I would have no reason to doubt their medical competence.'

'So, if four separate medical teams found nothing, then let's assume there was nothing to find.'

'As I said, I tend to work with facts and avoid assumptions.'

'Fair enough. Another question then. If these people were all perfectly healthy two weeks before they died, what are the chances that these diseases could appear from nowhere, spread rapidly, and kill them inside that time?'

She shrugged. 'You would need to ask a specialist in each disease.'

'Okay, but humour me and take an educated guess. Please.'

'Very well. I would say that the odds are vanishingly small. As near zero as makes no difference.'

'So how did they contract them?'

'One doesn't contract them in the sense you mean. These diseases are caused by the body's systems breaking down. With the exception of lung cancer, as I mentioned before, I know of no external agent which can cause any of these diseases. It's not like injecting someone with a smallpox or polio toxin.'

'So how do you explain it?'

'I don't, Mr Nightingale. It's not my job to explain why people die, it's my job to find out what they died of. I have done that. A pathologist in real life is not like Quincy or Kay Scarpetta, rushing round solving crimes. We just describe what we find. And there was no crime here. These people died natural, if very unusual, deaths. If you need to know why, I guess that's a question for God.'

'Or the Devil,' said Nightingale.

'She flashed him a tight smile. 'Well, you'll have to excuse me, I have yet another appointment with a dead body. Here's my card, should you have any more questions, but I doubt I'll have the answers.'

She passed over a business card. Nightingale thanked her and left.

CHAPTER 24

Nightingale wasn't at all proud of what he was about to do, but couldn't see any other way round the problem. He needed information, and there seemed only one place he might get it. The tennis star and the basketball player would have had an entourage of people keen to discourage access to them, which left the minor-league baseball player. Nightingale had memorised the address from the autopsy record, and so arrived outside the Gonzalez home an hour or so later.

He parked and looked over at the house. The Gonzalez home was a far cry from the Lattimore mansion. Nightingale assumed that minor-league baseball was nowhere near as well rewarded as the NFL. The little brick bungalow was clean, and the front garden well-tended.

The door was opened by a dumpy woman of around sixty, in a green and yellow nylon housecoat, an apron over the top. Her black hair was covered with a net and she held a polishing cloth in one hand.

'Mrs Gonzalez?' asked Nightingale.

'*No, soy yo la cria.*'

'Sorry, do you speak English?'

'*Inglés, no. No hablas espanol?*'

Nightingale had picked up precisely no Spanish in his time in the USA, with the exception of the words for the more popular folding systems for Mexican food. 'I don't speak Spanish,' he said. 'Mrs Gonzalez?'

'*Quién es, Anna?*' came a voice from behind the woman.

'*No sé senora, el no habla espanol.*'

'*Vale, sigua con la cocina. Arreglaré yo todo.*'

The first woman stepped aside, to be replaced by another, around fifteen years younger, with light brown hair, her eyes hidden by heavy dark glasses. She wore a black jacket over a black knee-length dress. She wore heavy make-up, but there were cracks near the eyes, where she might have been crying. She looked at Nightingale, but didn't favour him with a smile from her reddened lips. 'Can I help you?' she said, though her tone of voice was more irritated than helpful. 'If you are selling something, or a reporter, this isn't a good time.'

'Neither of those, Mrs Gonzalez,' said Nightingale, holding out the business card he'd been given an hour earlier. 'As you can see, I'm Dr Townsend from the coroner's office. The 'S' stands for Simon, by the way. I was wondering if I could just ask one or two more questions about Alejandro.'

Nightingale was feeling his way as carefully as he could. The woman looked too old to be the widow, but who could be sure?

The old woman frowned. 'My son is dead and buried, Dr Townsend. Surely all the necessary questions were asked at the inquest?'

'Probably,' said Nightingale. 'But in such an unusual case, we like to make sure of everything, so, if you had ten minutes to spare…'

She stood aside from the door. 'Okay, come in. We will sit in the back garden.'

She led him through the house and into an immaculately kept rear garden, the large lawn edged with well-ordered flower beds. At the near side of the lawn was a patio area, where a table stood, with garden chairs set round it. She waved him to one, and sat on another. 'Now, what more can I tell you that you didn't know, Dr Townsend…'

She frowned again as she said the name, as if trying to remember something, so Nightingale plunged ahead hurriedly. 'We know that Alejandro had never smoked,' he said, 'nor worked with pollutants like asbestos. When did he first have the idea that he had lung cancer?'

'He never had the idea. He had just been cleared to start playing again after a full physical, and the day after, he had a horrible cough, which just wouldn't go away. Eventually he started coughing blood, and could hardly breathe, so we drove him to the Emergency Room, where they gave him the X-ray. It all came on so quickly. He never gave a thought to any such thing, he thought it must be an allergy. I had warned him not to use that stuff…'

'What stuff, Mrs Gonzalez?'

'It hardly matters now. He'd been out of the team with an elbow injury for a while, which hadn't been clearing up very well. Couple of the black guys in his team persuaded him to see a Jujuman, who put him in a trance. Some sort of hypnosis, I suppose, and gave him some herbs to burn in his room at night.'

'I don't seem to have heard about that. Could these herbs have caused…'

She waved a hand to cut him off. 'No, nothing like that. The scientists tested them, They stank, but there was nothing toxic about the fumes. Funny thing is, the elbow problem seemed to clear up after he started using them. That was all he wanted, to get back to playing, maybe finally get a try-out for the Majors...and then he was gone, so soon.'

She took off her dark glasses, and dabbed at her eyes with a handkerchief. Nightingale hated what he was doing, but pressed on. 'Do you remember the name of the man he saw?'

'He just called him Habeeb, I think.'

She stopped talking, then looked hard at Nightingale. 'You said your name was Townsend...Townsend...wasn't the chief pathologist woman called Dr Townsend too?'

'Yes, my sister,' said Nightingale. 'We work in the same department.' He flashed her his most reassuring smile.

She gave a short nod, but didn't look too convinced. She stood up from the table. 'Excuse me a moment, I'll be right back,' she said.

Nightingale had a strong suspicion that her first call would be to the coroner's office, and her second to the police, so as soon as she had gone inside the house he let himself out by the side gate, and lost no time in putting some mileage between himself and the Gonzalez home.

Ten minutes later he pulled over to the kerb, took out his phone, and called the Lattimore home. Johnson answered, and put him through to Charmain.

'Mrs Lattimore, Jack Nightingale. Sorry to bother you, I just had one more question.'

'What would that be?'

'You said your husband considered going to a faith healer. Did he mention a name in particular?'

'No, I don't think he did. As I said, I told him it was a silly idea, and he forgot about it.'

'Thank you, I'll try not to bother you again.'

She hung up.

Nightingale rubbed the back of his neck. Had her husband forgotten about it, or had he gone looking for a Voodoo faith healer? That was a question that Nightingale needed answering.

CHAPTER 25

Nightingale had been warned about trying to drive through the popular areas of New Orleans, and, according to the concierge, taxis weren't too easy to flag down. So he left his rental car at his hotel and walked to the nearest Streetcar station. He waited a few minutes until the red and yellow car arrived,. Nightingale had ridden the Streetcars in San Francisco, but New Orleans used a very different system. Running a cable under the pavement would have been impossible due to the high water table, so the cars pulled electrical power from overhead lines via long electric trolley wires. Nightingale paid his $1.25 with the exact change and settled down for a view of the Mississippi river, for the short trip to the Dumaine Street station. A five-minute walk took him to the New Orleans Historic Voodoo Museum. He'd learned enough of the history of New Orleans to know that most of the buildings dated from the 18th century, and had been designed and built under Spanish rule, since the older French colonial architecture had almost all been destroyed by the Great Fire of 1788. Having paid vague attention to the news reports of Hurricane Katrina nearly a decade before, he'd expected most of the old buildings to have been swept away, but the French Quarter's distance from the breached levées had saved it from any serious damage. The district had even been lucky enough to escape the looting and violence that had followed the storm, leaving most of its art and antique shops untouched. Some day, maybe, he'd find himself in a city with time to stand and stare, but today wasn't likely to be that day. He needed information fast.

Half a block past Bourbon Street, Nightingale nearly walked past it. The Voodoo Museum was smaller than he'd expected, looking more like a small craft store. Nightingale hurried inside, seven dollars ready in his hand. The guy behind the desk was tall, around sixty and gave him a welcoming smile. None of which details grabbed Nightingale's attention. Instead his gaze was riveted on the long, pale yellow snake which coiled round the man's neck and shoulders, and poked its forked tongue out at Nightingale.

'Good morning to you, sir,' said the man, taking Nightingale's money. 'Welcome to the New Orleans Historic Voodoo Museum, my name's John T Norton and this here's Joli Vert. She's an albino python.'

'Pleased to meet you, both,' said Nightingale, reaching a tentative hand out to take his ticket, his gaze never leaving the snake. 'What does she eat?'

'Mice mostly,' replied John T. 'Hasn't had a human in days.' He rolled his eyes and laughed.

'That's reassuring,' said Nightingale, not feeling particularly reassured. 'Does she work here every day?'

'Every day I'm here. In fact she donates her spare scales to us, you can buy them in bags for a dollar a time, powerful medicine some folks say. Anyway, you go right on in, you won't need your jacket today, we turn off the air conditioning when Joli Vert's around, she likes it warm. Look around as long as you like, Mr Gandolfo's not in today, but Mrs Ledoux should be able to answer any questions you might have.'

Nightingale headed in, still casting mistrustful glances at the snake, though she seemed docile enough. He stopped at the entrance to the main room, trying to take in at a glance the riot of esoteric objects that met his eyes. The museum was certainly not organised in any kind of logical fashion. Skeletons fought for space with shelves of bottles containing all colours of liquids, highly decorated wooden masks, altars bedecked with photos and Voodoo dolls. The walls were mostly draped with netting, from which hung scores of home-made crosses, each one bearing a doll or effigy. In the gaps between the netting hung portraits of famous Voodoo practitioners, including one giant central portrait which he recognised as an image of Marie Laveau, the city's most celebrated Voodoo Queen. Even on his short acquaintance with New Orleans, he'd seen her face everywhere. Very little here seemed to be labelled or explained.

There were ten or so other visitors wandering around the room, and Nightingale tried to figure out which one might be Mrs Ledoux, who would be available to answer questions. He decided that the chubby blonde woman in the floral dress talking to the two schoolgirls was probably the likeliest bet, waited until the girls had finished, and approached her. 'Mrs Ledoux?' he asked.

She smiled and nodded. 'Call me Claire, how can I help you?'

Nightingale moved closer and dropped his voice. 'My name's Jack, I had a few questions. I was wondering if we could maybe chat somewhere a little more quiet for ten minutes?'

She nodded. 'Certainly, let's drop into the office.'

Nightingale followed her through a door marked Private, into a small office which clearly doubled as an overflow room for the museum, with more artefacts scattered on the floor and every other flat surface. Claire Ledoux moved a large black and red wooden mask off an old leather chair and waved Nightingale towards it. She found herself a vacant square foot on the edge of the desk and perched on it. 'Now then,' she said. 'What's on your mind?'

'Rituals,' said Nightingale. 'I'd like to know about Voodoo rituals. The serious ones.'

She frowned, opened and closed her mouth a couple of times before answering. 'Oh, well, yes,' she said. 'To be honest that's not really my strongest area. I tend to concentrate on the more positive aspects, the religious side of the faith, reverence for the ancestors, healing. I mean I know the basics, foot-track magic, love potions, *gris-gris*, roots and mojos, but the real serious stuff is outside my field.'

Nightingale had very little idea of what she was talking about, but it seemed she wouldn't have what he needed. 'Is there anyone you know who might be able to give me more information about serious Voodoo?' he asked.

'Might I ask why you want to know?' she replied.

'It's research, for a book I'm writing,' said Nightingale. Even as he finished the sentence, he was thinking about how weak it sounded, but Mrs Ledoux didn't seem to be bothered by it. She thought for a while.

'Well, Mr Gandolfo might be able to help, but he's on vacation for another two weeks. Of course, you could always talk to Mrs Devereaux…'

'Who's she?' asked Nightingale.

'Well, she's pretty much the number one lady when it comes to research into Voodoo and things like that. She's made a lifelong study of it.'

'She works here?' asked Nightingale.

'Not now, she used to do a day a week.'

'Would you have a number for her" he asked.

'I can do better than that,' she said. 'Why don't I call her for you, then you can talk to her right away.'

She took out a notebook from the top drawer of the desk, looked up a number, punched it into the office phone and Nightingale heard it ring at the other end.

'Hello, hello, Mrs Devereaux? It's Claire Ledoux at the museum. Yes, great thanks, and you? Oh. I have a gentleman here who's interested in some aspects of Voodoo I can't help with, and John's on vacation. Yes. Yes. Sure...hold on.'

She handed the phone over to Nightingale, mimed leaving the room at him and went out of the office. Nightingale said hello and gave her his name.

'Well now, Jack Nightingale, how can I help you?'

It was just about the sexiest voice Nightingale had ever heard. Soft, low and Southern, dark chocolate with molasses, he thought, though he wasn't sure what molasses really were. He forced himself to concentrate. 'I'd like to talk to someone about Voodoo rituals, serious ones.'

'Come now,' she said with a hint of laughter. 'You sound such a nice man. Why would you be wanting to talk about such things?'

Somehow Nightingale knew that the 'writing a book' line wasn't going to get him too far here. He looked around, but Ms. Ledoux was just leaving the room. 'A clergyman here has asked me to look into the death of his sister. She seems to have died twice. As ridiculous as that sounds.'

There was a short silence at the other end before she replied. The voice was still warm, but the playful tone had gone. 'Oh my,' she said. 'I think you'd better come and see me right away.'

Nightingale wrote down the address she gave him, and replaced the receiver. He thanked Ms Ledoux for her help, then headed for the museum exit. Once outside, Nightingale had intended to head straight back to the streetcar station, but he stood outside the museum for at least a minute, staring into space, then shook his head, trying to clear his thoughts. He turned left, and started to walk away from the parking

98

lot, his movements stiff and his eyes unfocused, until he came to the next left turning, which he took and walked down a quiet street, which was home to small shops on both sides. Fifty yards or so further on, he shook his head again, focused his eyes and looked around him.

'Where the f…' he began, then broke off to light the cigarette which he'd placed in his mouth without even thinking about it. He gazed round again, saw the main road fifty feet behind him and turned to retrace his steps. As he did so, his gaze fell on the display in the shop window next to him, his jaw dropped, and the cigarette fell unnoticed to the sidewalk.

The window contained a variety of seemingly random items, all with a vague occult connection. Astrology charts, small leather pouches of dried herbs, large black and white candles, crystals, African fetish dolls, and crucibles in a variety of metals, but Nightingale barely noticed any of them. His gaze fixed on a doll, maybe six inches tall, which stood in the very centre of the window. A female doll, the hair a mix of red and copper, the lips full and red, the pale, flawless complexion contrasting with the two patches of red at the cheeks. She was dressed in an emerald green dress, cut tight from bust to waist, but flaring out around the thighs, hanging loosely, as if waiting for a breeze to blow it gently around.

'It can't be,' said Nightingale aloud. 'Just can't be.'

He looked up at the simple red on black sign above the shop, which bore the words *Papa Dimanche* in large letters, with *Vodun Supplies* in a smaller font underneath. He took three steps and pushed open the glass door. A set of chimes announced his appearance, and he walked across the small store to the counter, paying no heed to the various displays around him.

There were no other customers, and the old man behind the counter raised his eyes from the book he had been reading, and greeted Nightingale with a warm smile. 'Good morning, Mr Nightingale. How nice to see you again.'

Nightingale took a long look at the old man behind the counter. He guessed his age at seventy or so, from the bald head with its liver spots, the large ears, with untrimmed hair showing, the rheumy pale-blue eyes and the wasted muscle tone. He wore an old v-necked sweater, somewhere between brown and green, over a white shirt with a rumpled collar, and a grey tie. When he spoke, he revealed a partial set of teeth which owed nothing to expensive dentistry. Nightingale caught a strong smell of alcohol on the old man's breath. "How do you know my name,' asked Nightingale, forcing his voice to sound as calm as he could make it, despite his complete confusion. 'And what do you mean about seeing me *again.* I've never been in here before.'

The old man frowned, as if puzzled. 'But of course you have, Mr Nightingale. Otherwise how would I have remembered your name?'

'Could be lots of ways. One thing I am sure of, I've never been down this street before, or inside this shop.'

The old man shook his head. 'But you were here two days ago, when you ordered the doll. And now you've come to collect it.'

'I haven't ordered any doll,' said Nightingale.

'But of course you have, I saw you looking at it in the window, and you came straight in. Though I say it myself, it's a fine piece of work. A really good match for the description you gave me, don't you think? You recognised her straight away.'

Nightingale put his hands on the counter, then leaned across, until his face was eighteen inches or so from the old man's. 'I have never been in this shop in my life before,' he said, enunciating each word clearly and separately. 'I never ordered that doll, I never gave you a description of it. I have never even seen you before in my life. I don't know what this is all about, but you're not telling me the truth.'

The old man took a pace or two backwards, his face betraying his fear. 'Well,' he said, 'perhaps there has been some mistake. But you are Mr Nightingale?'

Nightingale nodded.

'Well then, it really is a most astonishing coincidence, unless you have a brother, or somebody who looked enough like you to pretend to be you. But then, if it wasn't you who came in on Tuesday afternoon and ordered the doll, why are you here now, and why do you so clearly recognise her?'

'Tuesday afternoon, you said. What time?'

'Around three.'

Nightingale smiled. 'Not a chance. I was...I was asleep in my hotel room. Jet lag I suppose.'

The old man nodded. 'Of course. Maybe one of your friends is playing some kind of joke on you. Though he did look like you. He had the same coat too... Yes. That must be it, a joke.'

'Yeah, I suppose that could be it,' said Nightingale, trying to sound convinced. 'Look, I didn't mean to be rude, Mr...'

'Hargreaves. Melvin Hargreaves.'

'Mr Hargreaves. I apologise, it was all a bit of a shock. Perhaps that jet lag hasn't worn off.'

'Well, no harm done. Perhaps the other Mr Nightingale will be back for the doll in a day or so.'

Nightingale reached into an inside pocket and pulled out a business card, which just bore the two words *Jack Nightingale*. He took a pen from another pocket, and wrote down the number of his latest mobile phone under his name. 'Look, Mr Hargreaves, if the other guy does come back, I'd really appreciate it if you'd give me a call.'

Hargreaves took the card, holding it by the edges between the thumbs and first fingers of his hands, turned it over, gave a little frown of distaste, and put it in a drawer, under the counter. 'I shall certainly remember to do that. Is there anything else I can help you with?'

Nightingale shook his head. 'Not today, thank you.' He turned and walked out of the shop.

Three minutes later, when Hargreaves looked up from his book, Nightingale was still outside the shop, staring at the doll in the window. Their eyes met, Hargreaves raised his eyebrows, Nightingale threw down his latest cigarette, shook his head, and walked back up towards the main street.

CHAPTER 26

Guided by the voice of Google Maps, Nightingale drove his rented Ford Escape up to the stone-pillared gates of the Devereaux mansion. He stated his name to the intercom and the large, wrought-iron gates immediately swung open, allowing him to drive a hundred yards past immaculately tended lawns, flower beds and fountains to park in front of the large French colonial-style main house. It was painted gleaming white, and reminded Nightingale of a wedding cake, with its three stories of balustrades, balconies, outside staircases and dormer windows. He walked towards the front door which swung open as he reached it.

'Mr Nightingale? You are most welcome to our home, sir. My name is General Samuel Devereaux.'

Nightingale took the outstretched hand and tried not to let his surprise show on his face. Samuel Devereaux looked exactly like the posters of Colonel Sanders on the Fried Chicken outlets. His snow white hair was worn long and matched his beard and moustache. His suit and tie were also immaculately white, with the only splash of colour being the bright red shirt. He stood tall and straight backed, though Nightingale thought he couldn't have been less than ninety years old. His blue eyes were clear and looked directly at Nightingale. 'Won't you come inside sir. We do still run to a butler, but he's getting along in years, so I do most of the door-answering personally.'

Nightingale wondered how old the butler might be, if Samuel Devereaux felt the need to save his ageing legs, but kept his thoughts to himself. He followed the General inside and into a huge entrance hall, with a spiral staircase leading up to the second floor. Nightingale imagined it must look like a set from *Gone With The Wind*, though he'd never actually seen the film.

'Now, sir,' said the General. 'It's Hannah you've come to see, and she'll be down directly, I told her you'd arrived. Meantime, what can I organise for you in the way of refreshments? I do still make a mean

Mint Julep, though since you're driving you might prefer an iced tea or some coffee?'

'Iced tea will be fine, General,' said Nightingale. 'It's still a little hot.'

'Ha, not for us Southerners,' replied the General. 'I did think you were looking a little warm. You probably wouldn't enjoy summer here. I'll be back directly, if you'd care to take a seat here. I'm not quite sure where Hannah will prefer to take you.'

Nightingale sat down on a large cane plantation chair and looked up at the staircase. He assumed that Hannah was the General's granddaughter, and would be making a Bette Davies entrance down that imposing marble staircase.

Once again his expectations were not to be met. He turned his head at a whirring noise behind him and rose to his feet as the elevator reached the first floor and the door which he hadn't noticed before opened.

'Why hello, Mr Nightingale,' said that gorgeous voice. 'I am delighted to meet you, my name is Hannah Devereaux. My husband told me you'd arrived.'

She was certainly not the General's granddaughter. The woman looked to be in her eighties, her pure white hair contrasting with her dark skin, and her eyes hidden behind thick dark glasses. At a conservative guess, she must have weighed two hundred and fifty pounds. Nightingale bent down to take her hand as she moved the electric wheelchair towards him.

'Why don't you follow me into the downstairs library and we can chat there?'

The wheelchair rolled almost silently along a short corridor and through a large wooden door that already stood open. Nightingale looked around him with admiration. The room was huge, dotted with desks, side tables, old leather sofas and chairs. If the Lattimore mansion was the epitome of new money and modern taste, the Devereaux home was its complete opposite. Almost every inch of three walls was covered with shelves, packed tightly with countless books of all sizes and ages. Nightingale had been in extensive libraries before, but this stood comparison with any of them. And Mrs Devereaux had called it the 'downstairs library', perhaps implying there was more upstairs? Nightingale doubted that anyone could live long enough to read that many books. The fourth wall featured an enormous fireplace. Above it hung a military officer's sabre in its scabbard.

Hannah Devereaux coughed gently, to recapture his attention. She noticed him looking at the sabre. 'My husband's great-grandfather's. General PGT Devereaux, of the Confederate Army. Thankfully, my husband does not share his ancestor's views, though, to be fair to the old man, apparently he was quite a supporter of civil rights after the war.'

She waved Nightingale to a green leather Chesterfield chair in front of a low coffee table, and parked her chair opposite him. Samuel Devereaux came through the door at that moment, carrying a silver tray which he placed on the table.

'Iced tea for you, sir and I assumed you'd take a glass of milk, Hannah,' he said, placing his hand on her shoulder and squeezing very gently. 'Now I'll leave you in peace to talk.'

She placed her left hand over his, returned the squeeze. Looked up at him and beamed.

'Thank you so much, Samuel. You'll be in the garden?'

'I will indeed,' he said. 'That mimosa could stand to be cut back, and Hawkins is laid up with his rheumatics again.'

He turned and left, and Mrs Devereaux gave her attention back to Nightingale. 'You may, of course, smoke if you wish to, Mr Nightingale,' she said.

Something in her voice gave Nightingale the impression she'd rather he didn't so he gave a little shake of his head and sipped his iced tea. It was sweet and cool. He needed it, the General was right, he did seem to be sweating rather a lot.

'You'll excuse the chair,' she said. 'I fear a lifetime of good old Southern food and too much time in studying piled the pounds on me, and now I have heart trouble and diabetes too. I still have the use of my legs, but the chair makes things much easier. Slowly and surely I am wearing out.'

Nightingale tried to think of something positive to say, but she was clearly not a well woman. Her voice was incredibly young and warm, but every now and again she needed to pause to catch her breath. In the end, he said nothing, and she filled the gap herself.

'Still, I keep going. Something tells me you're not at your best yourself, Mr Nightingale. There's a lot of strain and worry about you, but it's more than that. Let me look at you properly.'

She took off her dark glasses, blinked at the light and focused her soft, watery brown eyes at him. Or maybe not at him, more around him, if that were possible. She gave a gasp, far more pronounced than the other small ones, and replaced her glasses. 'Oh, my,' she said. 'Oh my.'

'What did you see,' asked Nightingale.

'You're in trouble, aren't you?'

Nightingale took a deep breath. 'Not more than usual, I don't think. Why, what did you see?'

'Your aura is stranger than any I have ever seen. Tell me, when did you sell your soul?'

Nightingale gasped. 'How do you...' He left the sentence unfinished.

''Do you want to tell me about it?'

''I don't really,' said Nightingale. 'But it wasn't me who sold my soul. It was done for me without my knowledge. At birth.'

'The first time.'

Nightingale closed his eyes, and nodded. 'Yes, okay. The second time was down to me. There was someone I needed to save, and it seemed worth it.'

'Yet you still have your soul.'

'Yes. Seems I managed to find a loophole or two in the contracts.'

'A twice-pledged soul, yet still unclaimed.''I beg your pardon?'

'Nothing. Just an old half-remembered phrase I heard somewhere. I must find out where. You must be a remarkable man, Jack Nightingale.'

'I've never really felt that way. But you're certainly a remarkable woman. How did you know?'

'Your aura. I have never seen one like it. Nevertheless...still, let's move on. You have come to me seeking help. Tell me about it.'

CHAPTER 27

Melvin Hargreaves was in his workshop at the rear of the *Papa Dimanche* Vodun store, when he heard the sound of the door-chimes. Reluctantly he put down his pliers, turned away from his bench and walked through the strip curtain into the front area. 'Good afternoon, can I…I…' The words froze on his lips as he focused on the face of his visitor. The blood drained from his wrinkled cheeks, and his bleary old eyes shone with fear. He bent his head and started to kneel down.

'No need for that, Melvin, not in a public place anyway.' The voice was soft, almost friendly, but it stopped Hargreaves dead, and he straightened up again, though his gaze stayed firmly on his visitor's black shoes. 'He came.'

It wasn't a question, but Hargreaves still babbled a reply. 'Yes...yes...just as you said, he came and asked...'

'I know what he would have asked Melvin. And you told him what you were instructed to, no more, no less.'

Again, it was a statement of fact, and this time Hargreaves merely nodded.

'He didn't try to take the doll?'

'No, M…'

'Do not speak my name. Never speak my name.' The voice was still soft and calm, but there was no mistaking the warning note.

'Of course, my apologies. I meant no harm.'

'I know, but do not grow careless. Did he leave you anything?'

'Yes, a card, with his number, to call if the one who ordered the doll returned.'

'Ha. That seems unlikely. You took care with it?'

'Of course, I merely held the sides, not where he had touched it.'

'Good, Melvin. Show it to me.'

Hargreaves opened the drawer, and his visitor walked round the end of the counter, looked into the drawer and picked up Nightingale's card, handling it only by the edges, as Hargreaves had done. The green eyes closed, and Hargreaves heard a sigh of satisfaction. 'Oh yes, this will do admirably. My force of will enabled me to exercise a small amount of control, and send him past your store, but nothing of any note. With this, his hair, and with the doll you will make, my control can be complete.'

The card disappeared into the left-hand pocket of the black jacket.

'But surely, more than this would be necessary?' said Hargreaves before he could stop himself. 'Hair, blood, nails…'

'Hsssht. You are not addressing some old Voodoo priest now. You know who I am. You know my power. I tell you this will suffice, it bears traces of him. And I have his hair. It was arranged in advance.'

Hargreaves was silent, conscious that he had gone too far.

'Now, Melvin, the doll. You observed him perfectly?'

'Oh yes, you know I never forget a face. I could remember him perfectly ten years from now.'

The smile re-appeared, it seemed he was forgiven for his clumsiness. 'I know, it is a useful gift. So make the doll. I shall keep the card to infuse it with power.'

Hargreaves bowed his head in acknowledgement. 'I shall start right away, It will be ready in two days.'

The green eyes widened, and the nostrils flared. 'I think not, Melvin. I shall return to collect it in four hours.'

Hargreaves trembled, but dared not argue. He nodded weakly. 'It will be ready in four hours.'

'I know, Melvin. You always work so hard to please me.'

Hargreaves was staring at his own shoes now, and heard the sound of the chimes and the closing door as if they were streets away. He shuffled to the door of the shop, turned his sign to *Closed*, locked the door and headed back to his workshop, his face still a mask of fear. He needed a good inch from his bourbon bottle before his hands would stop shaking long enough to pick up his tools.

CHAPTER 28

There was a knock on the door, and the General walked in with a fresh tray. 'I thought you might appreciate a refill, sir,' he said, placing the tray on the coffee table and gathering up the old one and the two glasses. He looked down at Nightingale. 'My, you do appear to be feeling the heat,' he said. 'We generally don't bother with the air conditioning this early in the year, but I could switch it on?'

Nightingale did seem to be sweating rather more than normal, but shook his head. 'No thank you, General, I'll be fine.' The general nodded at Nightingale and left the room, closing the door again behind him. Nightingale sipped at his fresh tea. Mrs Devereaux ignored her glass of milk.

'I wonder, Mr Nightingale,' said Mrs Devereaux. 'Might you be more comfortable talking outside. I usually take a turn round the grounds every day about now, you might find it a little cooler.'

'That's fine with me.'

She started up her wheelchair, and Nightingale stood up to follow her. As they passed the grand piano, Nightingale noticed the photo of the handsome young black man in military uniform. 'Your son?' he asked.

'Yes, Edward, our only boy. He was killed in Iraq, Desert Storm, his plane was shot down by anti-aircraft fire.'

'I'm sorry.'

'It was a long time ago.'

'Does that help?'

She stopped the wheelchair and looked up into his eyes. 'No, it doesn't. Of course it didn't. The wound is still there, and it aches every day.'

Nightingale nodded, he had no idea what else he could say, but the woman had moved ahead, along the entrance hall and out of the front door. She drove her wheelchair along the tiled paths between the lawns with Nightingale walking by her side. Over to the left, Samuel

Devereaux waved as he pruned a bush. He'd swapped his immaculate white suit for some blue coveralls.

'It's beautifully looked after,' said Nightingale.

'Why, thank you,' she said. 'We have a little team to do the heavy work, but Samuel loves to tend to the details. I used to like gardening too, but at least I can still get out and enjoy it. Now, Jack, suppose you tell me what brings you here. and maybe I can be a little more help to you.'

'Well, as I told you, I've been asked to look into the death of a young girl, her name was Bethany Cole. Trouble is, she seems to have died twice.'

'Dead twice? I assume all the obvious explanations won't work. And you suspect some kind of Voodoo connection?'

Nightingale wasn't usually keen to share information, but this time he was in over his head, with nobody else to turn to for help, so he told her pretty much everything, from Bethany's double death and the murders of Delroy and Spike

Nightingale always claimed to be a good listener, but Hannah Devereaux was a class apart. He spoke for ten minutes, and she never interrupted once, staring straight ahead with just the occasional nod to show that she was following. Finally he finished, and she halted the chair and turned her head up to look at him.

'Now,' she said. 'You must understand, that while I have studied a great deal about Voodoo, I'm not a practitioner, nor have I been received into all its mysteries. My abilities, such as they are, derive from the practice of Wicca.'

'You're a witch?' asked Nightingale.

'Not a term I encourage, especially in Samuel's hearing. Perhaps a follower of the Right-hand path would be more accurate, something which has far more in common with Voodoo than you might imagine. They are both essentially practices of the natural arts to help, heal and bless. So what do you think is happening?' she asked.

'It sounds ridiculous,' he said. 'But it points to dead people being reanimated and used as killers. But is that really possible?'

'Reanimating the dead?' she said. 'I'm not at all sure it is. But the legends of Voodoo give another possibility.'

'Yes, I've heard about that.' said Nightingale. 'A drug that maybe simulates death. Must be very convincing.'

'A drug, or perhaps a curse,' she said. 'Apparently both are possible. You appreciate my knowledge is purely theoretical, I've never seen it done, much less of course, tried to do it myself.'

'But is it really possible?'

'I believe it is,' she said. 'The idea has been too persistent in the history of Voodoo for it to be purely myth.'

'I'm guessing it's not the sort of thing you could do with a few herbs and a magic wand?' said Nightingale.

'No, it's a very complicated ritual. There are two parts. First the victim needs to be cast into a trance that resembles death so closely that it would convince a doctor. Perhaps that's where Foot-Track Magic comes in.'

'Foot what?'

Mrs Devereaux smiled. 'Yes,' she said. 'It does sound a little strange if you've not studied Voodoo, but the feet are a vitally important part of the body. You want to curse someone, the best way is to put something in their shoes, collect the dirt from their footprints and mix up a potion or get them to walk over the symbols of the curse. Depending on which version of the legend you read, the death-trance curse can be administered by a poison on the soles of the feet or by walking over cross marks made with chalk and the victim's footprint dust.'

'It's that simple?' asked Nightingale.

'In theory, but it's not like baking a cake from a recipe. The stronger the curse, the more powerful needs to be the belief, power and expertise of the person placing it. You could follow all those steps and not even give someone a headache. So, that's one theory. The other is that the person is really killed, and completely re-animated.'

'Which one strikes you as more likely?'

'I have no idea, both seem unlikely, but it's an area in which an outsider would have no knowledge. And besides, that's the easy part.'

'You mean the reanimation is much harder?' asked Nightingale.

'As you'd expect,' she said. 'It involves a full Voodoo ceremony, with the body reanimated, the curse or poison counteracted, and the victim's true soul and personality captured away from their body.'

'Captured? How?'

'Well, again there's not much information available to the outsider. I've heard the souls and memories can be captured in something called a memory jug, or even imprisoned in a Voodoo doll. Once that happens, the victim has no mind of its own, and exists only to serve the Voodoo master.'

'Is there a cure?' asked Nightingale.

'Perhaps,' she said. 'It's said that smashing the jug or burning the doll will restore the victim's memories and soul. I doubt if anyone's ever proved that.' She paused. 'Far more likely that the reanimated body just endures for a while before deteriorating completely.'

Nightingale thought about it for a minute, then asked the all-important question. 'You said only a really powerful Voodoo practitioner could ever pull this off,' he said. 'You wouldn't have some names and addresses?'

She smiled again. 'Well, I don't think I do. New Orleans has plenty of Voodoo Queens and Kings, but they tend to be fairly harmless, not possessed of any great power. Certainly not practitioners of the more evil side of Voodoo. But then, it seems unlikely they would advertise.'

'Another thing, a friend of mine told me about a group of young athletes…'

Nightingale repeated the story Wainwright had told him. She frowned. 'This is unusual. I have heard of people being killed by a Voodoo curse, but they do not normally cause specific illnesses. Just a general wasting away. I have never heard of anything such as you describe.'

They arrived back at the front door of the mansion, and Nightingale was almost ready to say goodbye, with grateful thanks for all her help. But his curiosity got the better of him. 'Can I ask a personal question?'

She looked surprised, but gave a small nod.

'You and the General. It seems…' He wasn't sure how to finish the sentence so he just shrugged.

'You find it surprising? Yes, maybe it was, and not without its difficulties over the years. My mother was from Africa originally, my father a German, my colouring is a mixture of their races. I was a singer in a blues band, when Captain Devereux met me. It nearly finished him with his family and friends, but he never wavered. As I said, it was difficult in the early days. Back then, we couldn't even sit next to each other on a streetcar. Things are easier now.'

'Perhaps I shouldn't have asked?'

'Why not? We have nothing to be ashamed of, we are very proud of each other, and of our son.' She looked at him, clearly concerned. 'Jack, I think you may be in great danger, if what you suspect is true, but I wish you every good fortune in your quest. If you need any more help, you know where to find me.'

'Thank you,' said Nightingale.

She held up a hand. 'Wait. Danger may come in many forms with Voodoo. Take particular care where you walk, never walk over crosses made with dust or chalk, and don't let your shoes out of your sight. If I were you, I'd sprinkle a line of red brick dust outside your door, and keep it there at all times for protection.'

Nightingale grimaced. 'Not sure the hotel management would like that,' he said.

She looked him full in the face and dropped her warm voice to a whisper. 'Better an extra cleaning bill than losing that precious soul of yours. Bend down. Please.'

Nightingale bent forward, and she took a small heart-shaped silver locket from around her neck, then transferred it to his neck, peering over her glasses at the hook and eye and taking a while to fasten them with her stiff fingers. 'There. Now wait. There is more.' She placed her right hand over Nightingale's heart, holding the locket in the left and said a sentence in what sounded like Latin. Then she sat back in her chair again. 'Never take it off,' she said. 'And especially never open it. Its aura will help block the power of evil.'

'I get it,' said Nightingale. 'And thank you. How much…'

She frowned and held up a hand to stop him.

'Absolutely not,' she said. 'A protective charm must be freely given and accepted for it to work. I would have thought Mrs Steadman would have told you that.'

Nightingale gaped at her. He surely hadn't mentioned the name of the woman who'd been so much help to him in London. Hannah Devereaux laughed at his discomfiture. 'Oh come now,' she said. Ours is a small world, we know each other well and we talk. And Nightingale is a *very* unusual name.'

CHAPTER 29

Chris Dubois hadn't overstated her abilities. The following morning, Nightingale had a message on his phone, There was a photo of Bethany Cole with the name Crystal Carr underneath. There was also an office address for Dreamgirls International, otherwise known as Goldman Enterprises. Nightingale headed to the Plaza's hugely expensive parking garage to collect his rental car. By the time he'd found a place to park in the business district and handed over another twenty dollars, he was wishing he'd taken a taxi, and was beginning to get the idea that New Orleans wasn't a car-friendly city.

The office block he needed looked like any other in any city, and didn't run to a receptionist. The list of tenants included a couple of law firms who took entire floors, and a variety of smaller businesses. There was no listing for Dreamgirls but Deborah Goldman Enterprises occupied at least some of the third floor.

Nightingale ignored the elevator and hauled himself up two flights of stairs. The Goldman headquarters were down at the end of the corridor and looked to be just one office from the outside. Nightingale knocked and a female voice told him to come in. The office was bright enough, thanks to the large window in the far wall and the white colour scheme on the walls and ceiling. The desk was long and finished to look like teak, with a computer monitor in the middle and a printer to one side. Behind the computer sat a young blonde woman, dressed in a grey business suit and typing enthusiastically. Nightingale put her at late twenties. She stopped typing and looked up at him, giving him a practised professional smile.

'Good morning, how can I help you today?'

'Ms Goldman,' said Nightingale and gave his name. She repeated the smile.

'No,' she said. 'I'm Madison, Mrs Goldman's personal assistant. Do you have an appointment?'

The tone of her voice suggested she knew full well he didn't, but Nightingale played along. 'I'm afraid not, but I wondered if I could see her anyway?'

Madison looked at him discouragingly, and frowned. 'Well, I'm not sure,' she said. 'What would it be in connection with?'

'It's rather confidential.'

Madison widened her eyes at him. 'I am Mrs Goldman's *confidential* Personal Assistant,' she said. 'I doubt she'd want to see anyone unless she knew what it was in connection with.'

Nightingale gave in. 'I'd like to talk to her about Bethany Cole, I believe she used to work here.'

Madison gave no sign of recognising the name. 'I hardly think she worked here,' she said. 'But maybe in one of Mrs Goldman's other enterprises, perhaps.' She lifted a phone from her desk, pressed a button and told it Nightingale's name and errand. The person on the other end spoke, but Nightingale couldn't make out the words. Madison put the phone back down. She motioned towards the door in the left hand wall. 'Mrs Goldman will see you now, please go in.' She went back to her typing, as Nightingale opened the door and walked in.

This office was bigger, just as bright, but more tastefully decorated, with pale green walls and matching carpet. The desk was bigger, and might even have been genuine teak. The computer was more expensive, and the chair looked much more comfortable. The woman's hair seemed just as blonde as Madison's, and probably hadn't come from a bottle She rose from her chair, walked round the desk and held her hand out to him. 'Mr Nightingale? I'm Deborah Goldman, do please sit down. Coffee?'

Nightingale declined the offer, and sat in the client chair, as Goldman went back to her seat. She leaned back in her chair and studied him for a while, then gave a small nod, leaned forward, folded her arms and looked into his eyes. Nightingale said nothing. It was her territory, let her decide how to play it. She seemed to decide to go with flirtatious, gave him another smile, batted her eyelashes, licked her upper lip so quickly he almost missed it and spoke. 'So, what brings you here?' she said, in a voice that had dropped half an octave since her offer of coffee.

Nightingale couldn't help but be impressed with the performance, but he wasn't ready to start eating out of her hand just yet. He decided to play it tough. 'I'm making enquiries about Bethany Cole. I'm told she was one of your girls.'

She raised her eyebrows and put her head on one side. 'What can I tell you about Bethany that you don't already know? And what's your interest in her? I assume you're not a policeman, unless the NOPD have an English section.'

Nightingale allowed himself a pause, then leaned forward in his chair and laced his fingers together. 'Why don't you just tell me everything you know about her.'

Goldman wasn't biting. She leaned back, keeping the distance between them. 'Why should I be telling you anything at all, Mr Nightingale?' she asked.

'Please, call me Jack.'

She put her hands on the desk, palm down. 'Listen, *Mr* Nightingale,' she said. 'We've established you know the nature of my business. You're probably intelligent enough to realise that shooting my mouth off about it to any guy who comes in here with a persuasive act isn't going to do me any good, in fact it could do me quite a lot of harm. Now, I don't mean to be inhospitable, and I doubt I could throw you out of here personally, but I surely know some people who could. So, let's stop the tough guy act, tell me why you want to know about Bethany, and I'll decide what I feel like telling you.'

Nightingale held up his hands in surrender. 'Okay, I'm sorry,' he said. 'I've been asked to make some enquiries by her brother. She was killed in a car crash last week, seemed like she'd dropped out of sight for a year or so before that. This was her last known place of... er... employment.'

The softer approach seemed to work better. Goldman relaxed in her chair. 'My condolences to her brother. From what little I ever saw of her, she seemed a nice girl. But I'm a little confused, you say she was killed last week, I'd heard she died over a month ago. As far as I knew that was why she stopped calling in.'

'Who told you she was dead?' asked Nightingale.

She gave the question some thought. 'To be honest, I don't recall,' she said. 'It came via Trudy, Madison's predecessor, I guess, probably from one of the other girls. The girls usually call in on a Monday to fill their diaries with pre-bookings, and she just stopped calling. A shame, she was one of our most popular girls, plenty of repeat bookings.'

'And you never heard from her again?' asked Nightingale. 'Well, no. Otherwise I would have known she wasn't dead, wouldn't I?' Nightingale skirted around Bethany's two deaths, he could hardly expect Mrs Goldman to swallow that straight off. 'So, if she wasn't working for you, what might she have been doing?' he asked.

'To be honest, I have no knowledge of her resumé, her talents and any other way she might have made a living.'

'Let's imagine she continued to use her horizontal talents,' said Nightingale.

She smiled at that. 'Well, I don't have a monopoly of the hotel and high-end escort trade, but I feel fairly sure I'd have heard about it if she'd started to work for one of my competitors. It's a small world. Of course, she could have gone into business for herself...or maybe moved downmarket.'

'Downmarket?' repeated Nightingale.

'Well, yes. I like to think I cover the top end, but there are many lower levels. If she decided, or was forced, to move down, she would have come under the influence of less scrupulous people. Criminals.'

Nightingale avoided pointing out that her own business was strictly illegal too. She evidently didn't put herself in the same class as organised vice. 'Could you maybe give me some names?' asked Nightingale.

She shook her head. 'We are talking about people who wouldn't care to have their names bandied about carelessly, Mr Nightingale.'

'Like who?'

She bought herself some time by opening a gold box on her desk, taking out a cigarette, lighting it and blowing out some smoke. She pushed the box towards Nightingale, who hesitated. 'Is smoking allowed in offices here?' he asked.

She flashed him a tight smile. 'It would probably be the least of the charges if the police decide to prosecute me,' she said.

Nightingale lit up. 'So can you give me some names?' he asked.

'I would be very foolish to mention names.' she replied. 'Besides I heard nothing of Bethany working for anyone else. Honestly, I can't help. I've heard nothing from her and have no idea what she might have been doing other than in her working hours here.'

Nightingale decided to try another tack. 'So why did Bethany take to prostitution in the first place?' he asked.

She laughed. 'What do you think, Jack?' she said. 'She was trying to pay her way through college? Raising money for an operation for her sick brother? Chances are it was a way of making twenty times as much money as anything else. Not romantic, not the sob story, but pretty much the reason why most of my girls are in this business. I don't take junkies, I don't deal with criminals. My girls get good quality dates and I look after them. Further down the scale, it's a different story. They make no money, they take whatever Johns come along and they're kept on drugs. If that's the route she went down after she left me, I'm sorry for her.'

Nightingale was nearly out of questions, and wasn't about to try the Voodoo link. He tried a shot in the dark. 'She would have been early twenties when you heard about her supposed death. Have any of your other girls disappeared mysteriously?'

She gasped, and he knew he'd scored a hit. 'There were two or three. Girls I'd heard had died, but then there were rumours they were working on the street. Working for people I had no knowledge of, and no wish to know about.'

'Would you have names?' asked Nightingale.

'Names of the girls, I could manage, As for the people they might have been working for, I wouldn't wish to guess. Life is short, Jack, I have no wish to shorten mine further.'

She picked up a phone, pressed one button and spoke into it. 'Madison, could you bring in the green file, please.'

The young blonde arrived almost instantly and placed the file on Deborah Goldman's desk. She put on a pair of gold reading glasses, opened it, ran a finger down a sheet of paper, then copied three names and dates onto a yellow Post-It note. 'Here you are,' she said, passing it across the desk. 'Three girls who disappeared suddenly, and whom I heard were working elsewhere, plus the dates I last used them.'

Nightingale looked at the Post-it. All the dates were over the last six months. The names were Mystique DuMonde, Carla Storm and Suzette Starr. He guessed they might not have been baptised that way. He got up. 'Thank you for your time, Mrs Goldman,' he said. 'The card has my mobile number if you think of anything else that might help.'

They exchanged cards.

He'd been gone thirty seconds when Deborah Goldman picked up her phone and made a call.

CHAPTER 30

Nightingale had quite a distance to walk back to the parking garage where he'd left his rental car, but in the event his Hush Puppies weren't destined to suffer any wear. The black Lincoln Towncar pulled alongside him before he'd gone three hundred yards. The rear window rolled down and the large, shaven-headed black man leaned out. 'Good afternoon, Mr Nightingale. Mr Jefferson would like to see you. Please step into the car.'

Nightingale kept walking, and the car crept along to keep pace with him. 'I'm a little busy at the moment,' he said. 'Perhaps Mr Jefferson could call? Whoever he is.'

The black man laughed. 'No, sir. Mr Jefferson has asked me to bring you, and it's my job to make sure that his wishes are fulfilled. Step into the car, please, he doesn't care to be kept waiting.'

That was one thing you could guarantee about crime bosses, thought Nightingale. They never cared to be kept waiting. Maybe impatience was a necessary character trait for the job. He had no desire to be 'taken for a ride 'to some undisclosed destination so he shook his head. 'No.'

The car stopped and the rear door opened. The black man got out. Nightingale had pegged him as large at first sight, but huge would have been a better description. Very little of him was anything but muscle. He gave Nightingale a huge smile, showing two gold incisors. 'Enough procrastination, Mr Nightingale. You will be going to see Mr Jefferson now. It is entirely your decision how much blood you lose along the way.'

He pulled open his long leather coat and Nightingale saw the gun strapped just under his armpit. Nightingale looked through the open passenger door and saw a slightly smaller man, who was also smiling at him.

'I would be delighted to see Mr Jefferson,' said Nightingale. 'Thanks for the lift.'

'You're not armed, of course?

'I'm British.'

'Well now, maybe that isn't always a no, these days. Still, if you are carrying, it's not in either of your coat pockets, and I'm guessing you'd be dead, buried and the will read before you could unbutton it. So I'll take your word for it."

The car was quiet and comfortable. Nightingale sat between the two black men. Nobody spoke for ten minutes, until the car pulled up in front of a restaurant called the *Cajun Cave.* The bald man opened the door, got out and beckoned for Nightingale to follow him. They went inside, and walked to a booth at the back of the restaurant.

The only occupant of the booth was black, around fifty with short greying hair and dressed in an immaculately tailored black suit, with a matching tie, contrasting with the red shirt. The suit must have taken quite some work, since Harold Jefferson weighed around two hundred and fifty pounds. In his case there seemed to be little muscle, Nightingale guessed that he hired what he needed. Jefferson looked up from his plate of jambalaya as the bald man spoke. 'Mr Nightingale, sir.'

'Mr Nightingale, please sit,' said Jefferson as the heavy walked away. 'I assume you haven't had lunch?'

'I'm not hungry, thanks,' said Nightingale.

'Nonsense,' replied Jefferson. 'You will be once you smell the food here.' Jefferson raised a finger and a pretty black waitress appeared almost immediately. 'Chantal, jambalaya for my guest. And a bottle of Corona, slice of lime.'

He smiled at Nightingale, who nodded in acknowledgement. 'You're well informed,' said Nightingale.

'It's my business to be well-informed, sir. Very little happens in New Orleans that I don't know about. For example the fact that you've been making certain enquiries in areas of interest to me.'

Nightingale didn't like the way the conversation was going. Jefferson was polite, but there was no doubt that things could turn unpleasant very easily, and Nightingale was alone and defenceless. 'I hadn't intended to cause problems for you,' he said.

Jefferson waved his fork at him. 'And of course, you haven't,' he said. 'As can be seen from your continued survival.'

The waitress returned and placed a plate in front of Nightingale and a bottle of Corona to the right of it. He had eaten jambalaya before - a mixture of rice, meat and vegetables, similar to paella. As he looked down at the plate he saw andouille sausage, succulent prawns, and crawfish. Jefferson was right, it smelled delicious, and Nightingale started eating. Jefferson went on talking. 'No sir, you are not inconveniencing me, The nature of your enquiries, in fact, suggests that you may be of use to me. I understand you are trying to find information about Bethany Cole?'

Nightingale's mouthful of jambalaya prevented him saying anything, but he nodded.

'I know almost nothing of her,' said Jefferson. 'Except that she worked in Mrs Goldman's organisation, then stopped, was believed dead a few weeks ago, but was next seen slicing Delroy Parker's dick off last week, along with two other whores.'

'That's what I heard too,' said Nightingale.

'And what is your interest in this matter?' asked Jefferson.

'Her brother wants to know what happened to her,' said Nightingale. 'He knew how she made a living, but thought she'd died a while back. Was Delroy Parker...er...an associate of yours?'

Jefferson nodded. 'He was. And he is also not the first of my associates to meet an unexpected death in the last few months.'

'I would have thought that it's not a world where people have a high life expectancy,' said Nightingale.

'There are frequently casualties,' said Jefferson. 'But lately there seems to be more of a concerted campaign against my associates. Delroy was apparently killed by three hookers claiming to be sent from me. There have been other deaths involving hookers, fake postmen, fake police officers. Someone is trying to hurt me.'

'Isn't that normal?' asked Nightingale.

'Only in the movies,' said Jefferson. 'The idea of gang wars is mostly fictional. My business interests are generally recognised as my territory, and nobody would be foolish enough to set up in competition.'

'Until now,' said Nightingale.

'As you say, until now.'

Nightingale's plate was clean, and he pushed it aside. 'So, who's trying to muscle in?' he asked.

'That is indeed the sixty-four thousand dollar question,' said Jefferson. 'There has been no overt declaration of war, yet I keep losing people. There are rumours of a new power behind the scenes. But there is no name given to him.'

'It'll make finding him difficult,' said Nightingale.

'Indeed. At the moment his focus is on my entertainment businesses, a profitable area I control. Though if I continue to lose operatives, my control might be at issue.'

'You really know nothing about him?' asked Nightingale.

There was a pause. Nightingale took a sip of his beer and waited for Jefferson to continue.

'Nothing. I know nothing of his identity, nor of how he manages to recruit operatives.' He broke off, took a sip from his glass, which looked to contain bourbon on the rocks. Nightingale waited again. 'Also…' continued Jefferson. 'Tell me, Mr Nightingale, what do you know of Voodoo?'

Nightingale decided to play his cards close to his chest. 'Not much,' he said. 'You mean rituals and zombies. Stuff like that?'

Jefferson grimaced at that. 'You seem to have the tourist idea. Voodoo is an old religion, generally used for good. It's true it can have other uses, and the rumour runs that this new power has a powerful Voodoo connection. There is even a suggestion that he uses zombies for his hits.'

'You believe that?' asked Nightingale.

'There are more things in heaven and earth than are dreamed of in your philosophies, right?'

Nightingale had never anticipated hearing a New Orleans Mob boss quoting Shakespeare at him. Much less the same line he'd heard from the priest the day before. 'So what do you want from me?' asked Nightingale.

'I want you to share what you find out. If you discover the identity of this man, I will need to know, so I can…make arrangements.'

'You don't have your own sources?' asked Nightingale.

'I do indeed. But they are not helping me, and I have lost some good people.'

'Whereas I'm expendable?' said Nightingale.

Jefferson laughed. 'I guess you are,' he said. 'But when it comes to making enquiries, you also enjoy one other advantage over the majority of my associates.'

'Which is?'

'Whiteness.'

Nightingale frowned. 'You telling me that you think this guy is white?'

'As I mentioned, I have no idea of his identity, it's just something that gets whispered around. I do know that any of my operatives who have tried to find out more have been returned to me with several important body parts missing. My operatives are as loyal as anyone else's, and they have a healthy respect for my anger. But they are not impervious to the kind of pain some of them have suffered.'

'And you've never managed to get any of his operatives to talk?'

'A very interesting question. Perhaps I should show you something.'

Jefferson pressed his fingers together, and looked across at the heavy, who occupied most of the next booth. 'Percy, please ask Stanley to bring the large car round, and join myself and Mr Nightingale for a little drive.'

Jefferson must have caught the quick look of concern in Nightingale's eyes. 'Don't worry yourself, Mr Nightingale. If I meant you any harm, you would already be dead by now, and would certainly never have known my name.'

Nightingale forced a smile. 'Thank you, that's very reassuring.'

Jefferson nodded. 'Let's hope that happy state of affairs continues.'

That wasn't so reassuring.

After a short drive, the car stopped, and Percy and Stanley got out to look carefully around before opening the rear doors. They were parked in front of a modern upscale apartment block. Percy walked across to the front door, pressed the intercom, and spoke a seemingly random set of numbers into it. The door lock clicked immediately.

Jefferson laid a hand on Nightingale's shoulder.

'Any competent detective could discover this address very easily. You would be very ill-advised to return here except at my personal invitation, and with myself or Percy to escort you.'

Nightingale nodded. He had already noticed that there were very few white faces to be seen, and wondered how many of the seemingly casual bystanders were paid by Jefferson.

Percy held the door open, and the other three walked in. Stanley and Jefferson headed for the bank of elevators, and Nightingale stopped, looking for the stairs. Jefferson missed nothing.

'Is there a problem, Mr Nightingale?'

'I don't like elevators much, mind if I take the stairs?'

'It's the top floor, I would prefer you not to be in here unescorted, and none of us would appreciate the walk up with you. Indulge me this once.'

Nightingale looked at Percy, who gave him a huge smile, and, inevitably, Nightingale stepped into the lift. He did his level best to keep his breathing steady all the way up, but still had to wipe away the sweat from his brow when the door opened again.

'Thank you Mr Nightingale,' said Jefferson, 'I regret making you feel uncomfortable. Many of us have seemingly minor things that we avoid if at all possible.'

Nightingale thought about asking Jefferson for a list, but decided that British humour might be too much of a risk. The man was unfailingly polite, but there was no doubt that Nightingale's life would be over the minute Jefferson decided that he was a nuisance.

There were no numbers on the apartment doors on this floor, but Percy walked straight up to the first door on the right and knocked three times. The door opened on a chain, then closed and opened again. They stepped inside.

It wasn't an apartment at all, it was one huge room which ran the whole length of the building, down to the far wall, where a passage presumably led to the other half of the floor, across the hall. There were black leather sofas dotted around, a couple of huge-screen TVs, both switched off, but not a great deal else in the way of creature comforts. Nightingale kept looking round, but saw nothing to indicate why he'd been brought there. Three tall, heavily built black men stood in the centre of the room, looking at Nightingale with mild interest, but no warmth. They seemed to have been pressed from a very similar, if slightly smaller, mould to Percy.

Jefferson smiled at him.

'There are some advantages to designing, and owning, one's property,' he said. 'Gentlemen, this is Jack. At the moment he is of use to me, and should be considered a friend. You won't need to know these gentlemen's names, Jack.'

Nightingale nodded. As far as he was concerned, the less he knew about Jefferson's affairs the healthier he would feel.

Jefferson addressed the man in the middle. 'And how is our…guest?' he asked, with just a slight hesitation before the final word.

No change, was the answer.

'She has eaten? Has she drunk anything?'

'No, sir, She will not, and we had no instructions to force her.'

'Quite right, I would not wish her damaged...any more than has been necessary. Come with me, Jack, Percy, The rest of you stay here please.'

The three men walked to the far end of the room, turned left and took the narrow passage that led to the other side of the hallway. Again, this side was not divided into separate apartments, but there were several interior doors off a hallway. One or two were open, and Nightingale could see a kitchen, and two bathrooms.

'Nice place,' said Nightingale.

'It has its uses,' replied Jefferson. The large room and several of the bedrooms are effectively soundproof. Not that there is anyone living on the two floors below.'

Nightingale shuddered, as he considered what that might mean for Jefferson's 'guests'. He sincerely hoped he wasn't destined to be numbered among them.

Percy opened the door of the furthest room, with a key from a bunch he took from his pocket, took a quick look inside, nodded, and then stood to the left of the door for Nightingale and Jefferson to enter. Jefferson clicked on the ceiling light as he walked in. The first thing that Nightingale noticed was that the room had no window, and had been in total darkness when they entered.

The second thing was the naked woman lying on the bed.

CHAPTER 31

Madison DeWitt heard a knock at the door of her office, and, without looking up from her computer, called out. 'Come in.' She heard the door open and close, then finally looked up, a smile on her face, ready to greet her visitors. The smile froze, then turned to a puzzled look, as she saw the two black-robed figures standing in front of her.

The second last thing she ever thought was that she had never seen a black nun before, let alone two. Her final thought, as they walked briskly towards her, was that she'd certainly never seen any nuns with that amount of make-up, but, by then, one of them had grasped her wrist in a grip of steel, and the other was behind her, pulling the cheese wire tight and through her throat.

Neither of the nuns spoke a word, they just moved to the door on the right, one of them opened it, and the two walked quickly inside, closing it behind them. There was the sound of one voice speaking a few words, and then nothing.

CHAPTER 32

The naked woman on the bed looked to be in her mid twenties, black, with short straightened hair. The inside of both arms bore the track marks from numerous injections and there were half a dozen cigarette burns on the inside of her thighs, but otherwise she looked in pretty fair shape, She lay on the bed, her brown eyes fully opened, staring straight ahead of her, up at the ceiling. The only other blemish on her body was a huge bruise on the left side of her jaw. She gave no sign at all that she had noticed the men entering the room. She lay completely still, only the slight rise and fall of her breast betraying that she was still alive.

Nightingale took a good long look, then turned towards Jefferson, waiting for an explanation.

'She came for Percy, at his apartment. Brought a birthday card, meant to be from me. Wasn't, which Percy knew damned well, since I get him a new car for his birthday, every July. Percy's good at noticing things, and her necklace was a long strand of wire with two wooden toggles. Set him to thinking about Delroy and Spike. He took a swing at her, she went down.'

'I'm not surprised. I bet he packs a punch.'

'He does indeed, and he says there was plenty on this one. Force of it knocked her off her feet and down to the floor. Damned if she didn't shake her head and get straight back up again.'

Nightingale's eyes widened.

'Percy threw her on the bed, put plenty of his weight on her, wrapped her in sheets, tied them with a tie and belt, called me and I told him to ship her down here, That's three days ago, in that time she's eaten nothing, drunk nothing, and not said a word. Just keeps staring into space.'

'You tried persuading her to talk?'

Jefferson gestured at the cigarette burns. 'What you think? Makes no difference, she doesn't seem to feel any kind of pain, never says a word, never even changes her expression. You ask me, she doesn't know we're asking her anything. Doesn't even know she's alive. It's like someone programmed her to put a hit on Percy, and now she's shut down. We gave up pretty quick on trying to get anything out of her, it was like trying to get answers from a loin of pork.'

'Do you think there's anything medically wrong?'

'Got a tame doctor to look at her. He says she's okay, though her breathing and pulse is low. Says her skin's not in great shape either, almost as if it was starting to flake off.'

'And what do you make of that?'

'I don't make anything of it. Mystery to me, though seems to have a few connections to the affair of the late Delroy. Black girl, cheese wire. So does this help you with your case?'

'Not much, but it's all data. Anything else?'

'Yes there is, though I don't know if it means anything. Check her right shoulder.'

Nightingale's stomach lurched, and he lifted the girl's shoulder from the bed. He found exactly what he'd expected. A goat's head, the Goat of Mendes, and a seven pointed star. Nightingale kept his face as expressionless as he could. 'So?'

'Does that mean anything to you?'

'Should it?'

'Answering a question with a question,' said Jefferson. 'Some people might say you're evading giving a straight answer. Lots of young girls got tattoos now, thing is, they don't usually stop at one. Specially if they have an addictive personality. Besides, the doc says that isn't a tattoo, it's a brand. Done with a hot iron. Pretty recently. Must have hurt like hell.'

'Must have.'

Jefferson looked at him for a whole minute without saying anything. Finally he spoke. 'If you know something, maybe my boys could get it out of you.'

'If I don't, maybe I'd end up damaged, and then what use would I be to you?'

'There is that. Oh, one more thing. We ran her prints and DNA. I have friends in the NOPD.' He smiled. 'Jamella Carter, aged twenty-four. Three arrests for possession, two for hooking.'

'No great surprise there.'

'This might be. We went to her apartment. Her sister says she died of pneumonia two weeks ago. Looking at those tracks, maybe I know what brought it on. So what's she doing walking around and trying to kill Percy three days since?'

It was a fair question and Nightingale had no answer to it. Nor to the question of how and why a New Orleans street junkie came to be bearing the brand of the Order Of The Nine Angles on her shoulder.

There was a knock on the door, and one of the other large men walked in. He held up his phone and pointed to it, Jefferson walked back outside with him, and was gone for no more than two minutes, When he returned, his face was deadly serious. 'I sent one of my boys down to Dreamgirls,' he said. 'Thought I'd get Mrs Goldman's side of the story, just be checking you hadn't forgotten anything. He says the place looks like a slaughterhouse. Blood everywhere, her and the secretary garrotted it looks like. Seems you were the last person to see them alive.'

Nightingale shuddered, it was barely an hour since he'd spoken to the women. 'Second last,' said Nightingale. 'You're forgetting whoever killed them.'

'So you say. What proof do you have that you're not the killer?'

'Well, you know I didn't kill Delroy, or make a run at Percy. And you can't see any blood on me.'

Jefferson smiled again. 'There is that. Also the fact that Percy spoke to her just before he picked you up. You had no time. But it's a big coincidence that they killed them just after you left, and I don't like coincidences.'

'Maybe Percy isn't the only one following me around?'

'Could be. Look, this is getting way stranger than a little disagreement over territories. I'm no great believer in Voodoo or Hoodoo, but that doesn't mean it can't happen. You know something about it?'

'Not much,' said Nightingale, 'but maybe I could come up with one or two people to ask.'

'The way I see it, I lose nothing by letting you run with it a while. Anything you find out comes straight to me. Percy will give you his card when he drops you off back at your car.'

He nodded at Percy, and Nightingale accepted his dismissal. Then he turned back. 'You mind if I make a call first?'

'Knock yourself out.'

'It's a little private.'

'Step into the next room.'

Nightingale left them and called Wainwright. 'Joshua, I'm with a girl who seems to have gone the same route as Bethany Cole.'

'You mean she's dead twice?'

'Just the once so far, then she seems to have been resurrected to try to kill another hood. She failed, and they've caught her, but she won't talk. And they've been pretty persuasive.'

'If she's one of the walking dead, they don't have the power to speak, or so the story goes. And she won't feel pain, being dead.'

'What I really want to know, is how dead is she?'

'Usually dead is an either or thing, Jack.'

'I know that too, but this girl was walking and is still breathing. Where's her spirit, her self?'

'Beats me, Jack. Maybe it hasn't passed to Hell or Heaven yet, who knows, what difference can it make?'

'I was wondering whether it might be possible to get in touch with her some way.'

Wainwright let out a whistle. 'Shit, that's heavy stuff, Jack. Summoning back the dead, there's a lot of things can go wrong.'

'Yeah, I remember, but maybe there are different rules for the not quite dead.'

'You might try that Devereaux woman, she seemed pretty well up on Voodoo rituals.'

'I think she'd be horrified at the idea. She's more of a healer, a *herbalist.*'

There was a pause. 'Look, Jack, if there's a way to do this,it's going to be in a book I have here, but have never read. *The Grimoire of Doctor John.*'

'The musician?'

'Hardly. This was a New Orleans Voodoo king in the 19th century. A freed slave from Senegal. He was famous as a healer, in fact people said he was so good that he could raise the dead. I paid more money than you'd believe for his spellbook, it's the only copy there is. Leave it with me, I'll need an hour, but if it's in there, I'll find it.'

He ended the call and Nightingale walked back into the main room where he nodded at Jefferson.

'There might be a way to get some information from her,' he said. 'A good friend of mine's doing some research. It'll take him an hour or so.'

'You want to wait here?'

'I'll go and grab a coffee.'

'There's a coffee shop across the road.' He nodded at the driver. 'Henry can go with you.'

'I'm not planning on running.'

'That's good, because you wouldn't get far.'

'But I might need to collect some things, so he can drive me.'

'Whatever you need,' said Jefferson.

Henry escorted Nightingale out of the building and across the road to a small coffee shop. They sat in the window and drank coffees and Henry munched through three Danish pastries.

Wainwright called and sent full instructions to Nightingale's phone. He gave Nightingale time to digest the message and phoned back. He spoke very slowly and deliberately. 'Jack, this isn't like a recipe from Martha Stewart's cook book, I have no idea whether it might work or not. I do know that anything involving summoning the dead, or even the half-dead, is incredibly dangerous. You can never know for sure who's going to turn up, and what they're going to do. I've known people who died trying, and some who were never the same again after they tried it. And, whatever else you do, don't forget the crucifix.'

'Well, unless you're going to fly here and do it for me, I'm just going to have to do the best I can. And I won't forget the crucifix.'

Henry finished his pastries and then drove Nightingale to the Esoterica Occult store, where Nightingale picked up the items he needed easily enough.

Jefferson cast a curious glance at the brown paper bag in Nightingale's hand when he returned, but asked no questions.

'Mr Jefferson, I'm going to need to take a shower before I start. And then I'll need to be alone with the girl.'

Jefferson nodded and pointed at a door. 'Through there. As for being alone, that can be arranged, but you'll have no objection to our leaving the cameras running.'

'No, that's fine, but you might be a little surprised at what you see.'

Jefferson smiled thinly. 'Not much surprises me in New Orleans. Besides which, a mutual friend has already advised me that you can be quite a surprising guy.'

He could only have meant Wainwright, but neither man spoke his name. Nightingale thought it cleared up Jefferson's knowing his preference in beers. 'I wasn't aware you knew the gentleman.'

'He's a man it pays to know,' said Jefferson. 'I had a call from him soon after you arrived here. He figured that if you started asking questions and annoying people, you'd come to my notice sooner rather than later and he wouldn't have wanted us on opposite sides. Anyway, Mr Nightingale, the floor is yours. Help will be at hand if you call for it.'

Nightingale got to work. He showered and washed his hair, then put on a new white towelling robe and walked into the room where Jamella still lay motionless on the bed. He took five squat candles from his bag, arranged two on each side of the bed, and one at the bottom, then lit them with his cigarette lighter. He pulled seven hairs from the girl's head, and laid them on the bedside table. She never flinched or made a sound.

Nightingale took a copper bowl from the bag and set it on the table over a spirit burner, which he also lit. He opened a parcel of herbs, and poured them into the bowl and set fire to them The smell was unpleasant, and his eyes started to water.

Now, to remember his script. 'Archangels of Heaven, protect me. Gabriel in front of me, Michael behind. Rafael to my left, Uriel to my right. I summon the spirit of Jamella Carter.'

Now came the tricky part, Dr John's spellbook was written in French, Nightingale hadn't tried speaking the language since school, and it had never been a strength. He picked up the little vial of salt, which he'd been assured had been suitably blessed by a priest and emptied it into the bowl.

'Avec le sel, je t'appelle.'

The flame from the herbs shot up and shone blue.

He took the seven hairs from Jamella's head and added them to the bowl.

'*Avec les cheveux, je t'appelle.*'

This time the flame was green.

Nightingale took a bodkin from the bag and pricked his left index finger. He squeezed seven drops of blood into the bowl.

'*Par ce sang versé je t'appelle.*'

The flame died down, then rose again with a red glow. He took a deep breath.

'*Je t'invoque par ces mots, je t'invoque. Jamella Carter, je t'invoque.*'

Nothing.

'Concentrate,' he muttered to himself. 'Believe, Jack, believe.'

'*Je t'invoque par ces mots, je t'invoque. Jamella Carter, je t'invoque.*'

The girl's lips started to move, her eyes focused on him. He almost forgot the most important precaution, but then slipped the chain of the silver crucifix around her neck. The girl showed no reaction. Which was a good sign. If a demon from Hell had manifested itself, she would have screamed at the touch of it and tried to tear it off.

'Jamella, Jamella Carter, speak to me.'

The lips opened, and stayed parted. The words came out slowly, in a harsh metallic voice.

'Why have you summoned me from the Twelve Gates? I should not be here.'

'I have questions for you, will you answer me truthfully?'

'I am bound by the summoning. I must answer truthfully, but I can not remain here long.'

'Did you die of pneumonia?'

'No, I was sick, but I was murdered.'

'By whom?'

'By the Docteur.'

'What is the doctor's name?'

'Amede.'

'And he gave you life again?'

'No, it was not he. It was the *Roumwytha.*'

'Who is the *Roumwytha?*'

'I do not know, I never saw the face of the *Rounwytha*. Just the mask. And the hood.'

'Who sent you here?'

'It was the *Rounwytha*. I was sent here to cull the black man Percy. The Docteur brought me, and was to collect me, but I failed. I was to walk into the river when my task was complete, but now I have failed. The *Rounwytha* will be displeased.'

'Cull? You mean kill?'

'No. We cull. That is what we do.'

'Where can I find Doctor Amede, where can I find this *Rounwytha*?'

'I do not know, I do not know. I must not say. I can no longer stay here, the Twelve Gates are calling to me, I must go there...'

The candles flickered and died. The brown eyes lost focus and stared dumbly at the ceiling. The lips closed. The body was still breathing, but the spirit had deserted it again.

Nightingale heard the door behind him open, and Jefferson spoke. 'A most interesting performance, Mr Nightingale. It seems our mutual friend was correct, you are a very unusual man.'

Nightingale slumped to the floor, picked up his cigarettes from the table and lit one. He smoked in silence for a minute, before his hands stopped shaking. 'Well,' he said, 'we have two names. Amede and the *Rounwytha*. Not sure we're any further forward.'

'I never heard of a *Rounwytha*,' said Jefferson, 'but I am familiar with a Doctor Amede.'

'Yes, said Nightingale. 'maybe that name has come up before. I was told Habeeb, but maybe it was Amede. What do you know about him? He's a faith healer?'

''Oh yes, though faith healer falls a long way short of describing his sphere of activities. Voodoo priest, Hoodoo man, Juju peddler, quack, but well respected and feared by the more gullible folks. Makes a lot of money with potions, curses and anti-curses. Got quite the congregation for his little services too. Some people swear he's cured them of all kinds of stuff.'

'Got an address?'

'These days he don't take house visits. Tends to appear by request, and disappear afterwards. Though I could probably find out where he can be found, given a little time.'

'I'll be waiting. I need to talk to him.'

CHAPTER 33

The ritual had sapped Nightingale's strength and he was almost falling asleep when he handed his keys in at the hotel parking lot and crossed the street. He'd gone no more than fifty feet when he saw her, leaning against a street light, one leg bent and drawn up behind her, the sole of her boot pressed against the lamppost, like a caricature of a streetwalker. But he knew better.

She'd gone back to her old spiky fringe which hung low over her eyes and made the dead-white face look almost blue. The long black leather coat was missing, but she had kept the black leather shorts, torn, black fishnet tights and long studded black boots. Her T-shirt was also black, with a drawing in white of a top hat, with a long feather pushed into the band. The slogan was in purple, and read *The Voodoo That I do*. Her earrings were silver skulls, and another skull hung from the spiked dog collar round her neck.

The eyes always made Nightingale shudder. Black as night, the irises merging completely into the pupils, no expression, no warmth. Maybe no soul.

'Enjoying the weather, Nightingale? A little warmer than Wyoming.'

Nightingale flashed her a cold smile. 'Proserpine. Where's the pooch?' It was the first time Nightingale had seen her without the black and white sheepdog by her side.

'Pooch? I suggest you mind your manners, Nightingale, he wouldn't care for that term, and you've seen for yourself how difficult he can be when someone upsets him.' She ran a hand through her hair. 'He's not far away. He's running a little errand for me. He was rather hungry anyway, so, two birds with one stone.'

'So,' he said, 'still keeping tabs on me?'

She shook her head. 'Always the ego, Nightingale. I've told you before, you don't occupy my thoughts at all.'

'And yet you always seem to turn up wherever I am.'

136

She drew her lips back to show the vulpine teeth. It couldn't have been called a smile. 'Perhaps you have that backwards, Nightingale. Maybe you're the one intruding.'

'Intruding on what?'

She pressed her lips back together, and widened her eyes at him. It was like staring into twin pools of nothingness, and, despite himself, he shuddered. 'I really wouldn't be questioning me like that, if I were you. You've also seen how difficult I can be when someone upsets me.'

Nightingale surely had, and seen the corpses to prove it. 'No offence. Anyway, I had the feeling you kind of liked me.'

She shook her head. 'Don't delude yourself, Nightingale. You're a minor piece of unfinished business. Your soul was pledged to me, it is still owed to me, and I shall have it.'

'Not yet. And there are other people who think they have a claim too.'

'Perhaps people might not be the right word,' she said. 'But maybe that's all that's saved you so far. Though you seem to be keeping strange company at the moment.'

Nightingale said nothing. His police training had always stressed the importance of silence when a suspect was talking. Proserpine was in a different league, but maybe the same rules held. Besides which, he wasn't about to speak Lucifuge's name aloud.

She smiled slyly. 'Cat got your tongue, then, Nightingale? If you want to do the thoughtful silence bit, remember that I could stand here mute for a thousand years.'

Maybe police training didn't work with a Princess of Hell after all. But Nightingale had no idea how much she might know, and really didn't want to use Lucifuge's name. 'Wasn't it you who used that chess analogy?' he said. 'Sometimes we play white, sometimes black. Friends turn into enemies and vice versa.'

'I used it about my kind, not yours. You're far too simple a creature to make such distinctions. What have you been offered?'

'Why would you be interested?'

This time it was nearer to a smile, though without much humour. 'A question for a question. Same old Nightingale.'

'Well, I'd love to stay and chat,' he said. 'But you know, places to see, people to go…'

She held up the index finger of her right hand, and he stopped talking. 'Don't push your luck, Nightingale. My patience isn't limitless.'

'I know, you could kill me any time you wanted, without sparing it a thought. But still you don't. So tell me why you're here.'

'Just checking on my investment. And a warning. No point in telling you not to be fooled by appearances, it would be like telling a junkie not to take a fix. But choose your enemies carefully Nightingale. And your friends even more carefully. There are things happening here that you can't begin to understand. You get in the way, and it'll be like that kid at the Memphis Railroad Station. You'll just be crushed.'

Nightingale shuddered at the memory. 'So you have something big planned here?'

'You need to listen to what I say, Nightingale, rather than put words into my mouth. This could come out very badly for you, and for those who matter to you.'

'There isn't anyone any more. You and your friends saw to that.'

'Isn't there, Nightingale? Isn't there really? And, like I said, not everyone who claims to be a friend really is one. Not to you, or to me.'

'But the Nine Angles pledge allegiance to you.'

'Some do. But I don't pledge allegiance to them, or guide their every thought. You used to be a football fan when you were little, Nightingale. Manchester United, wasn't it? Red shirt, red scarf. That was your allegiance.'

'So what?'

'Just showing that a pledge of allegiance works one way. Do you think any of those players had the faintest idea who you were? When you were fifteen and shoplifted that half-bottle of vodka, do you think they knew about it, much less had instructed you to do it? You were just a vague follower, one among millions. Same goes here. I'm not responsible for every action of those who pledge allegiance to me.'

Nightingale was speechless. Was there anything she didn't know about him?

Her gaze passed over his shoulder. 'Ah, there you are boy…'

Nightingale heard a low growl behind him, and spun round. There was nothing. He turned back, and Proserpine had gone.

He forced his hands to stop shaking long enough to light a cigarette. 'Just when you think that things can't get any worse...' he muttered to himself.

CHAPTER 34

An encounter with Proserpine, following on from the long meeting with Jefferson, had left Nightingale's stress levels way too high, so he opened a beer from the minibar in his hotel room, and lay on the bed to try to unwind for a while. He'd taken no more than two sips, when his eyelids started to get heavy, and after the third, the can slipped from his hand, and he fell asleep.

He opened his eyes wide again, and focused on the road ahead of him. He was in his latest hire-car, but the two-lane road ahead of him was unfamiliar. He struggled to remember where he was heading, but couldn't even recall where he was coming from. There seemed to be no other vehicles on the road in either direction, so he pressed the accelerator until the display read sixty. Wherever he was headed, better to get there sooner, rather than later.

He hit the brake, as she stepped out of the bushes a hundred yards ahead of him, waving both her arms wildly at him. He skidded to a halt, twenty yards past her. If she'd walked onto the highway, he'd have hit her, for sure.

He opened the door, stepped out and looked back at her. The same woman, tall, red and copper hair, the same emerald green dress. She ran to him, threw her arms around him, and he could feel her warm breath in his ear as she spoke with that same soft lilt.

Oh, Jack. Save me. You must save me. You will come to me when I call. You must save me, or I shall be forever lost.'

'But save you from what? From who? Who are you, how do you know me? What are you doing in my dreams?'

She put her index finger on his lips. 'So many questions. You will have your answers soon. But you must be ready to come to me when I call. And you must bring the doll, Jack. We will need the doll, you cannot save me without the doll. Get it.'

There was real urgency in her voice now. 'Yes, I will get it,' he said. 'And bring it to you when you call. But who are you?'

She dropped her arms to her sides, took three steps back, and fixed her shining green eyes on his. 'Call me Brigid,' she said. 'And come when I call.'

Nightingale woke up on his hotel bed, soaked in beer from the dropped can. He headed for the shower.

He arrived by taxi outside the *Papa Dimanche* store thirty minutes later, pushed the door open and heard the chimes.

Melvin Hargreaves was standing behind his counter, looking as if he hadn't moved an inch since yesterday. He looked up as Nightingale entered, and gave him a weak smile.

'Ah, Mr Nightingale, how nice to see you yet again. Something told me you'd be returning quite soon.'

'A little bird.'

Hargreaves looked puzzled for a moment, then smiled again. 'Oh, I see, a little bird. Like a Nightingale, perhaps?'

Nightingale hadn't intended it for a joke, so pressed on. 'No sign of the man who ordered the doll in the green dress?'

Hargreaves gave him a long look, then shook his head. 'I fear not sir. He seems to have disappeared into thin air.'

'There never was another man, was there? Who fed you this story, who put you up to it?'

Hargreaves blinked and took a step backwards. Nightingale could sense his fear. 'Nobody sir. I promise you, you, or someone very like you, came in and described the woman to me and asked me to make the doll.'

Nightingale clenched his fists inside his raincoat pocket, but then relaxed. He'd never been the type to beat a confession out of a suspect. Except for that one time. Allegedly. Anyway, he heard the bell behind him, and a young couple entered the shop and started to look around. 'That doll isn't in the window now. Did you sell it?'

'Oh no, sir. I wouldn't have done that.'

'So can I buy it?'

'Of course you can, sir. It's yours.' Hargreaves bent down behind his counter, then straightened back up, a package wrapped in shiny green paper in his hand, He laid it on the counter, and pushed it across towards Nightingale. 'All wrapped ready for you, I hope you'll find it satisfactory.'

Nightingale pulled out his wallet. 'How much do I owe?'

'Why, nothing, sir.'

'Nothing? Why not?'

'You paid me when you placed the order, sir. All settled.'

'But that wasn't me.'

'Well...no, sir. But it does seem that the...er...other gentleman isn't coming back. I'm sure it'll be perfectly alright.'

The bell tinkled again.

'Maybe. Perhaps I'll come back and talk to you when you're not so busy.'

Nightingale gave it up, took the package and headed back to his hotel. Once there, he tore off the green paper, opened the black box with *Vodun* written on it, and took out the doll. He held it in both hands and stared at it. It was Brigid, no question. As he held it, he stroked the hair and gazed into the green eyes. They seemed to widen and deepen as he looked at them. He felt a tingle run up his arms, and settle in the pit of his stomach. He shuddered, closed his eyes, opened them again, took the doll and placed it on the bedside table.

CHAPTER 35

Miles away, two black-gloved hands held another doll. A similar size, but this one was dressed in black jeans and a black shirt, a battered beige overcoat over the top, On its feet were scuffed shoes of brown suede. The hair was untidy and in the right hand there was a tiny cigarette, the red tip looking as if it would burn anyone who touched it.

A quiet voice spoke. 'It is done. The dolls are connected, and my control is established. He will be mine to use as I wish now. But not yet, there are still preparations to be made.'

Another voice, sounding nervous. 'Yes. Concerning the other matters…'

'Tell me.'

'The woman Goldman and her secretary were successfully culled. The two who carried it out were showing signs of deterioration, so their usefulness has ended, and I have ordered them disposed of. Then the river.'

'Yes, it was unfortunate that we could not deal with the other three properly, but one cannot foresee everything.'

'The one sent to cull the bodyguard has not returned, and he still lives."

'We must assume failure, and probably that they still have her. They will learn nothing, but I shall advance her time.'

There was a silence in the room, and the black-gloved hands took up a small, black, wooden doll in one hand, and a viciously sharp stiletto in the other.

'Sleep forever now, Jamella.'

The stiletto was pushed straight into the soft wooden head.

'And the shopkeeper?'

'Yes, he is a loose end. He told the story we gave him, but he is weak, It would not be difficult to make him tell what he knows if he were threatened. I shall pay him a visit, and explain this to him, It will be a useful test of my powers.'

CHAPTER 36

Melvyn Hargreaves had no urgent commissions to work on, so was making an inventory of his stock in the back room, when the bell rang in the shop. He stood up from his computer and walked out into the front, flexing his fingers to unstiffen them. His attempt at a welcoming smile froze on his lips when he saw the visitor. His hands started to shake, and there was a tremor in his voice. 'I...I was not expecting you to call, though...of...of course, I am delighted to see you. How may I serve you?'

The *Rounwytha* smiled at him.

'Calm down, Melvyn, there is no need to be frightened, you know I would never harm you. So, did the Englishman return for the doll?'

'Yes, it was just as you predicted. I told him what you ordered me to.'

'And he seemed satisfied?'

'I am not sure. He said he might return later, when the shop was not so busy.'

'Yes, it seems likely that he would, he is quite determined, and he knows the story you told him is untrue. He would press you for the truth.'

'You know I would never betray you. He would learn nothing from me.'

The *Rounwytha* nodded. 'I have every confidence in your loyalty to me, Melvyn. Perhaps not so much in your strength.'

'I will tell him nothing.'

'How old are you, Melvyn?'

Hargreaves paused at the sudden change of subject. 'I am seventy-three.'

'A long life. You have served me well in these past years, and you deserve your reward.'

'My...my reward?'

'Yes. Look at me, Melvin and listen to my voice. Listen to my voice. Listen to my voice.'

Hargreaves felt himself growing tired as he listened to the low insistent voice, and gazed into the deep, green eyes which seemed to draw him into their depths. He could not look away, he couldn't ignore that voice.

'Yes, You are tired,Melvyn. Life has been long and wearisome, You have served your masters well, and now it is time to seek your reward. Go, Melvin, go to your reward. Leave your pain and cares behind you. Go to your reward.'

Hargreaves nodded, but said nothing. In silence, he showed his visitor out of the shop, and turned the sign on the door to *Closed*. Inside the shop, he lowered the blinds on the windows and door, then walked into the back workshop. He took a length of the rope which he generally used to tie up crates from the corner of the room and tied one end into a noose. He took the step-ladder from in front of his bookshelves and leaned it against the wall, just under the small, steel-barred window set high in the back wall. He climbed up six steps of the ladder, then tied the free end of the rope around the bars in a secure knot. He pulled on it to test his work, slipped the noose over his neck, climbed up one more step, turned and jumped.

The drop wasn't long enough, nor the knot placed accurately enough to break his neck, so Melvyn Hargreaves took ten minutes to die from occlusion of his jugular veins. In all that time, as his face turned bluer, he made no sound or movement, except for a gentle slow spinning at the end of the rope.

CHAPTER 37

Nightingale's mobile phone rang There were now a few more people who knew his number, but he didn't recognise this caller. He pressed the green button, but said nothing.

'Mr Nightingale, this is Percy. I have been asked to give you some information.'

'I'll get a pen.'

No need, I'll send you a message. We've been told where the Voodoo man who calls himself Docteur Amede can be found. He operates from an old farmhouse down by the bayou. It can be reached by road, a track off the interstate. 'Perhaps I should pay him a visit.'

'I wouldn't recommend that. He's surrounded by armed guards.'

'And Mr Jefferson doesn't feel like arranging a visit?'

'My boss has no wish to get involved in a shooting war just yet. Not on the basis of you talking to a dead girl.'

'I see his point. Maybe I can find a way in that's a little less dramatic.'

Nightingale ended the conversation and called Chris Dubois. 'Can I see you, as soon as possible?'

'Joshua Wainwright's paying me enough to make you a priority, can you find Jill's again? In forty minutes?'

'I'll be there.'

Nightingale needed to pass Hargreaves's store on the way to Jill's, so decided to see if it was empty, and whether he could persuade the man to come up with the truth. The front window was dark, the door screen pulled down and nobody answered when he rang the doorbell. He gave up and went to Jill's.

Nightingale walked over to the booth when he spotted Chris Dubois behind a glass of tomato juice. He sat opposite her and ordered coffee. She looked up, but didn't bother with a welcoming smile. 'What do you need?' she asked.

'I think I may have a lead on a guy who caused Bethany Cole's death.'

'Which death?'

'The second one. The permanent one.'

'And who is he?'

'Apparently he's a Voodoo medicine man. Name of Docteur Amede. Does that ring a bell?'

She shook her head. 'No, but then I told you, I'm no Voodoo expert, so I'm not up on the names. What makes you think he's involved?'

'I had a tip-off from some guys who might not want their names known.'

She stared at him, and Nightingale tried hard to keep his face straight. He didn't much like lying to her, but the truth would be hard to swallow.

'How do you think he's involved?' she asked eventually.

'I'm not certain. Maybe there's some drug he gives the girls.'

'Girls?'

'Yes,' said Nightingale. 'I ran into another ex-escort turned hit-woman recently.'

'My, you do move in interesting circles. Who did she kill?'

'This one was a misfire. You probably don't need to hear the name.'

'You're not a man who shares confidences easily, are you?'

'It might be in your own interests not to know,' said Nightingale. 'I have an address and some details.' He showed her his phone screen, with the map and location that Percy had sent.

'I've never been there,' she said, 'but I know where it is. Looks pretty isolated, out between the bayou and the main highway. You planning to make an appointment?'

'Maybe not. My sources say it's invited guests only.'

'And you figure his list won't include nosy Englishmen?'

'Something like that. I was wondering if there's any way to scout the place out, before I figure a way in.'

She smiled. 'Well now, maybe I can help you there. You want to do a little reconnaissance, you need the eye in the sky.'

CHAPTER 38

Nightingale was bone-tired by the time he got back to his hotel room. Chris Dubois was nowhere near convinced of the zombie idea, but had agreed to keep searching for any agency that Bethany might have worked with in the period between leaving Dreamgirls and her first death. Nightingale wasn't at all hopeful of any results, since the girl wouldn't have been using her real name, and any photos were probably long gone, but the more threads they pulled at, the more chance of something unravelling.

He sat on his bed and called the Reverend Elijah Cole on his mobile phone. 'Reverend Cole. Jack Nightingale, sorry to call so late. This is a little awkward, but it could be important. When you identified Bethany the...the first time, did they just show you her face?'

'No, they didn't. They wanted to be very sure, of course, so in addition to her face, I was able to point out one or two particular features. An appendectomy scar when she was sixteen, a small red birthmark on her inner left thigh, and an incipient bunion on her left foot, from too many ballet classes as a kid. They were all present and correct.'

'Did you notice anything else about her body?'

'It was thinner than when I had last seen her, maybe the effects of the disease. And she had acquired some tattoos.'

'Lots of them?'

'Not so many. I suspect they didn't really work so well with her dark colouring. On her lower back, she had what I believe they call a 'tramp stamp', a Y-shaped floral design. On her right shoulder was a blue dolphin. On her left shoulder blade there was...an animal, and a star.'

'What kind of animal?' asked Nightingale.

The priest paused for a moment, obviously trying to picture in his mind something he had dismissed as insignificant a few weeks ago. 'A ram? A stag? I know it had horns.'

'And the star, could you describe it?'

Another pause. 'No, I'm sorry, it just registered as a star. Is it important?'

'It's okay, I think I've got the idea. Would you have any idea when these tattoos were done?'

'None at all, I'm afraid, my sister and I bathed together as kids, but it's been decades since I saw her undressed. The animal one looked somehow...deeper, I don't know if that would make it more recent?'

Nightingale ended the call and lay back on the bed, staring at the ceiling. He was almost asleep when the phone rang. It was Jefferson. 'Nightingale, that girl up and died on us.'

'How?'

'She just stopped breathing. Doctor can't really explain it too well. He seems to think that she died of pneumonia. But get this, he says she died at least two weeks ago.'

'Well, we all know that's not possible. She was talking today.'

'Something was keeping her going. You ask me, whoever sent her decided it was time she checked out.'

'You think that someone could kill her from a distance?'

'Beats me. That's your department, Mr Magic Man.'

CHAPTER 39

Nightingale woke early after a dreamless sleep. He ordered breakfast in his room and showered, shaved and changed into fresh clothes before it was delivered to his room

Once he'd finished his eggs and bacon and drunk the last of his coffee, he called Joshua Wainwright. He answered on the first ring. 'Jack. How's it going?'

'I'm not sure I'm getting anywhere. I seem to be firing off in lots of different directions. I think Cameron Lattimore and Gonzalez might have consulted the same faith healer. Some self-styled doctor by the name of Amede. His name came up when I called back the dead girl's spirit. I'm going to try to take a look at his place from the air later today.'

There was no reply.

'You still there?' asked Nightingale.

'Yeah. This sounds pretty bad. Bringing back the dead isn't cabaret magic, Jack, It would take an Adept of immense power to do it. Unless the dead woman wasn't dead, but had been given some drug to put her into a catatonic state.'

'Wouldn't a doctor be able to tell the difference?'

'No idea. But then of course these people might have a tame doctor in tow. Shame the girl isn't still around.'

'Her body's still around, but it's empty again. She gave me the name of Amede, and someone or something else. You ever heard of a *Rounwytha*?'

'Can't say that I have.'

'Join the club.'

'Jack, it looks like they're using reanimated corpses to hit Jefferson's people.'

'Maybe,' said Nightingale, 'but I'm not interested in being in the middle of a gang war. I'm meant to be looking into some unfeasibly early deaths, next I get asked to investigate some girl who died twice, now I have a mobster wanting me to stop his henchmen getting butchered, and all the while Luce…'

He broke off.

'Loose what?'

'Loose ends, Joshua. That's all I have. I'm not sure what I should be doing now.'

'We have two sets of highly unlikely, borderline impossible, things going on in the same place at the same time. Much easier to assume one prime mover. Rather than several. No law says they have to concentrate on one thing. Your new friend Jefferson deals with drugs, whores, numbers, extortion, protection, plus a hundred or so legit businesses topping up his coffers. I say both cases will lead you to the same source.'

'So far, all I know is that both girls bore the brand of the Order Of The Nine Angles.'

'Well that's not good at all if they're involved, they don't wish either of us well. The Order has plans to bring about some huge changes in this world. Maybe this is the start of them.'

Nightingale ended the call and took a cab to Lakeside Airport, a few miles north-east of downtown New Orleans, where Chris Dubois kept her plane. His cab dropped him in front of the square, pink art deco terminal building. There was no sign of her so he lit a cigarette. He was halfway through it when a large black Harley Davidson pulled up in front of the terminal. He did a double-take when the biker flipped up the tinted visor of a full face helmet. It was Chris Dubois, wearing blue jeans and a brown leather zippered jacket. 'Let me park this and then I'll take you inside,' she said.

He held up his half-smoked cigarette. 'Take your time,' he said.

'Those things will kill you,' she said.

'Says the girl on a death machine.'

She grinned, flipped the visor down and drove off towards the car park. When she returned on foot, she led him through the building at a brisk pace, leaving him little time to appreciate the famously ornate interior décor.

'Maybe you've seen it in the movies,' she said,'They used it for a James Bond, and in *Green Lantern.*'

'I never saw the *Green Lantern*, but I remember *The Blue Lamp.*'

Chris Dubois grunted, but showed no sign of recognising the reference or the joke.

She led him to the private area of the airport, and into a hangar where light planes stood waiting. She nodded to a mechanic who was standing next to a blue and white high-winged Cessna Skyhawk. 'All set, Luis?' she asked.

'Sure, Ms Dubois.'

She opened the door of the plane and motioned Nightingale inside. 'Wait a minute,' he said.

'What's the problem?'

'It's only got one engine.'

'How many do you need?'

'What happens if it cuts out?'

'We land.'

'Can't we use one with two engines? It would be safer.'

She sighed. You ever flown a plane?'

'No.'

'Well let's make the assumption that you have no idea what you're talking about. Statistics show that a single-engined plane is just as safe as a twin. If you lose an engine on a twin, the extra drag unbalances the plane, and makes it a real pig to fly or land., Besides, this is the plane I have shares in. Are you in or out?'

Nightingale paused, remembering names like Buddy Holly, John Denver, John Kennedy, Graham Hill. On the other hand, he needed to look at Docteur Amede's place of business, and this seemed the only way it might happen. 'I'm in,' he said, swinging himself into the passenger seat. 'Just be gentle with me.'

Chris Dubois settled herself into what Nightingale thought of as the driver's seat, and started to check her instruments.

'Hey, I've got a steering wheel too,' said Nightingale. 'Am I supposed to do something?'

'The plane has dual controls for training purposes. You are very much supposed to NOT do anything. Unless I have a heart attack and die, in which case you'll have thirty seconds to teach yourself how to fly and land a plane.'

'I don't like my chances.'

'Me either. Comfort yourself with the knowledge that I had a physical last month, and my ECG was just fine.'

She handed him a headset that matched her own. Having finished her pre-flight checks, Chris Dubois contacted the control tower and was given permission to taxi onto the apron, and soon afterwards was cleared for take-off. Nightingale's contribution to the process was to sit in silence, his fists clenched and the knuckles white. He was never an enthusiastic flier, even in a passenger jet, but the little Cessna reminded him way too much of his dislike of elevators.

Chris Dubois managed the take off perfectly, then turned east and followed the Mississippi for a while, before branching off along the Interstate. About twenty minutes later she gestured downwards, and Nightingale had his first look at Docteur Amede's base. It was fairly small. Consisting of four or five large fields, separated by fences, bordering the bayou. In the middle was a large red-brick plantation style house, with a drive leading from it over to a gate, which connected to the side-road from the main highway. Even from this height, Nightingale could see two men, armed with rifles, stationed at the gate.

'I don't see any animals or tractors,' he said to Chris. 'No sign of any crops in the fields. And the only building apart from the house is that big barn thing.'

'Guess there's not much actual farming going on,' she said through his headset. 'Those cars would look more at home in the city than out here.'

Nightingale had noticed the three long, black sedans pulled up outside the main house next to a white Humvee. As he watched, the front door of the house opened, and a black man and a blonde woman came out. Those were about the only details he could pick out from their height. The woman pointed upwards at the plane, and the man took something out of his pocket and pointed it at the plane. Nightingale heard a faint crack. 'He's shooting at us.'

'No shit?' said Chris. 'He won't be hitting us at this range with that pea shooter.'

As she finished speaking, a second black man emerged from the house, carrying what looked like a rifle in one hand. The woman raised a pair of binoculars to her eyes, and again pointed upwards. This time the crack was much louder, but the rifleman missed his target.

'He'll need to be lucky to hit us, but I'm not in the mood to gamble,' said Chris, banking the plane to the left. 'This bird's heading back to its nest. You learn anything?'

'Well, we know that's no ordinary farm down there, and the warmth of their welcome leaves a lot to be desired. We also know that driving up unannounced won't work.'

'Let's hope they don't feel inclined to take it any further,' she said.

'I doubt they can do that. Seeing as we're up in the air and they're not.'

'Oh no? That woman had field glasses and there's a very big registration number written on this plane.'

CHAPTER 40

The *Rounwytha* sat alone in her sitting room, on the long leather sofa she had inherited from her parents, along with the rest of the magnificent mansion. The money and the house had been very useful, and a source of great pleasure to her. But that had been many years ago, and now she craved far more than money or possessions. And soon she would have it.

She picked up a small silver bell from a side table, and rang it twice. The door at the far end of the room opened, and Gabriella walked in. She was a tall blonde woman in her early thirties, her green eyes shining with pleasure at the summons from the *Rounwytha*.

'You called me, *Rounwytha?*'

'Indeed. I hope I have not disturbed you from your studies?'

'Oh no, I study every morning, as instructed. I know how important it is to perfect my skills. Just now, I have been walking in the gardens. This is a magnificent house, I do so enjoy being here.'

'I have always lived here. Now it is mine, inherited from my parents, together with a great deal of money, which has helped our cause considerably.'

Gabriella raised her eyebrows in surprise. 'I have never heard you speak of your parents before.'

'I rarely do, only to those close to me.'

Gabriella shivered with pleasure. 'Have they been dead a long time?' she asked.

The *Rounwytha* thought for a moment. 'It must be twenty years now. They were on vacation in the Hamptons, when intruders broke into their cottage and bludgeoned them to death.'

'How awful.'

'Not really, I arranged it.'

'You?'

'Yes, it was necessary. They were *Opfer*, heathens, heretics. They would have disapproved of our order, had they known of it. And I

156

needed their money and possessions. My only regret is that I was unable to perform the cull personally, and gain power from their death. But it was essential that I could not be connected with the deed.'

'So it was not your mother who introduced you to the Order?'

The *Rounwytha* clicked her tongue contemptuously. 'Not her. She gave herself to a man early in life, and never developed any power. It was her sister, my aunt who introduced me to the Order. A *Rounwytha* like myself, untouched by men. She recognised the power within me, and helped me to develop it.'

Gabriella smiled and licked her lips. To be taken so deeply into the *Rounwytha's* confidence was a rare honour for one of her rank. It could only bode well for her prospects of advancement. But the *Rounwytha* was speaking again.

'Gabriella, the African Doctor has been in contact. A small plane flew over his home this afternoon, made a pass or two, then left, after his men fired at it. It is hard to think of anything which would arouse more suspicion. Still, it will pique our enemy's interest.'

'So this is good?'

'All is proceeding as planned. But a lesson can still be taught. The plane is owned by a woman. Her name is Dubois.'

Gabriella said nothing, the name was unfamiliar.

'She is a half-breed. Her father married a savage.'

Gabriella's mouth curled in disgust,

'She must be culled,' said the *Rounwytha*.

'Shall I send an undead?'

The *Rounwytha* shook her head. 'I have something else in mind, Gabriella. Your powers are increasing, someday soon you should move up in rank, It is time you performed a cull personally.'

The younger woman's face lit up with pleasure. 'Oh, thank you. Thank you so much. I will not fail you.'

'I know. Now listen, I have a suggestion.'

CHAPTER 41

The tall dark woman was halfway through a TV dinner and an episode of Game Of Thrones when the doorbell rang. Her apartment was in an older part of town, and didn't run to an entryphone. She walked to the door and took a look through the peep-hole. A blonde woman in a New Orleans Saints baseball cap was standing on the doorstep. She opened the door on the chain. 'Yes?'

'Ms Dubois?'

'That would be me.'

'I have a delivery for you.'

'It's a little late.'

'We have to work all hours these days.'

She closed the door, took off the chain and then opened the door again to usher the woman in. As she did so, she gave a puzzled look. 'Shouldn't you have a unifo...'

The question was never finished. The blonde snatched the long-bladed knife from inside her jacket and slashed it across the side of the tall woman's neck. She collapsed to the floor, as the blood pumped out of her carotid artery.

Gabriella bent down and began to drink, lapping at the expanding pool of blood the way a cat would drink milk from a saucer.

CHAPTER 42

Nightingale's phone woke him from a deep sleep and he had been holding it to his ear for several seconds before he realised it was Joshua Wainwright. 'Have you seen the papers?' asked Wainwright.

'Yeah, because I always read the papers in my sleep.' He sat up and rubbed his eyes.

'I'll send you a link to their website. Call me back once you've read it.'

Wainwright ended the call. After a few seconds Nightingale's phone beeped and he clicked on the link to the *NOLA News* website.

The body of 26-year-old Francoise Dubois had been discovered in her apartment the previous evening. The body had been identified by her sister, Christina. Foul play was suspected.

Nightingale called Wainwright. 'Do we know what happened?' he asked.

'Valerie's been making a few enquiries at *NOLA*, we have a few contacts there. Someone or something made a hell of a mess of that girl.'

'My fault,' said Nightingale. 'I should have guessed they'd trace Chris through the plane. Ten to one the sister was killed by mistake.'

'Who do you think could have done it?'

'Yesterday Chris took me over Docteur Amede's place. We were seen and they shot at us. She was one of the owners of the plane, it wouldn't have been too hard to track her down. I guess the sister was in the wrong place at the wrong tme.'

'You need to make sure that she's safe,' said Wainwright.

'I will,' said Nightingale. He went to shower and was zipping up his trousers when his phone rang with a number he didn't recognise. 'Nightingale? Detective Matt Johnson here. I'd like you to come downtown, we need to talk.'

'About what?' asked Nightingale, though he had no doubt he knew the answer.

'The late Francoise Dubois. Where are you staying?'
Nightingale told him.

'There'll be a cruiser outside in fifteen minutes to bring you down to Royal Street. The city of New Orleans appreciates your co-operation.'

One of Jack Nightingale's ambitions was to have just one conversation with a police officer during which he could tell the plain, unvarnished truth, would be completely believed, and offered all the help he needed. Some day it might happen, but surely not today. He sat in yet another police interview room, opposite Matt Johnson, who had removed his suit jacket and hung it over the back of his chair. To his left sat a younger officer, wearing his jacket. Johnson had introduced him as Dan Hall, or maybe Horne, Nightingale hadn't really been listening. Johnson did all the talking.

'So, Mr Nightingale, how do you come to know Christina Dubois?'

'Aren't you supposed to advise me of my rights first?'

Johnson smiled. Perhaps it was meant to be friendly and encouraging, but Nightingale doubted it. 'Not necessary, Sir. You're not under arrest or in custody, and this is not an interrogation. We're just trying to establish a time-line here, figure out who saw Ms Dubois last, where and when.'

Nightingale nodded. 'Okay. So, I never met Francoise Dubois. I do know her sister, Chris. So how come you connected her to me?'

'We went through her sister's movements yesterday, your name came up. I remembered your name from your visit here. There can't be too many Jack Nightingales in town. Now, your turn.'

'I told you that I'd been asked to look into the death of Bethany Cole, by her brother. Being a stranger in town, I thought I could use a little help finding my way around, so I picked a detective agency out of the Yellow Pages, and I went to see her. Tried to get her to find some background on Bethany, figure out what turned an escort into an alleged murderer.'

'Did she get anywhere?'

'Not really. She was trying to find out who Bethany worked for, maybe see if there was a pimp around. And there was some talk of her having joined a cult.'

'What cult?'

'Can I smoke in here?'

'No, of course not. Now, what cult?'

'It was never established. I guess there are quite a few around.'

'None that I know of that practise dick-slicing on a regular basis. Did you mention that to Ms Dubois?'

'No, I didn't. I was being sensitive.'

'A shame someone else decided to treat her sister with a lot less sensitivity. She was practically decapitated. You were with Christina yesterday. What time did you leave her apartment?'

'Nice try, I was never there, no idea where she lived. I got the impression she was pretty careful around men she didn't know.'

'So where did you meet her?'

Nightingale gave him the bars and the times.

'So Jill's Bar at four on Thursday was the last time you saw her?'

Nightingale paused. The murder was bound to make waves all over the city, and chances were that people at the airport would come forward to say she'd taken her plane out on the afternoon of her sister's death, accompanied by a mystery man. Nightingale's appearance wasn't all that distinctive, but the mechanic might remember the English accent. If Johnson found out later, the next session might be a lot less friendly. He had to tell the truth, even though it would lead to questions that he would rather not answer. There was also a chance that Chris had already told the cops about the flight. He was going to have to tread very carefully. 'No, the next afternoon, she took me for a trip in her plane.'

'Where to?'

Nightingale couldn't tell if Johnson knew about the flight or not. 'Nowhere really, just out along the river, over some bayou country. A little sightseeing.'

'Why?'

Nightingale thought that was a pretty good question, but he was ready for it. He forced himself to speak slowly. 'I'm not really all that sure. Once we'd moved on from Bethany, we started to talk about the area, she offered me a quick trip in her plane. Maybe she wanted to show off a little?'

'You think she wanted to impress you?'

'Probably not the way you might be thinking. She was very clear that she was immune to my boyish charm.'

'Hard to believe,' said Johnson, his voice loaded with sarcasm.

'Imagine how I felt. Perhaps men aren't her thing.'

'Perhaps just you. Still, you'll get over it. So, after the flight, you drove her home?'

'I told you, I never knew where she lived. I took a cab back to my hotel, as far as I know she left the airport on her motorcycle. She didn't offer me a ride as I had no helmet. Louisiana law apparently mandates helmets, and I'm a very law-abiding citizen.'

'I'm sure you are. Law-abiding, I mean.'

'Anyway, that's the last time I saw Chris. Is she okay? I read that she found her sister's body.'

Johnson grunted. 'She's fine. Okay, for the record, where were you between eight and ten last night?'

'Eating in the restaurant at my hotel. Alone.' Nightingale fumbled in his wallet. 'Here's the check, I paid cash. My server was Juana.'

Johnson took the receipt and placed it on the table.

'Assuming she remembers her English guest, that should rule you out. Thank you for your co-operation. You can go now, but please don't leave New Orleans without telling me.'

'Do you have any leads?' asked Nightingale.

'You used to be a cop, you know there's no way I'll be answering that question.'

'Okay, let's try another one. Where is Chris Dubois now?'

'She's in a place of safety.'

'Are you guarding her?'

The cop's eyes narrowed. 'Why would you say that?'

Nightingale shrugged. 'Because I'm guessing you don't have a motive for the sister's murder. Which means that she might also be at risk.'

'We'd considered that, obviously. So yes, we're taking good care of her.' He tilted his head on one side. 'You still here?'

Nightingale took the hint.

CHAPTER 43

Gabriella stood before the *Rounwytha*, her head bowed, tears in her eyes. The television set in the corner was still recapping the news of the previous night's killing. 'I failed you,' said Gabriella between sobs. 'You trusted me, and I failed you.'

The *Rounwytha* smiled and stroked the young woman's hair, as if reassuring a child. 'It is of no consequence. A halfbreed *opfer* has been culled and her death strengthens us. If there is blame, it lies with me for not discovering the existence of this sister. You were not to know. The message has been clearly delivered, and the Dubois woman will be dealt with soon enough.'

'Let me finish what I have started,' said Gabriella. 'Let me attend to her personally.'

'When the time is right,' said the *Rounwytha*. 'For the moment, she will be well-protected and on her guard. I dare not risk you again so soon. We have another to cull in the meantime. Go and see to his preparation.'

The *Rounwytha* sat on an ornately carved wooden chair, to the left of the large wooden altar which dominated one end of the old factory. Behind the altar was a crucifix, eight feet tall, upside-down and bound in grasses. A marble slab stood in front of the altar, with a smaller wooden table by the side. A small group sat in wooden chairs, in a semi-circle, a few feet in front of the altar. There might have been twenty of them, male and female, with ages ranging from early twenties to late sixties. All of them were dressed in long white robes, the hoods pulled down over their faces. Only their hands betrayed their age and racial origins. All were white.

The *Rounwytha* turned to the tall woman standing next to the throne, and gave a quiet order. 'Bring in the *opfer*.'

The woman walked to a side door, opened it and stood aside. Five people entered. Four large white men, all of whom clearly spent a good deal of time in the gym, and, dragged between them along the floor, the bound and gagged figure of the Reverend Elijah Cole. The four men deposited him in front of the marble table.

'Let him stand,' said the *Rounwytha*.

The four men dragged Cole to his feet, two of them holding him by his bound arms. The *Rounwytha* rose from the throne, took a long, sharp curved knife from the marble table, and held the blade against the priest's throat. At a nod of command, the gag was removed.

'Do not speak until you are asked a question,' said the *Rounwytha*. 'You come to us as an *opfer,* one who has selected himself for culling by his low worth, and by his obstruction of our purpose. But it is necessary to ensure that the decision is correct. Are you, indeed, a priest of the Nazarene heresy?'

Cole looked into the *Rounwytha 's* probing green eyes, and tried to force down his fear. 'I preach Jesus Christ crucified and resurrected, I preach him as my redeemer. I defy whatever evil you are perpetrating here, and call on God to strike you down. And I demand to know what you did to my sister.'

The *Rounwytha* nodded.

'*Opfer*. You select yourself. Condemned from your own mouth. To the table with him.'

It was all over within a minute. The four thugs dragged Cole to the marble table, spreadeagled him across it, holding one limb each, and the hand flashed down and across, with the knife slicing through the priest's throat. The tall woman filled a large brass bowl with the pumping blood, and offered it to the *Rounwytha*, who held it up, and drank deeply.

'From the death of those unworthy to live, we gain strength. Drink of this blood, my friends, and be strengthened too.'

The bowl was passed around the semi-circle, each one taking a sip. When it reached the tall woman, she drained off the remaining blood. The *Rounwytha's* soft, commanding voice spoke one final time.

'The sacrifice is made. The omens are good. Soon we shall celebrate our latest *conjure de Dhahibu,* my friends, and then our power will be complete. On that day, I shall embody the spirit of Vindex, the avenger, and usher in the next Ayeon of mankind.'

CHAPTER 44

Nightingale tried to call Chris Dubois, but her mobile phone was switched off. It was a relief in a way, as he had no idea what he could have said. This was his fault, if he'd never involved her, Francoise would still be alive.

He phoned Jefferson and explained that he needed to get a closer look at Docteur Amede's residence. He told him about the flight and the fact that his men had shot at the plane.

'It's clear that he doesn't welcome your interest.'

'Looks that way but it's not much to go on, and I can't see any way of getting closer to him to find out any more.'

'There might be a way,' said Jefferson. 'I will get Percy to send you the details.'

It was an hour later that the instructions arrived on Nightingale's phone. He collected his rental car, turned on Google Maps and followed Percy's directions out onto the interstate, turned off onto a minor road and finally a dirt track which led him down to a collection of shacks next to a small weed-jammed creek. He parked the Escape in front of the largest shack, which bore the sign *Scott's Bayou Fishing & Tours* over the large double door. An old man with a long grey beard, dressed in camouflage jacket and pants, sat on a bench outside, repairing a fishing reel. Nightingale got out of the car and walked across to him. The old man looked up from his task and gave Nightingale what might have passed for a smile if he'd had enough teeth for the job. 'Help you, son?'

'I'm looking for Duane.' That was the name Percy had given him.

'That's my daughter's boy,' said the old man. 'My name's Caleb, Caleb Scott. Hey, Duane, come out here.'

What the old man's mouth lacked in the way of teeth, it made up for in volume, and his yell echoed across the bayou. A minute or so later a much younger man appeared, dressed in oil-stained, blue mechanic's coveralls, an Exxon baseball cap on his head. Every visible piece of his skin except the face was covered in a riot of indistinguishable tattoos.

'You'd be Jack, huh?' he said, showing a mostly complete set of teeth. 'Percy said you'd be dropping by. Out for a little...fishing, then?'

This last remark seemed to be more for his grandfather's benefit than Nightingale's, and the old man grunted and went back to his repairs.

'That's right,' said Nightingale.

'No problem at all, if you got the cash.' said Duane. He took a long look at Nightingale, widening his eyes at the Hush Puppies. 'Course, you ain't exactly dressed for fishing,' he said. 'Still, I do believe we can rent you a better outfit. Come on in the store.'

The store turned out to be a smaller shack, crammed with a variety of hunting and fishing equipment and clothing. Duane picked out a pair of camouflage pants, matching jacket and cap and some black lace-up boots, which he placed on the counter and pushed towards Nightingale. 'Here you go. Y'all can change just over there.'

'Thanks,' said Nightingale, making to pick up the pile of clothing.

Duane held up a hand. 'Be fifty dollars a day for the clothes,' he said. 'Thousand a day for the boat. Payable in advance.'

Nightingale pursed his lips. 'Seems a lot for hiring a fishing boat,' he said.

Duane smirked. 'Surely does,' he said. 'But then that ain't no fishing boat you renting. And seems to me you don't plan to do no fishing or duck shooting neither. Tell you what, call it an even two thousand and let's be on our way, huh?'

With Wainwright footing the expenses bill, money was never likely to be an issue, so Nightingale counted out two thousand dollars, and went to change his clothes.

'Meet you outside in ten minutes,' Duane shouted after him. 'Need to get me cleaned up and into some huntin 'duds myself.'

Duane's version of huntin 'duds was an almost exact duplicate of Nightingale's outfit, though he was carrying the jacket and the khaki singlet he wore showed off more of his inkings. He waved Nightingale over to another wooden shack at the far end of the compound, this one equipped with a metal up-and-over garage door. Duane took a key from his pants pocket, unlocked the door and shoved it upwards. 'Here you go,' he said. 'Here's Suzy Q. Fastest little girl on the bayou.'

It was obvious he expected his client to be impressed, so Nightingale gave a low whistle and a nod of appreciation straight away, and then took a good long look at the craft. It was the first time he'd seen an airboat close up, and his first impression was how small it was. It seemed to consist of little more than a metal sled, painted in camouflage colours and with two elevated padded seats. Behind the seats sat an enormous gleaming engine, connected to what looked like an aircraft propeller, housed inside a giant wire cage, presumably to stop body parts or other debris flying into the prop. There was a large storage box in the space under the seats, and Duane opened it.

'Y'all got stuff to take, put it in here,' he said.

Nightingale went back to the Escape, opened the trunk and took out the black bag with the equipment he'd brought. He dropped his clothes in the trunk. By the time he got back to the boat garage, Duane was cocking what looked very like a machine gun, which he then placed in the box.

'You carrying?' he asked.

Nightingale shook his head.

Duane walked to the back of the garage and returned with a hunting rifle, which he checked and also put in the box.

'We'll bring along a little extra firepower, case you change your mind,' he said.

A large brown bloodhound dog ran out of the office and leaped up at Duane's chest, resting his forepaws on the young man's shoulders. Duane and the dog slobbered at each other. 'Say hello to Hubert, the best hunting dog on the bayou. He always knows when I'm taking a trip.'

'Nightingale held up a hand and waved, but made no move to get any nearer. 'Good to know you, Hubert. Will Hubert be joining us?'

'No Sir. You take Hubert anywhere near that house and he'll be up and howling so loud you could hear him in Mississippi. Dogs can't stand the place.'

Nightingale nodded. He'd heard about dogs and Satanists before - not a good match.

'Down you go, Hubert,' said Duane. 'Now, let's get Suzy Q on the water.'

'We have to pull her down there?' asked Nightingale, who couldn't see a trailer.

'I can see you got a lot to learn about airboats, mister,' said Duane. 'This here's the ultimate all terrain vehicle. We just start her up, and drive her down there. Suzy Q can go anywhere, water, weeds, grass, ice even, not that we get much ice hereabouts.'

'Anywhere but the highway, eh?' said Nightingale, smiling.

Duane shook his head. 'Well, I don't recommend the highway, tear up the bottom after a while, and kinda slow. But there's people who take these things to drag strips and race them. Not me, though I've taken her racing on the water, over to that *Thunder on the Loup* race meeting in Nebraska. Placed first in class.'

'Versatile. But it seems a little small for a fishing boat,' said Nightingale.

'Well, like I said, we don't generally use Suzy Q for hunting and fishing, we got others, bigger and slower for that. We use Suzy Q for when we might have merchandise to deliver quickly, or when we might want to get out of a situation in a hurry. Now, you put your bag in there and we'll get going.'

Duane pulled the boat out of the garage, shut the door and waved Nightingale to a seat. He handed over a pair of ear defenders. 'Might want to put these on, Suzy Q's got a pretty quiet prop, but that's a 424 cubic inch big block Chevy V8 just behind your head, and we got an hour or so to go.'

Nightingale put them on, Duane turned the key, the engine roared into life immediately, he pressed the gas pedal gently and Suzy Q slid slowly forward, across the grass and down towards the water.

'So how fast can this thing go?' Nightingale shouted above the noise of the engine.

Duane turned his head to look at him, pursed his lips, then spat a stream of tobacco juice into the water, before answering. 'Probably a whole lot faster than I'd ever have the guts to push her,' he said. 'Maybe up to one-thirty, one thirty-five, but anything over sixty on water is asking for trouble. You hit anything at that kind of speed, log, gator, and you're airborne, and little Suzy Q ain't designed to fly. Maybe racing on clear water, you can push things a lot further, but I still see plenty of these things turn over at meets.'

Nightingale looked around. The bayou stretched forward as far as he could see, but was barely fifty yards wide. There were clumps of reeds and weeds lining both banks, trees with their branches dipping in the water. Duane had assured him that there were plenty of alligators around, but Nightingale hadn't seen any so far, just a couple of turtles on shore, basking in the afternoon sun. There were plenty of birds around, some that looked like herons and maybe storks, but, despite the name, Nightingale was no ornithologist, and didn't have enough interest to ask Duane about them. It seemed this was one of the less touristy bayous, so far they hadn't seen another boat. Duane had told him that most of his fishing trips went in the opposite direction.

Duane eased off on the gas, and the boat slowed immediately 'You want to try?' he asked.

Nightingale certainly did.

'Couldn't be much easier,' said Duane. 'You just press down gently on the gas, and off she goes. The lever controls the rudders, push it forward for left, pull it back for right. But remember, it ain't a car, the flow of the water and the boat speed will change the way it moves, so keep it slow and gentle till you get a feel for it.'

He stepped down from the driver's seat, walked round and stood behind it as Nightingale shuffled across. He put his right foot on the gas pedal, and pressed as gently as he could. The note of the idling engine changed immediately, as the drive shaft engaged and the prop started turning. The boat lurched forward and headed towards the left bank, Nightingale pulled back on the stick, but over-corrected and the boat lurched right.

'Where's the brake?' he shouted.

'Don't got no brake,' said Duane. 'Just ease back on the gas, man.'

Nightingale took his foot off the pedal and the boat slowed immediately. He tried again, barely stepping on the pedal to get the boat moving, then gentle movements of the lever to get it heading in a straight line. Duane nodded. 'You getting it now, man. Nice and easy, till you and Suzy Q get properly acquainted. Never rush a lady.'

Within ten minutes Nightingale had the hang of the little craft, and was feeling confident enough to push the speed up a little. The speedo said he was doing fifteen miles an hour, but the wind and the noise made it feel like three times as fast. For a few minutes the world of zombie killers and Voodoo curses melted away, as he revelled in the exhilaration of zipping along the water. Duane broke the mood. 'Maybe better back off the gas now, let her drift into the bank. We nearly there, don't wanna be arriving at full volume and attract attention.'

Nightingale nursed the boat slowly into the bank. It came to rest against a tree root, and Nightingale climbed down from the driver's seat and stood in the bow. He lit a cigarette and looked around him. 'I don't see anything,' he said.

'Just around the next bend,' said Duane. 'That's where the guy has his place. So what's your plan?'

'Thought I might go ashore, check the place out. Hopefully without being spotted.'

'Suggest you find a new plan,' said Duane. 'I told you it's not a good place, and it ain't. More snakes between that house and the bayou than the whole of the rest of Louisiana. Cottonmouths, copperheads, rattlers. Full o 'gators too. Big ones. Wouldn't last two minutes. I heard folks say he talks to them, feeds them, keeps them around as guard-dogs.'

'So they're alligators, not crocodiles?'

'You don't know the difference?'

Nightingale shook his head.

'It's easy, the one you'll see later, the other you'll see after a while.' Duane slapped his thigh, roared at his own joke, and Nightingale forced a laugh. 'Actually it's a whole lot easier than that. Louisiana got gators, crocodiles only in Florida. Ah don't recommend you try to introduce yourself to either of them. Crocodiles a whole lot more aggressive. Folk say gators will generally just leave you alone if you don't bother them. I never cared to test out that theory.'

'Looks like plan B then,' said Nightingale. 'I don't want to be arguing with reptiles. How about we moor a couple of hundred yards away from the house, on the other side of the creek and I can maybe watch the place for a while?'

'What you expecting to see?'

'No idea just yet, I'm hoping to see a few people who've gone missing. Maybe talk to the owner at some point?'

'Talk to Docteur Amede?' He shook his head. 'He don't welcome visitors. Specially not white folks. What else you think he keeps the reptiles for?'

'Look, I don't have a lot of time,' said Nightingale. 'Let's take a look at the place, then maybe you can land me a little further up and I can come at the place by road.'

'Don't recommend that either,' said Duane. 'I heard rumours he got all kinds of things waiting for unwelcome visitors. Things that used to be dead people, you get my drift? I don't believe in such things...but I don't need to go looking to prove it neither. Still, can't do no harm to take a look. I'll pull her round the bend, you get yourself some fishing tackle out that box and look busy.'

CHAPTER 45

Night was beginning to fall and the bayou temperature was dropping. Duane opened his magic box and took out a couple of heavy jackets. The Suzy Q had been moored against the bank, in the shade of a couple of overhanging trees, about two hundred and fifty yards down from Docteur Amede's house. The only movement came from a black jet boat, a little larger than the Suzy Q, with four seats, which bumped gently from time to time against the makeshift wooden jetty to which it was tied. For three hours now they'd watched it from the boat, pretending to be interested in fishing. Not that there were many fish to be seen, since Duane had also been right about the number of alligators who'd made the place their home. They were everywhere, basking in the sun, prowling the bank looking for food and floating in the water. They'd shown no sign of trying to get onto the boat, but Duane had his rifle laid on top of the box, just in case.

An hour of pretending with the rods had landed them no fish, and no information either. No one came or went and they couldn't glimpse anyone inside. Nightingale had taken out a camera with a telephoto lens and snapped off a few shots, and had even tried focusing a parabolic microphone on the windows, but there was nothing to hear.

'How long you figurin 'to stay here doin 'nothin', mister,' asked Duane eventually. 'Won't be seeing much here in the dark, and we neglected to pack dinner.'

'Guess you're right,' said Nightingale. 'We could be here days, and I don't have days. Nothing to see, let's move along.'

Duane put the rods away, climbed into the driver's seat and put the key in the ignition.

'Wait,' said Nightingale, holding up a hand. 'Listen.'

Across the water came the sound of a car, and as Nightingale peered through the dusk he saw twin headlights moving slowly down the unlit track to the side of the shack. Quickly he fixed an infra red lens to the camera and strapped the night-vision goggles. In the greenish glow of the goggles he saw a long dark car draw up in front of the house. He clicked off as many shots as he could manage as the doors opened and four people got out.

The two in the front were tall, young and black, in dark suits, and Nightingale pegged them as the hired help. It was the back-seat passengers that interested him more. An older, tall, bald black man, wearing a cream suit and carrying a matching fedora, and a white woman in her sixties, from what Nightingale could judge. She was tall, walked with a slight limp, her white hair worn longer than most women of her age. She was formally dressed, in a dark pant suit, over a white high-necked blouse. Doctor Amede in the white, unknown woman in the black, thought Nightingale, who stopped clicking his camera as the party went inside.

He took out the parabolic mike and focused it on the front left window, but picked up nothing. He switched to the right one, which seemed to be a living-room, and immediately picked up some conversation. The distance was too great for absolute clarity, but the more strongly stressed words came across.

'...Saturday night...without fail...initiation...more people.'

'Guarantee...need money...victory.'

'Money no problem...power...dark he do ...Vindex...'

'Duane, pull her into that landing stage over there, I've got to get in closer.'

'I don't recommend it, I don't see no welcome mat out for strangers.'

'Please, Duane, I need to know what's going on, and I'll never pick up enough from here.'

'It's your ass, mister.'

Duane unclipped a paddle from the side of the boat, and silently propelled the little craft up against the wooden jetty. 'Here we are, mister. I was you, I'd be taking this rifle along with me.'

'The noise would bring them running.'

'Some gator takes a liking to you, you'll be making enough noise to rouse the dead. Take it.'

Nightingale slung the rifle over his shoulder, looked in as many directions as possible and saw no life-threatening animals. He jumped ashore and crawled awkwardly towards the house. He stopped three times to listen to rustling noises in the undergrowth, but saw nothing.

He stopped about ten yards from the lit window, and focused his microphone on the glass. The woman's voice, high and strident, came across clearly.

'... worked to perfection, my X-rays are clear. The doctors cannot understand it.'

The other voice was deeper and lower. 'As you were promised. But you should not have come here.'

'Nobody will find out,' said the woman, 'my security detail are loyal only to me. And I have news, a suggestion.'

'Indeed?'

'A military man. Here are his details, given to me by one of my doctors.'

'He is dying?'

'Yes, but is not aware of it yet. He would make an ideal recruit.'

'I shall advise the *Rounwytha*. We will need a suitable sacrifice, but that is easily arranged.'

'Good. Now I must leave.'

'Wait!' He hissed the command, then there was silence, and Nightingale's night vision lenses let him watch, as the window was thrown open, the tall black man looked out, sniffed the air, then pointed straight at the Suzy Q. He screamed an order, and slammed the window again. Nightingale got to his feet and ran back to the boat. He watched two dark figures emerge from the shadow of the house, their gait a stiff mixture of a walk and a run.

Nightingale reached the jetty, stumbled onto the airboat and turned to Duane. 'Okay, time we were gone, Duane,' he said. 'Here's where Suzy Q earns her money.'

'Sure thing, mister,' said Duane, springing back into the driver's seat. 'Hold on to your ass.' He turned the ignition key and the Chevy engine sprang to life. Nightingale kept his night vision goggles on, even after Duane had thrown the switch for the Suzy Q's powerful headlights. The mike was back in the metal box now, Nightingale slipped the memory card from the camera into his pocket, then the camera joined the rest of his equipment in the box. By the time he reached the passenger seat, Duane had turned the boat round, the prop was whirling and they were headed for home.

Five seconds later, Duane's head exploded, showering Nightingale in blood, bone and brain matter, simultaneously with the roar of a powerful gun. What was left of Duane slumped sideways, fell from the seat, bounced on the edge of the boat and fell into the water. Instantly Nightingale heard a ghastly threshing sound and the water seethed with movement as the alligators fought for a share of the unexpected meal. The Suzy Q lost power and slowed rapidly.

Nightingale kept his head as far down as possible, shuffled desperately across into the driver's seat and floored the gas pedal. The boat responded like a thrashed horse, tearing across the water like a skimmed stone, veering from one side to another as Nightingale desperately over-corrected with the rudders.

In fact his incompetence probably saved his life, as he heard the crack of the rifle twice more, but neither shot came near enough to cause a problem. By now he just about had the boat in the middle of the water and pointed straight ahead. He rounded the bend that put him out of sight of the house and out of range. He breathed a sigh of relief, throttled back enough to bring the airboat under complete control and headed back to the Scott's fishing store and his car. He wondered who the old white woman had been, but identifying her would need to wait until he could study the memory card.

The chatter of machine-gun fire banished all other thoughts from his mind, and he heard the ping of a bullet hitting some part of the boat. Instantly he gripped the rudder stick tight and floored the gas pedal. Again the Suzy Q responded immediately, the prop revs increased and the boat took off, but in a straight line this time. Nightingale screwed his head round to look through the whirling prop, but could only see two powerful lights a few hundred yards behind him. He heard the sound of another propeller being pushed hard. Naturally Docteur Amede would have had an airboat, and it was heading his way.

Nightingale looked upwards. 'Well, Duane,' he whispered. 'Let's see if she really is the fastest thing on the bayou.'

It occurred to Nightingale that his straight line trajectory made him an easier target, so started using the rudders gently to travel in a series of long wide parabolas from one side of the water to the other. He could still hear the occasional burst from the machine gun, but his pursuers would have to get very lucky at that range. Nightingale

175

cursed himself for leaving Duane's firearms in the box, but it quickly occurred to him that it would have been suicidal to return fire backwards through the prop. Anyway, getting involved in a gunfight always worked much better for the hero in the movies than in real life. He heard the crack of the rifle a couple of times, but nothing hit the boat. He assumed firing at a moving target from a speeding boat didn't make for accuracy.

Nightingale forced himself to forget his pursuers and focused his gaze on the water ahead. The speedometer was already pushing eighty, and Duane had told him that anything over sixty was playing Russian Roulette. He peered through the gloom, desperately trying to spot any debris, sandbars or even an alligator that could transform the speeding craft into an airborne projectile. He prayed he wouldn't meet another boat coming in the opposite direction.

Reaching Docteur Amede's house at a slow meander had taken nearly an hour, but the return trip lasted no more than fifteen frantic minutes. Nightingale kept twisting around to keep track of his pursuers, but they seemed to be dropping slowly back, and no bullets reached him. He knew the chase couldn't go on forever, the fuel gauge was reading just below a quarter full, and he couldn't allow himself to be caught drifting helplessly. He'd have to put enough distance between himself and the other boat to buy enough time to reach his car.

The lights of the Scott's fishing store appeared in the distance. Nightingale gave the throttle one final push, the speedo leaped past eighty and he eased the rudders to the right.

Fifty yards from the shore, he cut the throttle, the boat slowed rapidly, and he blipped the gas pedal one more time to take the boat up the slope towards its garage. He leaped out before it stopped and sprinted for his car, expecting every second to hear the chatter of machine gun fire to spell out his final moments.

It never came. Instead, as his hand reached the handle of the Escape, he heard a huge roar and spun round to see a much bigger black airboat race up the bayou pointing straight at him, obviously aiming to crush him and the car.

Whatever speed the other boat was travelling, it was far too fast to make the transition from water to land. The bow hit the side of the bayou way too hard, then slowed down almost instantly while the power of the prop continued to force it forward. The front of the boat flipped up into the air, the whole craft flipped over backward and landed upside down on the grass, the prop still spinning and the engine still roaring. Nightingale didn't wait around to check for survivors.

CHAPTER 46

The two young men who rang the doorbell had short haircuts that looked as if they'd been done that morning by the same barber. They wore matching dark grey suits, white shirts with button-down collars and neatly knotted striped ties. They each carried an attaché case, and wore name badges, identifying them as Brother Ephraim and Brother Matthew. 'Mormons,' was Mario's educated guess as he looked through the peep-hole at them, though he added a somewhat unnecessary adjective before the word. 'This time of the morning?'

'Just give them ten bucks and tell them to get lost,' shouted Mickey The Horse from behind his computer screen.

'Sure, sure,' grumbled Mario. 'What are the chances of me seeing the ten bucks again?'

He fumbled the security chain off, unbolted the door and pulled it open, reaching for his billfold even before the young men had chance to speak.

'Here you go, buy a new Bible, and goodbye,' he said holding out the bill to the nearer of the two, who made no move to take it. Mario dropped it at the floor by his feet, but the young man ignored it, keeping his eyes fixed on Mario.

'What's the matter with you? You don't want my money?' He ducked back inside and made to shut the door, but the young man's foot was holding it open. 'You gonna lose that foot if it's still there in five seconds,' growled Mario, and put pressure on the door. The young man didn't seem to notice the pressure on his foot, but began to push on the door steadily. Mario must have outweighed him by fifty pounds, but the Mormon's strength was incredible, and Mario found himself moving backwards. He darted his right hand under his armpit, but the two men were inside now, and one of them gripped Mario's wrist, squeezed and twisted it and the gun fell to the floor. His companion took a silenced pistol out of his case, pressed it to Mario's forehead and pulled the trigger.

Both men were holding pistols by the time they walked into Mickey The Horse's office. Mickey was hunched over his computer, his glasses pushed up on top of his bald head, an unlit cigar clamped between his teeth as he stared at the list of runners at Gulfstream Park, calculating odds and percentages. In front of him, the five girls in varying skin and hair colours were all taking phone calls and writing down bets. His illegal bookmaking generally netted tens of thousands a day, with a pretty heavy rake-off to Jefferson for permitting him to operate. He looked up as the two Mormons walked in, his mouth hanging open at the sight of the guns.

'What the f....' was all he managed before a bullet from each gun took him in the face, and he slumped across his desk. The girls barely had time to react as the two men turned the weapons on them, placing a bullet through each forehead with robotic accuracy.

When it was all over, the men placed the two guns on Mickey's desk, picked up their briefcases, walked back along the corridor past Mario's body and back outside, carefully pulling the door behind them. They crossed the road, and climbed into the back of a grey SUV, the engine running. The vehicle pulled away.

CHAPTER 47

Gabriella walked over to the *Rounwytha,* relieved that she finally had some good news. 'The bookmaker and his staff have been dealt with,' she said.

'And the two men?'

'The bayou, I doubt they will be found, there were alligators nearby.'

The *Rounwytha* laughed. 'It is so amusing to use real Mormons for our purpose. When I read of their asphyxiation from the faulty heater, it felt like a direct gift from Vindex. The Nazarene heresy brings about its own destruction. It is inevitable.'

Gabriella nodded. 'Will Jefferson's operation be weakened sufficiently yet?'

'Not yet, but his followers will be nervous. They are primitive people, fear will take root easily among them. He will know now that his people are our target, but he has no idea of who we are, what our aims are, or where we may strike next.'

And where may that be?'

'For the moment, let them wonder. We have more important work on hand, but uncertainty will do our work for us. Let the fear grow amongst them.'

CHAPTER 48

Nightingale's call to Jefferson was an uncomfortable one. It seemed Duane and the Suzy Q had been very useful in some of the mobster's transportation undertakings, and he would find the young man difficult to replace. Fortunately, he didn't seem to hold Nightingale responsible, since neither of them had anticipated such an extreme violent reaction from Docteur Amede.

'Seems there were things going on there they didn't want seen or heard,' said Jefferson.

'I rather gathered that. But all I got were a few photos of a guy I assume to be Amede, some woman and a couple of bodyguards. That and a snatch or two of not very informative conversation, before things turned very nasty.'

'So who is the woman?'

'No idea,' said Nightingale. 'Never saw her before.'

'But you got photos, right? Send them over to me, I've got someone who can run them through facial recognition.'

Nightingale ended the call. He managed to find the memory card slot in his mobile phone, and surprised himself by typing a message to Jefferson, and attaching the three clearest photos of the woman. The phone rang thirty seconds later. 'That was quick,' said Nightingale.

'Won't be needing no technology, just my own eyes. You probably the only person in the state doesn't recognise her. That there is Madeline J Crenshaw. Governor of Louisiana.'

'What the hell would she be doing there?'

'Beats me, you're the detective. Talking of which, I'd surely appreciate some concrete information soon. I'm losing a lot of people lately. They hit one of my bookie operations yesterday. Things are getting beyond a joke. I know I said I didn't want a war but I got some urgent questions I want to ask this Docteur Amede. I'm going to send some people in.'

Nightingale would have preferred to interview Docteur Amede himself, but couldn't see a way of getting to him, and Jefferson would probably be far more persuasive than he could be.

I'd be grateful if you'd tell me what you get out of him,' said Nightingale.

'You'll be the first to know,' said Jefferson.

CHAPTER 48

The *Rounwytha* rarely allowed emotion to influence decisions, but this time the anger was plain to see. Gabriella was an Adept and a dedicated psychic, but now she was trying to avoid closing off her mind to the anger, in case it overwhelmed her senses.

'Gabriella,' said the *Rounwytha*, 'you saw Docteur Amede. How did he strike you?'

'A mixture of anger and fear. He was angry that the Dubois woman had flown over his dwelling, and her sister's death filled him with fear, in case the police should learn of her last flight and question him. The visit of the Englishman also angered him, and left him frightened that he might be exposed.'

'You calmed him?'

'I think so. His Voodoo power makes him a more difficult subject than most, but I was not trying to make him do anything specific, just to set his mind at ease.'

'He overreacted to the Englishman's presence?'

'Yes, he panicked. Had he done nothing, the Englishman might have had no real reason to suspect him. Sending his men to try to kill him showed that he had things to hide. The Englishman will not go away, I fear.'

'One man can achieve little, but the Englishman has been seen with Jefferson. Jefferson has resources and could mount an attack on Docteur Amede's house. Amede knows too much about our operation, and it would not be hard for Jefferson to persuade him to talk. This could inconvenience us. I have always felt uneasy about Amede playing such a vital role in our work, the lower races cannot be trusted. It is time we severed our connection with the so-called Docteur.'

'So Amede should be silenced? But do we not need him for the rituals? It is he who finds the sacrifices, and summons the Loa?'

'This need not be a problem. We need just one more sacrifice for the moment, and it will present itself. After that, we can make other arrangements. As for the other ritual, I have studied it, and can perform it.'

'But we need the Loa? And Docteur Amede must summon it.'

'Anyone with the necessary knowledge can summon the Loa, but the Loa alone decides with whom to work. The Loa will be more ready to work with me than the Creole Amede, since our aims coincide, and I am of purer race. I have already summoned the Loa once, and it has been discussed.'

Gabriella gasped. She had never suspected her leader might be capable of such power. 'So Amede must be eliminated? Will I send an undead?'

'No, that is a system Amede knows far too well, the sight of such a creature would put him on his guard immediately. Besides, when he dies it will be beneficial to our aims for me to absorb his power, and that can only be done personally. A visit is in order.'

'But he is protected.'

'Less so than previously, two of his men are dead now. And we have no shortage of members. Yes, a visit is in order.'

CHAPTER 49

Nightingale called Wainwright, and passed on the news of his surveillance at Docteur Amede's headquarters. He could hear a female voice in the background, and guessed that Valerie,Wainwright's right-hand woman, was probably listening on speakerphone, and feeding him information.

'You sure there's no mistake, Jack? It was definitely the Governor?'

'I'm sure of my photos, Jefferson spotted her right away, and I've taken a look at loads of shots of her on Google now. It's her for sure.'

'But, shit, she'd have one of the biggest security details in the state. There's no way she could just turn up down by the bayou all on her own.'

'Well she managed it somehow...'

'Maybe. Valerie's telling me she checked into a private health facility a few days ago for some rest and checks. Not too far away from where you saw her. Maybe someone pulled a switch.'

'If they did, she was in on it all the way. She didn't seem under any kind of duress. Seemed very happy to be there, all smiles.'

'Maybe this guy Amede is treating her, and she doesn't want folks to know she's seeing a medicine man?'

'Looks that way,' said Nightingale. 'Any clue what the tests are for?'

'Valerie can't find anything, but the lady's sixty-two, and been smoking two packs a day since she was old enough to ask for a light.'

'So an old woman who's a lifelong smoker. Just like Alex Gonzalez...wasn't?'

'Looks that way,' said Wainwright. 'Which means exactly what, Jack?'

'Damned if I know,' said Nightingale. 'I'd better find someone who does.'

''You do that. Meantime, check your messages, Valerie sent you over a list of Louisiana's elder statesmen and women, with as much background on their health as she could get. Could be some stuff ties up. Have a look and see if anything jumps out at you.'

CHAPTER 50

It was three in the morning when Nightingale's mobile phone roused him from a mercifully dreamless sleep. Hannah Devereaux's voice was as low and sweet as ever, but this time there was an urgency to it that compelled his attention. 'Mr Nightingale? Are you still in the city?'

'Sure, yes. What can I do for you, Mrs Devereaux?'

'I have someone here you need to meet, urgently.'

'As in right now?'

'Yes. Exactly.'

Nightingale sighed. 'I'll be there in twenty minutes.'

He pulled on the previous day's clothes and was in his rental car heading west inside five minutes. Mrs Devereaux hadn't struck him as a woman who was imprecise with words, and her tone suggested that 'urgently' was no exaggeration. Two minutes inside the promised twenty, he was at the gate of the Devereaux mansion. This time, there was a young black man in a private security firm uniform waiting inside the gatehouse. He used the intercom to ask Nightingale to hold his ID up to the camera, then the gate swung open, and the man appeared at his door long enough to wave Nightingale inside. One more minute, and he was walking through the front door which Samuel Devereaux held open for him. 'This way, please. Hannah's in the library with our visitor. I'll bring you in some coffee directly, unless you'd like something stronger?'

'No thanks, General. I'm driving. Are you okay?'

The old man smiled. 'I'll be fine. Married to Hannah all these years, nothing surprises me. Mr Nightingale's here honey.'

He said the final words as he held open the library door, shutting it quietly behind Nightingale.

Hannah Devereaux was in her wheelchair, and she turned her head towards the doorway to greet Nightingale with a thin smile. Facing her, on the same sofa where Nightingale had sat the day before, was a blonde woman, dressed in a dark blue skirt-suit over a light blue blouse, the collar open at the neck. Nightingale guessed she'd be about 5 foot 6 standing up. He put her at early forties. Her shoulder length hair was immaculately dyed, and her make-up had probably been perfect, though the fear on her face had left it cracked around the eyes and mouth. There was an inch left of the cigarette she was smoking, and the silver ashtray on the sofa arm showed that it was her fifth or sixth.

'Please sit down, Mr Nightingale,' said Mrs Devereaux, indicating the chair next to her, and opposite the sofa. 'This is Doctor Stephanie Bell.'

Nightingale nodded. 'Pleased to meet you, Dr Bell.'

The woman nodded a curt acknowledgement, but said nothing. Nightingale sat back in his chair and awaited developments. Hannah Devereaux spoke again. 'I have known Stephanie for some years, via charitable institutions, ladies committees and just generally socially, though not so much in recent years, as my mobility has decreased. I had no idea she was aware of my...er...area of special interest, until tonight. She came to me with an extraordinary story, which, it seems to me, ties in with what you are investigating.'

The woman's small, dark eyes darted from Mrs Devereaux to Nightingale as if she were looking for a way to escape, but could find none. Still she said nothing, but licked her dry lips.

She was given a moment's respite by the reappearance of Samuel Devereaux, who set down a tray of coffee on the side table next to Nightingale. It seemed the two women must have already declined the offer, as there was just one cup. As he left, Mrs Devereaux spoke again. 'Stephanie, I can guarantee that Mr Nightingale is to be trusted, And it is very likely that he will be able to help you. But you have to tell him what you told me, he needs to hear it from you.'

This time the woman did speak, her words coming out too quickly, as if holding them in had built up to an intolerable pressure. 'I will tell you. But first, you must promise to get me away from here at once. Out of New Orleans, out of the USA, as far away as possible. Somewhere I have never been, somewhere nobody knows me. You must promise, because if they find me now I am dead.'

Nightingale looked at her. In his police days he had been trained to tell when suspects were lying or when they were telling the truth. It didn't always work, but he would have bet his non-existent pension that this woman was in genuine terror for her life. Mrs Devereaux had heard her story, and backed it, so he decided to take a leap of faith, and show the woman a gesture of trust. He took out his phone and called Wainwright. 'I need somebody taken care of, Joshua. She'll need protection and probably new ID.'

'It's the middle of the night, Jack.'

'This is important. Life threatening.'

'Give me the address.'

Nightingale gave him the address and ended the call. 'Alright, Dr Bell, it's done. In an hour, a car will take you from this house and drive you to a private airfield. From there a plane will take you wherever it takes you. Not even I or Mrs Devereaux will ever know where, so we can't tell anybody. The man who is arranging it can be trusted and he'll pay whatever needs to be paid.'

The woman inhaled deeply on her cigarette, crushed it out, and her shoulders rose and fell in a heavy sigh of relief. 'Thank you,' she said. 'You have probably saved my life. Or, at least, postponed my death.'

'Please, we don't have much time. Tell me what you're so afraid of, and how it ties in with what I'm investigating.'

Dr Bell lit another cigarette, again the small brown eyes darted around the room, and she took a couple of short puffs before finally speaking. 'I am a member of an organisation called the *Order Of The Nine Angles*. Mrs Devereaux had heard of them, I know you have too. Your name is known to me, to us.'

A cold hand clutched at Nightingale's throat and his breath caught in his throat. He tried not to show his surprise.

'I was invited to join through...a lover of mine, some years ago. She is now dead, so her name doesn't matter. At college she and I were brought together by a mutual interest in right-wing politics. My families original name was Böll, we left Germany after the war. I suspect that my great-grandfather's role in the war might have led to recriminations had he stayed there. But enough of my history, it only serves to explain why I found the Order appealing.'

'It was a Nazi organisation?' asked Mrs Devereaux.

'Far from it. I was told it had its beginnings in your country, near Shrewsbury, in the 1960s, though its founding priestesses stressed that it is a modern manifestation of an ancient, timeless belief system.'

'Priestesses?' echoed Nightingale. 'The Order was founded by women?'

'Indeed, the role of women has always been very important in the Order, though the leaders are shadowy figures, their real names unknown. From the early beginnings, the Order has spread, and now has its nexons worldwide, though each is self-contained, there is no controlling force, no guiding hand. Each nexon know only its own members, and works to further the Order's aims entirely by itself.'

'And what are those aims?' asked Nightingale.

Her answer flowed out without pause, like a script she had learned by heart. 'To bring about the evolution of humanity into its next stage, to facilitate the arrival of the next Aeon, the Aeon of Fire, in which an Aryan society shall colonise the Milky Way galaxy. And to destroy utterly the Jewish-Nazarene ethos, to crush the cultural distortion brought about by the Jews and their Christian followers.'

'So what has all this to do with what's been happening in New Orleans? Girls coming back from the dead? And what's brought you here in such a state of terror?'

'The leader of our nexon has learnt how to extend the life of members of the Order, And by increasing their lifespan, and by culling unbelievers, now it is believed that our leader can become Vindex, incarnate on Earth, in human form.'

'Vindex,' repeated Nightingale, remembering the snatch of conversation he had heard when he was eavesdropping at Docteur Amede's house. 'What is that?'

'It is the avenger,' said Dr Bell. 'The entity who will lead the Order in the destruction of the Nazarenes, and in the establishment of the new order.'

'And your leader plans to become this creature? How?'

'By extending their life, by absorbing the life energies of those who are culled, and by the help of a Loa to achieve immortality.'

'A what?'

It was Mrs Devereaux who answered Nightingale's question. 'A Loa. It is a God, or Goddess in the Voodoo tradition. There are many of them, mostly kind and helpful, but there are some who are mischievous, and a very few who embody pure evil.'

Nightingale nodded. 'Okay,' he said. 'So I have two questions. First, who is your leader?'

'I don't know.'

'Why not?'

'I have been a member for decades, but still only risen to the level of an *External Adept.* Anyone of a higher level, an *Internal Adept, a Master, a Mistress,* or a *Grand Master* is masked and robed at our meetings. I could not even say if the *Rounwytha* is male or female.'

'That's the name they use?'

'Yes, though of late, they have started to speak of themselves as Soon-To-Be-Vindex.'

'Alright then. Next question, and the most important. You've been a member for decades. Why are you running out on them now?'

'It is the culling. For years the Order seemed mainly symbolic, the local nexon held its rituals, members flourished, our old leader did not follow the doctrine of the cull. But the old leader ceased to attend, a new leader presented.'

'How? I'm assuming they didn't advertise and hold interviews?'

'No, the *Rounwytha* appeared from within a ring of fire at a meeting, produced all the regalia necessary. And our direction changed. Culling became the norm, both out in the wider world, and at our ceremonies. And my role...my role...'

She took several deep breaths to calm herself before continuing.

'The Order is an Aryan order. It denies the Holocaust, it despises the Jews and inferior races. Blacks were used as tools to cull those deemed unworthy to live. They were given the brand of the Order to show ownership, and then made to seem dead. It was sometimes my role to write the death certificates.'

'And were they dead?'

'To all intents and purposes, yes. But there was a ceremony that we never saw, something carried out by the Voodoo priest, or maybe the Loa. They could be revived, for a short while, though their will was gone. They were made to serve as weapons, to spread fear amongst those they were sent to cull.'

Nightingale nodded. 'And you didn't approve, is that it?'

'I didn't, but I was too deeply committed. But the culling at our ceremonies was worse. A day or two ago, it was a priest, the sister of one of the girls who had been used. He had interfered in our work. His throat was slit, and his blood drunk.'

Nightingale's knuckles were white as he clenched his fists. She could only mean Elijah Cole. He fought to control his emotions. 'So that brought you here? The killing of a priest?'

'No, not even that. It is more personal. I have a secret, have had for years. I have a lover. A woman. A Jewish woman. I will not speak her name, but it is well-known in this city. The leader discovered my secret, and I was punished with a scourging. But now I am told that there is a greater punishment. I must lead my lover to a meeting, and once there cull her myself, and pass her blood among the associates of the Order. I cannot do it. I have sent her warning, I ran to Mrs Devereaux, whose name is known to me, and she offered your help.'

Nightingale tried to conceal his disgust, but didn't do a very good job and she saw the contempt on his face.

'We are what we are, Jack Nightingale. I cannot excuse what I have become. And now my weakness has betrayed my own beliefs. I doubt I will survive for long.'

'I doubt you deserve to.'

She nodded. 'You have your own beliefs, no doubt. They are weak, and will not survive.'

'We'll see. And tell us why you chose to come to Mrs Devereaux.'

'I told you, her name was known to me.'

'How?'

'Her name had been discussed as a possibility for culling. The leader said she might present a danger.'

'Another thing, Dr Bell,' said Nightingale.

Yes?'

'What do you know of people having their lives prolonged?'

'This too was part of my role. I am an oncologist. A cancer specialist. My role for the Order was to pass on the names of high-ranking political, administrative or military figures who were seriously ill with cancer. And to use the Medical Record search system to find others. The names were given to the *Rounwytha*.'

'And then what?'

192

'That was the end of my function. Though I am aware of at least three of my patients who later made almost miraculous recoveries.'

'But you just had knowledge of cancer patients?'

'It was my speciality. Other members might have done the same for sufferers with other diseases, but I would have no knowledge of that.'

'Have you ever seen any healing ceremonies happen within your group? Older people having their lives prolonged?'

'I have not. Above my rank, there is the rank of *Master* or *Mistress*, then there is *Grand Master* or *Grand Mistress*, and finally *Immortal*, but I have no knowledge of how one may gain such status, and I would not be permitted to attend their rituals.' She frowned and put a hand up to her mouth. 'Wait, as I said, I have no knowledge of healing ceremonies, but I once heard an *Internal Adept* mention a phrase to the *Rounwytha,* in my presence, who immediately silenced them. A phrase I have never heard before or since. It was *conjure de Dhahibu.'*

Nightingale looked at Mrs Devereaux, who shrugged her shoulders and shook her head.

'Where do ceremonies take place?' he asked.

'In a variety of places, rarely the same one twice, and I was not present at many. Usually a place of ill-repute was chosen. Once the abandoned Mental Hospital for Adolescents, another time at a disused theme park. Until recently in the barn at a farmhouse just outside the city. I was told that they will be moved to a new place I was told that I would be given directions before the next cull, but I only know of a name they used. *The Plantation,* but I have no idea where it might be found.'

'*The Plantation?* Is that a generic name? Or is it a specific place?'

'They just said *The Plantation.* That's all I know.'

The telephone next to Mrs Devereaux rang softly. She picked it up, said a quick thank you, then replaced it.

'The car has arrived, Dr Bell. Godspeed.'

'Your God will have no use for me,' said Dr Bell, her voice loaded with bitterness. 'My own will doubtless punish me.'

CHAPTER 51

The Gulfstream jet taxied to the far end of the runway, turned around and brought its engines up to full power before starting its take-off run, The runway at the little airfield was barely long enough for a jet, but the two pilots were highly experienced, and the plane was carrying a very small payload. It would be refuelling before too long at a proper airport. The jet roared down the strip and off into the Louisiana night.

Five minutes later, the tall blonde woman in the blue hostess uniform got up from her seat at the rear, and walked forward to where the only passenger sat.

'You can unbuckle your seatbelt now, madam,' she said. 'You may smoke if you wish. Would you care for a drink? I can serve dinner in thirty minutes, if you wish.'

'No thank you,' said the woman. 'Nothing to eat or drink, and I feel like I have smoked quite enough for one night. I think I'll just try to get some sleep.'

She reclined the white leather seat as far as it would go, took the offered blanket, wrapped it around herself and turned her face towards the shuttered window. The stewardess went back to her own seat, dimming the cabin lights on the way.

Three hours or so later, as they started their final approach into their next stop, she went forward again, to wake her passenger and get her to fasten her seatbelt. She was well trained, so, although her eyes widened with fear, she neither shrieked or panicked when she felt the woman's icy cold-hand, and failed to find a pulse. She took the intercom and gave the news to the pilots, who decided, after a radio conference with their principal, not to pass the information any further.

CHAPTER 52

The *Rounwytha* looked at the tiny black doll with the lock of blonde hair attached to its head, and the sharpened stiletto which lay next to it on the small wooden table by the side of the leather chair.

A soft voice came from across the room. 'She will have told all she knew?'

'I think so,' said the *Rounwytha*. 'She was always weak, and it just took a little pressure in the right area to send her in the direction that we wanted. It will suffice to bring him to us, I am sure.'

'I can bring him to us anytime I choose.'

The *Rounwytha* nodded, respectfully. 'Of course, your power is far superior, but for the strength of the *conjure*, it is best he come unsummoned.'

'It is so amusing,' said the voice. 'So much fun to play with the creatures.'

Again the *Rounwytha* nodded, then noticed she was alone. The Loa had departed. She walked out into the corridor and opened the door of a bedroom. Gabriella, dressed in black slacks and a long-sleeved white T-shirt, rose to greet her, her eyes shining with pleasure.

'Doctor Bell is no longer part of our order,' said the *Rounwytha*.

Gabriella smiled. 'I sensed her passing, twenty minutes since.'

'Your powers are increasing almost daily, Gabriella, soon you will also achieve the rank of *Rounwytha*. I shall be proud to have you as my consort, once I am transformed. Now, advise me, Gabriella, what shall we do about Doctor Bell's lover?'

'She no longer has any relevance to us, might it not be better to expend our energies on more deserving candidates for the cull?'

The *Rounwytha* nodded. 'I agree. She cannot harm us. What then of the halfbreed woman, Devereaux?'

Gabriella smiled. 'A far more deserving candidate. She embraces the Nazarene heresy, she pays lip service to the false Satanism of

Voodoo and Wicca. The Englishman has consulted her. But she is old, her time must come soon anyway.'

'True. But perhaps a lesson needs to be taught to the halfbreed and her old fool of a husband.'

'We have no undead to send.'

'No matter, we have plenty of foot-soldiers who will be happy to shed blood for our cause. Despatch two.'

Gabriella nodded.

'Those who have no place in the Sixth Aeon must be culled. The man Jefferson must be disposed of soon too, without him it will be easier to take possession of his network.'

Again Gabriella nodded, and made to leave the room.

'See to it quickly, Gabriella, then return. I have needs to share with you.'

Gabriella smiled, and shivered in anticipation of the pleasures to come.

CHAPTER 53

General Devereaux had entered and left the room again, taking with him Nightingale's stone-cold, untouched cup of coffee, and Stephanie Bell's full ashtray. Nightingale suddenly noticed that he himself hadn't even thought about smoking since he'd entered the room. Maybe a little longer wouldn't hurt him, if only out of consideration for Mrs Devereaux. He looked across at her, Her eyes were closed, and her breathing was shallow and rhythmic, but he would have bet anything that she was still fully awake.

'So how do you like Dr Bell's chances?' he said.

She opened her eyes, and focused on him. 'Not good. Not good at all,' she said. 'This is not an organisation you simply leave. In fact…'

She stopped.

'Go on, finish the thought.'

'I was just wondering how it came about that she made it as far as she did,' said Mrs Devereaux. 'Unless it were that she was sent to us, to you maybe, with a message.'

'She'd have to be one hell of an actress.'

'I don't mean in that sense. More in the sense of winding up a little clockwork train, setting it on its track and giving it a push in the right direction. No doubt the *Rounwytha* would know the weak areas of an Adept, and where to put the pressure to bring about the right result.'

'Maybe it was all just a little too convenient,' said Nightingale. 'Breadcrumbs, more breadcrumbs. But why would they want me to know their plan?'

'But you don't, do you? You know what they've done, but not how they plan to proceed, or where to find them.'

'True enough, and a lot of what she said just confirmed what I already thought I knew, and filled in a little of the philosophy behind it. What about that last thing she said. *Conjure de Dhabihu* or whatever.'

'*Conjure de Dhahibu,*' she corrected. 'Conjure, is easy enough, it means spell or ritual. *Dhabihu* is not a term I am familiar with. I can do some research on it for you in the morning, but I really am about as weary as it gets now, so, if you'll excuse me…'

'And *The Plantation?*'

'Again, I would need to research it, it could denote many places, though the name would not be used by anyone with a trace of sensitivity, It resounds with too many echoes of past evils.'

Nightingale got up. 'I'll see myself out,' he said. 'You surely deserve a long rest. Thank you.'

'I just have one more thing to do before I sleep,' she said, 'and that's pray for the soul of Stephanie Bell.'

Nightingale had only enough energy to shower and clean his teeth before falling into bed and he fell asleep as soon as his head touched the pillow.

Minutes later, he was awake again, back on the same cliff, overlooking the storm tossed ocean hundreds of feet beneath.

'Oh no, not again,' he shouted. 'Show yourself!'

There was a crack from mid-air, time and space seemed to fold in on themselves, and when they unfolded, and there he stood. The coat was green this time, and he held a wicked looking rapier instead of the riding-crop, but there was no mistaking the malevolent sneer.

Nightingale glared at him. 'Do you have any more conjuring tricks to show me, or shall we just get on with it?'

The dwarf twisted his features into what might have been an attempt at a smile. 'I almost begin to find your insolence amusing, given how horribly you will be made to suffer for it in the long run. But, as you say, let us get on with it. You have made some progress.'

'Some. Pretty much the same way I always progress, by following the trail of dead people you and your followers leave behind.'

'Omelettes and eggs, Nightingale. How many of you creatures infest your world? Seven billion and increasing every second. The dead will not be missed. You have found the ones offering immortality?'

'Not yet. there's talk of a *Master* or *Rounwytha* of the Order Of Nine Angles raising themselves to the level of an *Immortal,* of embodying an entity known as *Vindex.'*

'*Vindex?* I know of no such creature.'

'Nor me,' said Nightingale, 'in fact it sounds like something you'd clean windows with, but I long ago gave up laughing at daft names. *Bimoleth* sounded a pretty stupid name, but it nearly destroyed the East Coast.'

The dwarf frowned. 'I *am* familiar with Bimoleth, and the world is a safer place while such a creature remains trapped where it is.'

'No argument there. But there's a Voodoo connection too, apparently a Loa is involved.'

'Loa, Schmoaa,' sneered the dwarf. 'Merely another name you ignorant creatures use for one of my kind. Loa, Demons, Princes of Hell, Demigods...each of us has different names in different places. Which one? Which Loa? There are many.'

'No idea, not met him yet. Or her. Or it. Can't you tell if you're missing one?'

'If I could, you would be suffering the torments of the damned right now, instead of serving as my assistant. I am not omniscient, Nightingale.'

'Good to know.'

'Still, it seems you grow closer to the centre of this mess. No doubt you will blunder into it soon, and discover that you are in deadly peril, and have no idea how to stop them. Summon me then, Nightingale, and I shall take them and all their works back to Hell with me. You remember the words you need to summon me?'

Nightingale had used the words three times in his life, and knew that he would never be able to forget them now. 'I do. But I remember using them from within the protection of a very carefully drawn protective pentagram every time. I get the feeling these people might not wait around for three hours plus shopping time while I construct one.'

'Nonsense, Nightingale, you have nothing to fear from me. Once you are in the presence of the Loa, summon me. Their plan will be stopped, and our pact can be completed.'

Time and space unfolded, then folded in again, and Lucifuge Rofocale was gone.

'Sure, our pact will be completed, if I'm alive to see it, and provided I spot all the loopholes you'll have included,' said Nightingale, then he realised he was lying in bed, talking to himself.

CHAPTER 55

It was nine o'clock in the morning when Nightingale woke for a second time, and once again it was the insistent buzz of the mobile phone that woke him. It was Wainwright. 'Joshua,' said Nightingale. 'What's happening?'

'The plane landed at Dallas to refuel, and your lady was stone dead. Not a mark on her.'

'What do the doctors say?'

'I didn't ask for a medical opinion, nobody much felt like explaining a dead woman to the cops, so the plane took off again, and made a short detour over the gulf of Mexico, where the lady left us. I'm guessing she wouldn't have missed a Christian burial service. So, fill me in.'

Nightingale gave Wainwright a report of Dr Bell's story.

'I tend to agree with Mme Devereaux,' said the Texan. 'She'd never have got as far as the house if they hadn't wanted her to. Something big is coming up, much bigger than knocking off a few hoods and pimps. Are you getting anywhere with the dead athletes?'

'Maybe yes, maybe no. I'm pretty sure this guy Docteur Amede is mixed up in it, whether he works for the *Rounwytha*, or, more likely he is the *Rounwytha*. Hannah Devereaux is working on this *Conjure de Dhahibu* idea, or will be as soon as she wakes up.'

'Let's hope she can find out something, it's a new one on me.'

'I'll keep you informed.'

Nightingale ended the call and almost immediately his phone rang again. It was Hannah Devereaux. Nightingale was tempted to say speak of the devil' but decided against it.

'Mr Nightingale, I think I might have found what we're looking for,' she said. 'Can you come to the house?'

'I could, or you could just tell me.'

'I'd rather not speak of it on the telephone.'

'I'll be right there.'

Nightingale headed for his rental car and drove to the Devereaux mansion. General Devereaux answered the door, once again looking immaculate in a light suit, and giving the impression he'd slept a solid eight hours. Again he offered to bring coffee into the library, which Nightingale gratefully accepted, since he hadn't got round to breakfast yet. As he opened the library door, it occurred to him that he hadn't got round to dinner last night either. He'd need to be more careful about eating, no sense in running out of energy.

Hannah Devereaux was looking far from fresh and well-rested. Even behind her dark glasses, the rings round her eyes were clear to see, and her complexion looked a little too yellow to be healthy. She seemed to be finding breathing more difficult today, and coughed sharply as she waved Nightingale to the sofa.

'Is this tiring you out?' asked Nightingale. 'Really, it's not up to you to make yourself ill over it, whatever's going on here is my affair, not yours.'

'Oh shush,' she said. 'I can't forget what I know, nor what I heard last night. If this *Rounwytha* character sent Dr Bell to me, then I'm in this as much as you are.' She fixed her gaze on Nightingale's eyes. 'You've heard something about her, haven't you? She's dead?'

Nightingale nodded. He should have been surprised, but he'd become used to old ladies knowing things they shouldn't be able to. 'On arrival. Not a mark on her.'

'There wouldn't be. Still, I think she knew that she couldn't hope to run far or fast enough, She made her choice a long time ago.'

'We did what we could. On the phone, you said you had an answer for me.'

'Yes, I think I do.' She gestured at a small, leather bound book, which lay open on her lap. Nightingale could see that it was written in pen, or quill, and ink which had once been black, but had now faded to such a light grey that it looked almost like pencil. 'I found it here, I knew if it weren't here, it probably wouldn't be anywhere.'

'And where's here?'

'*Li libre di Marie Paris.*'

'Marie Leveau's book?'

'Yes, she often used her married name, long after her husband's disappearance. This is one of two manuscript copies in existence, as far as I know. I was told that this is the only one in her own handwriting, but that may not be true. She speaks of the *Conjure de Dhahibu,* though she herself never performed it.'

'So how did she come to know about it?'

'She found out about it from another Witch Queen, since she suspected it had been performed on her husband, Jacques Paris, by a Satanist named Dr Jones. A man who claimed to be an African Prince, and who was suspected of causing the deaths of several people who stood in his way, and in the way of those who hired him.'

'Sounds a real charmer. So what is this thing? This *Conjure de Dhahibu.'*

'It is an African ritual. *Dhahibu* is a word from an African language, and it means sacrifice. So, it is the Sacrifice Ritual.'

'So a human sacrifice?'

'In a sense, but probably not in the way you think. It is used to help someone of importance, who is old and sick. A younger, healthier person sacrifices his health and remaining years for the benefit of the recipient. In return, he gets infirmities, sickness and imminent death.'

'Sounds a lousy deal. Why would anyone want to do that?'

She gave a very weak smile. 'The description of the ritual says nothing at all about the victim needing to be willing. It seems very unlikely that would be the case. If it happened to Jacques Paris, perhaps for the benefit of this Dr Jones, then I strongly doubt he would have known what was happening, or, if he did, would have been unable to stop it. No doubt Dr Jones had his own group of followers, on whom he could rely for physical assistance, and for silence afterwards. Marie Laveau speaks of this Jones as suffering badly from congestion of the lungs for a while, then making a full recovery, around the time her husband disappeared.'

'Is there any reason he chose Marie's husband? If he did?'

'First because he was young and strong, with many years ahead of him. The second reason… well, you can probably guess.'

'Jones wanted Marie for himself?'

She smiled. 'It seems so. Not that it did him much good. Marie was convent school girl, a good Catholic, but she turned away from Christianity after the presumed death of her husband. Another chapter of the book tells how she put the fix on Dr Jones, and he died of a wasting disease.'

'So this ritual basically transfers diseases from old sick people into young healthy ones, and the young ones sacrifice their lives to keep the older ones alive. Whether they know it or not.'

'That's what Marie Laveau writes, yes. Exactly.'

'And it ties in with those athletes dying of diseases of old age. Maybe I already figured out one beneficiary, and perhaps there are more on a list I've been sent. But if this ritual is so obscure, how would the *Rounwytha* find out about it?'

'Maybe they didn't. There are many people in New Orleans who claim direct descent from Marie Laveau, and who might have access to her writings. One you have seen, Docteur Amede.'

'But if Amede can do this, how come it's only started recently?'

'First it is a ritual which is forbidden by the Loa of Voodoo, since it brings death to the innocent victim. But secondly, how do you know it has only been happening recently? It doesn't seem the sort of thing anyone would advertise.'

'Not until now, and maybe there's a reason why they've been using famous people lately. Leaving that trail of breadcrumbs to be followed. Offering virtual immortality seems to set quite a few warning bells ringing, up here and in...other places. Anyway, it looks like this confirms quite a few guesses. Now all I need to do is find a way to stop them doing it.'

'I suppose it's useless to suggest the police?'

'Ha. What could I tell them that wouldn't get me committed? No, if I'm going to call for help, it won't be from the boys in blue. Did you have any thoughts about *The Plantation?* Any idea where it is? Or what it is?'

'Nothing too helpful. There were many sugar, cotton and tobacco plantations around here in past centuries, but I have no idea which one Dr Bell might have meant. These days, they tend to be called farms, and are not worked by slaves, of course.'

'Maybe I'll be able to find it some other way, though it would be a lot easier if I knew who I was looking for. Amede might be a good place to start, but I hear he's hard to track down these days.'

'If I can help in any way...'

'You wouldn't happen to have a large room I could use undisturbed for a while, preferably one without too much furniture. And a wooden or tiled floor would be best.'

'Would our ballroom do? It's rather a grand name, but it's not all that big, we haven't used it much in recent years. Actually, we rarely used it at all, people were never keen to accept our social invitations.'

'Sounds just right. I'll need to do some shopping, be back in an hour.'

'Should I ask what you're planning to do?'

'You might be a lot happier if you didn't.'

'That's what I figured. Be careful, Jack. Be very careful.'

CHAPTER 56

Nightingale had long since ceased to be surprised at the ease with which he seemed to be able to buy occult paraphernalia in almost any American town. An hour at Hex on Decatur Street provided everything he needed, and he had placed it all in a large cardboard box near the table. He sat on a chair for ten minutes, running over everything he needed to do. It was a ritual he had carried out many times, but it was vital that he didn't overlook anything. One careless slip when summoning a demon could result in his destruction. Or damnation.

He started by heading to one of the Devereaux's bathrooms, showering and washing his hair twice, with new soap and shampoo, scrubbing his hands with a new nailbrush. He dressed himself in a newly-laundered white towel robe.

He took a piece of consecrated white chalk and drew a circle with it, around six feet in diameter on the wooden floor. He used a fresh birch twig to brush round the outline of the circle as an extra safety measure. With a fresh piece of chalk, he drew a pentagram, the ancient symbol of a five-pointed star, inside the circle, with two of the points facing north. Then came a triangle to enclose the circle, again with the apex facing north. At the three points of the triangle, he wrote MI, CH and AEL to spell out the name of the Archangel Michael.

The next item was the freshly blessed flask of consecrated salt water. Nightingale took the bottle and sprinkled water around the circle, being careful not to leave any part of it untreated.

He took five large white candles and placed them at the points of the pentagram, then lit them all with his lighter, being sure to move clockwise round the circle. Then he took out plastic bags containing herbs, and a lead bowl. Again moving clockwise, he sprinkled the herbs over the flames, until the air was filled with pungent smoke which caught at his nose and irritated his lungs. The remainder of the herbs were placed in the lead crucible, which he put down in the centre of the circle. He took his lighter and set fire to them too.

This time the smoke was almost unbearable, and set Nightingale coughing furiously, but he choked it back down, and composed himself. He looked around his circle, checking that he had forgotten nothing, and that there were no gaps in any of the chalk lines. Any mistake could be fatal.

Or worse.

He took a deep breath, and began to recite the Latin incantation which he knew by heart, after using it more times than was probably healthy. He still didn't know what the words all meant, but he took care to pronounce each one carefully. Almost without thinking about it, his voice grew louder as he spoke, and was at full volume when he shouted the final three words, which were in a language which long pre-dated Latin.

'Bagahi laca bacabe.'

The fumes grew thicker, it felt as if the floor and ceiling were shaking, and, despite being indoors, there was a flash of lightning and a roll of thunder.

His eyes were streaming, and the fumes caught horribly at the back of his throat, but he concentrated on remaining motionless as he used what little breath he could muster to shout again the final three words of the summoning incantation.

'Bagahi laca bacabe!'

Again the room shook, there were two more flashes of blinding lightning, then the air in front of him shimmered. One moment there was nothing in the outer circle of the pentagram, the next the air flickered, time and space seemed to fold in on themselves, and then out again.

Then nothing.

There was no sign of Proserpine.

The flames of the candles flickered and died,

Nightingale stood alone in the darkness. 'Well, that could have gone better,' he muttered to himself.

CHAPTER 57

Nightingale stopped at a pizza restaurant on his way back from the Devereaux mansion. He had no great interest in food, but knew that he'd need the energy before long. As he pushed aside the final slice of his pizza, and waved away the waitress with the dessert menu, he felt a warmth and a throbbing sensation from his jacket pocket. He slid his right hand inside, and felt his pink crystal through its leather bag. It was warm to the touch, and he could feel it vibrating gently.

The crystal had come from Mrs Steadman's London shop. She had shown him how to use it for a Spell of Propinquity, which allowed the user to locate someone using something strongly associated with them. She'd hinted that the crystal could be of use for many more things to a skilful owner, but Nightingale had never had time to learn much more about it.

It had been all but destroyed by an occult charge in Memphis, but Mrs Steadman had recommended a Wiccan specialist in Salem, who had been able to regenerate it over the course of several weeks. Perhaps it was throbbing at him to tell him it was time he used it to locate the leader of the Order. Or maybe Proserpine.

CHAPTER 58

Lamont Sherman gazed down at the scar on his left leg, just above the heel, bent down and rubbed it. It wasn't tender to the touch, the surgeon had done a good job on his Achilles tendon, and the skin had healed quickly. But it wasn't perfect. He could jog on it without any problem, but at full sprinting speed, it ached just a little, and slowed him down. And with a personal best of 9.85 seconds for the hundred metres, a fraction slower made the difference between a medal and an 'also ran'.

Life had all been going so well, a sports scholarship at University, followed by selection for the USA Junior team, and then, finally, as an alternate on the senior team. With the Olympics not far away, and his personal best improving regularly, he had every hope of performing on the World's biggest stage, maybe even returning to New Orleans with a medal. Then had come the injury, a nagging pain at first which never improved, and the doctors had told him surgery was his only hope of getting back to the top level. He'd done as he was told, waited patiently for the surgery to heal, and followed his rehabilitation programme to the letter. Recovery went well, very well, according to his doctors and trainers.

Just not quite well enough.

Lamont had tried everything possible, from weight exercises to cryotherapy but nothing had worked well enough to give him back his competitive edge. His family and friends had tried to keep him positive, but the young man had begun to sink into depression, when a conversation with a friend of his sister had given him a new hope.

'Lamont man, you got to try some alternatives,' she had said. 'All those doctors done what they can, but maybe they don't know everything.'

'Louise, they know more about Achilles tendons than anyone else in the world.'

'In their world, maybe,' she had said. 'But there are older medicines around.'

'Come on, what do you mean, berries and leaves?'

She had looked at him scornfully. 'Of course not. But there's other healers I've heard of. When my Mother hurt her back, doctors wanted a fortune and couldn't promise anything. She saw another guy, he put her right.'

'What kind of guy?'

'A Voodoo Doctor.'

'Oh, come on. Brick dust, love potions and dolls with pins? Might as well call the tooth fairy.'

'It's not all black magic and drumbeats, Lamont. A lot of these guys have remedies that go back years, natural remedies. Help your body heal itself. I heard about people they helped when nobody else could.'

'So, do I pick one from the Yellow Pages?'

'I heard of a guy. Via a friend of mine, He doesn't advertise, but they say he's the best.'

'And who is this friend?' He might have been clutching at straws, but Lamont had been desperate.

'I can't tell you,' she had said. 'The Docteur doesn't like his patients to talk about him, the police get antsy about traditional medicine, but he was an athlete, just like you. Injured, but he's back to his best now.'

'Docteur?'

'Yeah, that's the name I was given,' she'd said. 'The Docteur. Just the Docteur.'

'You got his number?' he had asked.

'It doesn't work like that. He chooses who he helps by recommendation. I could talk to my friend, get him to tell the Docteur about you. Then maybe he'll get in touch.'

'It sounds like made-up nonsense to me, Louise,' he'd said. 'But I guess I have nothing to lose. Why not give it a whirl?'

'I'll see what I can do,' she'd said, and Lamont had all but forgotten the conversation when his mobile phone rang three days later.

'Mr Sherman? a soft male voice had enquired.

'Yeah?'

'I have been given your name, I think I might be able to help you with your injury.'

'Who is this?'

'I am called Docteur Amede. I practice the traditional healing arts.'

'Mister, some of the best doctors in Louisiana haven't been able to get me back to my best, what makes you think you'll be any different?'

'I use a completely different approach. Traditional medicine, to induce your body to heal itself.'

The man's voice had been soft and oddly hypnotic and Lamont found himself beginning to trust this stranger a little. But there had still been doubts.

'This isn't some kind of scam, is it, mister?' he had asked. 'You going to want some heavy payment for a few herbs?'

'Not at all. I never charge a fee, you are welcome to pay what you consider appropriate, but only after the treatment has been successful.'

'Mister, I figure I could be desperate enough to try anything now. Where's your place of business?'

'I prefer not to advertise my location, not everyone is understanding about my...talents. I can arrange for you to be brought to me.'

'Well, OK, I guess.'

The man had told Lamont to wait outside the New Orleans Union Passenger Terminal at three on Thursday afternoon, and that he would be collected. Lamont had stood outside the Passenger Terminal for a full hour that Thursday, but nobody had paid him any attention. He never heard from Docteur Amede again, which was unsurprising, as the Docteur was dead by then. Lamont never did make the USA Olympic team, but took a job in a local bank, at which he did pretty well. He married one of the tellers and they had three children together. In time Lamont got over the disappointment of his truncated athletics career.

To his final day, he never once realised that he had narrowly escaped dying of emphysema in his early twenties.

CHAPTER 59

The trouble with occult rituals was the amount of preparation necessary, but at least this one didn't demand the space to construct a pentagram. Nightingale hung the *Do Not Disturb* sign on his hotel room door. Nightingale had showered, and he was wearing another brand new white cotton robe that he'd bought that afternoon. He lit two white candles and switched off the room light, then took off the robe and placed it on the bed next to the small brown leather bag. He untied the bag and took out the pink crystal, by its silver chain, being very careful not to touch the stone itself yet.

On the floor he'd placed a large road map of Louisiana. He took the red-headed doll in its green dress out of his raincoat pocket. Placed it in front of the map closed his eyes, and said a short prayer, the crystal now pressed between his palms. When he had finished he opened his eyes and let the crystal swing free on its chain. He pictured a pale blue aura around himself as he took slow, deep breaths. He began to repeat her name.

'Brigid, Brigid.'

Nightingale focused all his attention on the name and stared hard at the doll. He whispered a sentence in Latin, and imagined the blue aura entering the crystal, helping it to show the direction in which she might be found, opening his mind to an image of the woman and her whereabouts.

The crystal didn't move by even a fraction of an inch.

'Brigid, Brigid.'

Nothing at all. It appeared there was no signal for the crystal to pick up. That meant Plan B.

Nightingale cleared his mind, put the doll back in his raincoat pocket on the bed, and tried to refocus his attention. He had nothing of hers to concentrate on, not a fragment of clothing, or even a photo. Just his memory and the force of his will.

'Proserpine, Proserpine, Proserpine.'

The crystal started to move slightly left, then slightly right. Nightingale concentrated on his aura, and the crystal started to spin in a small circle. Clockwise, then anti-clockwise and finally stopped dead and hung down motionless.

Nightingale scowled at the unhelpful crystal.

CHAPTER 60

The man who now called himself Doctor Amede held no doctorate from any University in any subject, but neither his followers or those who feared him challenged his right to the title. He had arrived in Louisiana some ten years previously, from Haiti, or so he claimed, He quickly built himself a formidable reputation as a practitioner of the arts of Voodoo, generally for good, particularly for healing. He claimed descent from the legendary Witch Queen Marie Laveau, though that was almost routine in New Orleans, and impossible to prove or disprove. For years, he had operated inside the city, from an expensive soundproofed penthouse apartment, where the recordings of traditional drums could cause no bother to the neighbours, and where the building's, and his own security, had ensured that his rituals were not disturbed. He had studied to perfect his knowledge of Voodoo, concentrating on areas forbidden to less daring practitioners. He had uncovered the darkest secrets of the old religion. He had earned a degree of respect in the city, and the law and the lawless left him in peace to practise his craft.

In recent months, that had changed. Unsavoury rumours had begun to run around concerning some of his activities, and while there was nothing that could be pinned down or proven, his reputation began to suffer, doors were closed to him, and he was made to feel unwelcome in his former haunts. Not wishing to wait until the background chatter hardened into anything more dangerous, he had taken himself and a small entourage down to his home on the bayou, where only carefully selected guests were seen, brought by word of mouth, and where the unsavoury reputation of the alligators, snakes and his own guards could keep him safe and his rituals private.

But this would only be temporary. Soon his work with the *Rounwytha* would have reached its end, and he could return, enriched and more powerful, and rebuild what he had lost. The leader paid well for his services, and his victims were happy to make large donations, whilst conniving at their own premature deaths.

He smiled at himself in the full-length mirror. The black suit fitted him to perfection, the shirt was dazzling white, and the bootlace tie was held in place by a silver skull the size of a man's fist. He wore round, mirrored glasses, their shine matching the gleam of his polished shaven head. The stigmata on his cheeks were the mark of a true African prince, or so he told people, though only he knew how genuine they were. He nodded at the mirror, pleased as always with what he saw. Soon, now, it would all be over. He had broken many rules, invoked the most dangerous of the Loa for forbidden purposes, but it would all have been worth it.

A frown wrinkled his high forehead, as his sensitive ears caught the sound of an approaching car. He was not expecting visitors, and very few would dare to arrive unannounced. Even fewer would be allowed through the gate by the two large Creole men stationed there.

Docteur Amede strolled to the verandah, just as the white Hummer with the mirrored black windows rolled to a halt outside. The frown relaxed into a smile, as the *Rounwytha* and Gabriella climbed down from the driver's seat. No mask, since Docteur Amede was well aware of his associate's true appearance. It was a warm enough day, but the *Rounwytha* wore a floor-length black coat. Gabriella's coat was shorter and grey. They walked onto the verandah, where he met them.

'Good afternoon. I was not expecting to see you until our next ritual,' said Docteur Amede.

'I know,' replied the *Rounwytha*, the voice, as ever, soft but commanding. 'But you will not be needed for that now.'

'What do you mean? I understood that this was to be the culminating *Conjure de Dhahibu*, at which you...'

The *Rounwytha* silenced him with the wave of a hand. 'You will not be needed. I shall perform the *Conjure* myself.'

'You? But you have no experience, no grounding...'

'How little you know. My grounding is equal to your own, and now I have studied the ritual, watched you perform it, and, most important of all, I have the trust of the Loa.'

Docteur Amede flushed with anger under his copper skin.

'What foolishness is this, the Loa comes at my summons.'

'Far from it, the Loa and I now work together to bring about a joint purpose. A purpose in which one of your race can never share. You were useful for minor rituals, you cannot be permitted to defile one of such importance as this.'

Docteur Amede stamped his foot in rage.

'Defile? My race? My race? How dare you? Voodoo was alive in Africa when your ancestors lived in trees in European forests.'

'Enough.' The *Rounwytha*'s voice rose just a little, but the command cut off Docteur Amede's rant straight away. 'The next Aeon will bring the dominance of the Aryan race. Your words select you as *opfer,* a follower of a degenerate heresy, and worthy only of culling.'

Docteur Amede gasped. 'No. I..."

The movement was too fast for the eye to follow. The right hand came out from under the long coat, and the razor -sharp knife flashed across Docteur Amede's throat before the Voodoo priest knew what was happening. He fell to the ground twitching, and was dead in seconds.

The *Rounwytha* raised the dead man's head, took a small lead bowl from a pocket of the robe, and filled it with the still-pumping blood. The bowl was raised high, then drained with one swallow.

'Thus do I drink thy blood, thus do I gain thy power. The Loa shall come at my command, I shall be Vindex. Drink, Gabriella.'

The *Rounwytha* handed the bowl to the younger woman, who filled it with blood, and also drank.

'Now,' said the *Rounwytha,* we have one more task to perform. We must find and destroy his *pot tet.'*

'What is that?'

'It is the single most important item in the life of a Voodoo initiate. A small pot which contains a fragment of their soul and other sacred items, sealed from the day they pledge themselves to their Voodop Loa. We must find it and destroy it, so that his power may fully pass to me. We shall look first in the *djevo,* the room he used as a temple.'

It took then just ten minutes to find it, hidden in a small cupboard behind the altar of Docteur Amede's *djevo.* The *Rounwytha* took the small, plain white earthenware pot outside, held it up to head height, then hurled it onto the concrete path, where it shattered into fragments. Quickly the *Rounwytha* knelt down and inhaled the cloud of dust which rose up. 'Now, his essence is no more, and his power shall be mine. Come, my dear.'

The *Rounwytha* climbed back into the Hummer and drove away, pausing briefly at the gate to collect the two large white men with the close-cropped hair who waited there. The bodies of the two Creole men were left where they had died.

CHAPTER 61

Nightingale was fairly sure of the response he would get, but decided to try anyway, and phoned Alice Steadman, at the Wicca Woman shop in London. He had occasionally managed to contact her on the astral plane, but it was never something he was comfortable about initiating. Too much could go wrong for a novice, and he had no wish to end up out of his body for good. The mobile phone was easier, so he punched in the number and she answered on the third ring.

'Good evening, Mr Nightingale,' came the thin wavering voice.

'How did you know it was me?' He always used burner phones and never kept a number for more than a month.

'One instinctively knows. I hope you're not in trouble again?'

Nightingale chuckled. 'I don't really know whether I am or not. I don't think anyone has it in for me personally, but there seem to be a lot of deaths around.'

'Oh dear, how very upsetting.'

'Well, not me so far, anyway. But I have a question, and I can't think of anyone else who might be able to answer it.'

'I can but try.'

'Well, as usual, I'm in over my head, so I tried to get some help.'

'From whom?'

Nightingale paused before saying the name as he knew that Mrs Steadman wouldn't be impressed. 'Proserpine.'

There was a silence that lasted nearly a minute. 'Oh dear me, I do wish you wouldn't try to contact creatures like that. You are risking so much every time you do. These are forces you cannot understand, much less control. Still, it is too late for lectures now. Did she offer help?'

'Well, not this time, as it happens. I followed the ritual to the letter, just like I've done before, but there was nothing.'

'What? She didn't appear when summoned?'

'No, not a trace. What could cause that?'

'I'm sure I can't think. Her kind come when they are summoned, it's the law. Unless…no…'

'Go on.'

'Well, unless someone else, or something else prevented her from coming.'

'Who or what could do that?' he asked.

'I really dread to think. Something of almost unimaginable power, but I couldn't say what.'

Nightingale decided to change tack. 'Tell me, Mrs Steadman, what do you know about Voodoo?'

'Not a great deal, I fear. It's rather similar to Wicca in its simplest and kindest form, using plants, herbs, filtres and potions for healing, to produce good outcomes. Why do I have the feeling that it's the darkest side that you are dealing with, Mr Nightingale.'

'Seems you know me too well. I think I might be in the realms of curses, and some very nasty rituals involving dead people.'

'Quite out of my area of expertise, I fear. I can't help you.'

'Can't or won't, Mrs Steadman? We've had this discussion before, I know.'

'Indeed we have, Mr Nightingale, and, as I told you then, it comes to the same thing. My role is not to interfere unless the essential state of things seems to be threatened.'

'The Balance?'

'If you like.'

'So, I am on my own again?'

'Not necessarily. There are people nearer at hand who will know far more than I do. I think you have met one of them. And it may well be that help is on its way, and will arrive when you least expect it.'

'What does that mean exactly?' Sometimes it felt as if Mrs Steadman spoke in riddles just to make his life difficult.

'I am afraid that you will have to wait and see. But remember Mr Nightingale, that you can never overcome evil with evil, or use darkness to defeat darkness. That way your soul will be lost. Use the light, Mr Nightingale. Use the light. I wish you luck.'

Nightingale heard the click as Mrs Steadman hung up her receiver.

CHAPTER 62

Nightingale finally found time to peruse the list that Valerie had sent him, but found it pretty useless. The only name he recognised was Madeleine J Crenshaw, Governor of Louisiana. Underneath was printed '*heavy smoker, rumoured to be suffering from emphysema and lung cancer.*' The other names were also of prominent politicians, judges, union leaders and even a police commissioner. All of them were over sixty, all rumoured to be suffering from serious illnesses, according to Wainwright's sources. It wasn't much to go on, and Nightingale couldn't see how he could use the information. His chances of getting an interview with the governor and asking her if a Voodoo doctor was treating her seemed remote.

He decided to phone Jefferson.

'I need to talk to a doctor,' said Nightingale.

'What are your symptoms?'

'Let's say I'm an old woman with cancer, who would I be talking to?'

'Possibly the oncology department at the University Medical Centre, though, no doubt there are other specialist centres. It's not a area that I concern myself with in my business dealings. Or my personal life.'

'What would be the chances of getting to talk to a doctor who treats any of these people. I need to ask a few questions.' Nightingale read him the list that Valerie had sent him.

'Fairly remote, I should think. Most of them would probably pay for very expensive medical treatment, most of those providing it would take their duties of patient confidentiality very seriously indeed. I can't see them wanting to discuss their patients' affairs with a random Englishman.'

'Yeah, I thought it might not be easy.'

'Leave it with me. My own medical practitioners may move in the same circles, I may be able to call in a favour or two. People often like to do favours for me.'

'I'll bet they do,' said Nightingale, but he said it after he hung up.

CHAPTER 63

If Matt Johnson was pleased to see Nightingale walk into his office, he hid his enthusiasm pretty well. 'You come to confess to something? Siddown.'

'Not really,' said Nightingale. 'I just stopped in to ask whether you were making any progress in the Dubois murder.'

Johnson sighed heavily, steepled his fingers, put his head on one side and sighed again. 'Listen, pal…' He broke, then continued in a more professional tone. 'Look, Mr Nightingale. I'm trying to be helpful, but I really can't discuss an ongoing investigation with a civilian. I appreciate your interest, given you were on very friendly terms with the lady's sister…'

Nightingale smiled. 'You're fishing, Detective.'

'Hah, a little, I guess. Anyway, all I can tell you is that our enquiries are proceeding. Anyway, it was a pleasure seeing you again,"said Johnson, indicating the door with his left hand. His face showed no signs of pleasure.

'Okay, thanks anyway.'

Nightingale got to his feet, then hesitated. By the way, do you know of a man called Jenson D Hart?'

'You been drinking?'

'It's a little early for me. So that's a yes?'

'Of course it's a yes, he's New Orleans's Superintendent of Police, has been for four years, well all except for two months.'

Nightingale raised an eyebrow. 'What happened?'

'You could have read the papers, he was off on sick leave recently.'

'Who took over?'

'His deputy of course, Maureen Wilde. But Hart's back now, Why would you be interested?'

'I'm not really, I just knew a guy in the Met who mentioned having known him. They were on an exchange visit or something.'

It was thin stuff, but the best Nightingale could come up with. Johnson grunted, but showed no further interest.

'Two months?' repeated Nightingale. 'Something serious?'

'Beats me,' said Johnson. 'Between him and his doctors. I heard rumours it might have been the Big C, but he's back at work looking fine, so I guess not.'

'Maybe just a face lift,' said Nightingale.

'English humour, eh? Don't give up your day job. If you ever find one.'

Nightingale guessed he'd worn out his welcome, so headed for the door, mentally putting a mental tick next to the name of Jenson P Hart on the list that Valerie had sent him.

Back in his office, Matt Johnson made a note for himself, to run a discreet check on any exchange visits his Police Superintendent might have made to London. He wasn't about to take Nightingale's word for anything.

CHAPTER 64

Doctor Li-Chen Yang was a small woman with black hair and round metal glasses. She fidgeted nervously in the booth as she sat opposite Nightingale, a glass of ice water untouched in front of her. Nightingale took a sip from his Corona, and looked into her green eyes, trying to put her at ease. The green eyes had surprised him but he assumed she was wearing contact lenses. 'Thank you for meeting me, Dr Yang. I appreciate this is a little irregular.'

'Far more than that, Mr Nightingale. If word of this conversation ever got out, my career would be over. And I should probably be sued for damages. My patient has considerable influence and wealth, it would not be pleasant for me.'

'I understand that. This conversation will never be reported. I promise you.'

She nodded. 'Mr Jefferson has given me his personal guarantee, which I accept.'

'You are also treating Mr Jefferson?'

Dr Yang stared into the distance, her lips pressed together. Nightingale took the hint. 'Forget that question,' said Nightingale. 'That's not why we're here. You were part of the team treating the...er...gentleman that Mr Jefferson mentioned?'

'I was.'

'Can you tell me, in layman's terms, what you were treating him for, and his prognosis?'

She nodded. I have agreed that I will do so. For the last three months, the gentleman has been treated for advanced prostate cancer, which was discovered too late for surgery. It had metastasised to his bones, lungs and liver, and our best efforts could do little for him other than pain relief.'

'So he's dying. How long has he got?'

'If you had asked those questions last month, I should have agreed, and told you that he had a matter of weeks left. Now, I do not know how to answer your question.'

'Why not?'

'Because his cancer appears to have gone. He discontinued his treatment a few weeks ago, and x-rays and scans we took at the time revealed no trace of the cancer.'

'It disappeared?'

'It seems so. There was no longer any trace of it.'

'Surely that's not normal?'

'In my experience, it is unprecedented, the man was at death's door, now he seems perfectly healthy.'

'Did Mr W...did the patient have any explanation?'

'None that made sense. He told my colleagues he had been following a special diet, but refused to give details. He also refused to allow us to report the development, share it outside the team or to run any more tests. And then he told us he wouldn't be needing our help any more.'

'You're sure there couldn't have been a mix-up in the initial diagnosis?'

'We are not talking about a mis-labelled X-ray here, Mr Nightingale. The man was examined by several colleagues, with hands, cameras, scans, X-rays. There was no possibility of an error. I have no explanation for this development. None at all.'

'And, just one more thing, you haven't heard of any other miracles like this recently?'

'No, I have not. Not so much as a rumour.'

Nightingale nodded, drained the last of his Corona and put ten dollars under the bottle for the waiter. 'Thank you for your help, Dr Yang. Mr Jefferson and I are very grateful.'

'I have no idea why. And for future reference, we have never met, and this conversation never took place.' She stood up, turned and walked away without a backward glance.

As soon as she had left the building, Nightingale phoned Joshua Wainwright and brought him up to speed.

'So, Jack, we have an ageing congressman cured of prostate cancer, and a young athlete suddenly dying of it. And a baseball pitcher who never smoked dies of lung cancer, while a chain-smoking

Governor in her sixties appears to be doing just fine after a health scare. Plus a Police Superintendent who may, or may not, have had cancer, but seems fine now.'

'I know it's not much to go on, Joshua, and I doubt we'll be able to get much evidence about any of the others on that list with rumoured health problems. And that list probably just scratches the surface.'

'Evidence, Jack? We won't be going to a jury with this. We both know what we think is happening here, the question is how we stop it.'

'I guess we cut off the head.'

'And who's the head, Jack?'

'Beats me, there's over a million people in the New Orleans area, care to pick one?'

'That's your best suggestion?'

'I guess I just keep annoying people, and see who reacts.'

Nightingale had barely finished the call when his phone rang again. It was Percy. 'Mr Nightingale? Percy. I have some news for you.'

'Good news or bad news?'

'Well, the Saints won in overtime. But the news isn't so good if your name's Amede. Mr Jefferson sent a car or two around to his place, maybe ask him a few questions. There won't be any answers forthcoming. Place looked like a slaughterhouse. Him and his so-called bodyguards, all with their throats slit.'

'Were the cops called?'

'Hell, no. Besides, there's no evidence, the boys rolled the bodies into the bayou. Alligators musta thought it was their birthday.'

Nightingale shuddered at the image. 'Did they find anything interesting in the house?'

'I'm afraid not. Doesn't look as if the good Docteur was too meticulous in keeping files on his clients. Not a computer or a phone in the place, Plenty of jars of herbs, liquids, knives, bowls, syringes, other Voodoo shit, and who knows what else, but they won't help us any. Still, if you think the boys might have overlooked something, you welcome to drive on down and take a look for yourself.'

'You know, I think I might take a rain check on that Percy.'

Nightingale ended the call. He had just stepped out onto the street when his phone rang, with a number it didn't recognise.

'Jack? It's Chris Dubois."
'Chris. I'm so sorry, I...'
'Save it, Jack. There's nothing you can say.'
'I know, I just feel responsible.'
'Me too, but I never had any idea things might turn out that way. The detective business had never felt dangerous before. But those bastards will pay for Frankie. Was it Docteur Amede?'
'I doubt it, more likely to be whoever he was working with. But he won't be telling us now. They found him with his throat slit. Same as Frankie.'
'Jack, I need to see you.'
'No way. Bringing you into this has been a big mistake, they killed your sister and I'm sure they still want you dead. I've got enough on my conscience already, Chris.'
'It's not your call, Jack. They murdered my sister. I'm going to make sure they pay for it. I won't get in your way, but I'll see these bastards in Hell.'
'Not happening.'
'You have no choice, if I have to, I'll find you and follow you every step you take in New Orleans.'
'Chris, please.'
'I meant it. You're not the only one who knows people in this city.'
'Alright, alright, I give up. Where are you?'
'Never mind that, I need to shake myself loose from my protection. 'll call you when I've done that, we can meet somewhere safe and you can bring me up to speed.'

CHAPTER 65

Annoying policemen was Nightingale's special talent, but it rarely achieved anything useful, so he decided to switch to bothering journalists. He headed down to Charles Avenue, to the offices of the *Times Picayune New Orleans Advocate* and tried to bluff his way in to see the editor. The middle-aged blonde lady receptionist seemed unimpressed with the idea. 'Mr Henman doesn't see anyone without an appointment,' she said.

'It's really quite important,' said Nightingale.

'I'm sure it is.'

She picked up a pen and notepad. 'May I take a name and ask what it's in connection with?'

'It's in connection with a murder.'

'Well then, surely, you should be talking to the police.'

'I am the police.'

'Indeed?'

'Yes, Inspector Jack Nightingale.'

'Of the NOPD? Can I see a badge?'

'Well, actually I'm British, from the Metropolitan Police. In London.'

'I guessed from the accent. Do the London Police have badges?'

'No, we have warrant cards. Here.'

Nightingale flashed his wallet open and closed it too quickly for her to read his San Francisco Library Card. She wasn't buying it. 'I'm sorry, Mister Nightingale.'

'Inspector.'

'Of course, but Mr Henman really is very busy at the moment. He has a lot of work to catch up on.'

'Oh? Why is that?'

''He's been off work for a little while, only just got back.'

'Oh, nothing serious, I hope?' Nightingale tried to sound concerned.

'Well, nobody's really sure. Some of us were pretty worried for a while, but whatever was wrong, he managed to shake it off pretty quickly. He looks so much better now.' She stopped speaking abruptly, perhaps realising that she was gossiping too much. 'Anyway, I'm sorry, Mr...er...Inspector Nightingale, but perhaps it would be better if you made your request via the NOPD. Then I'm sure Mr Henman would be happy to cooperate.'

She lifted her gaze towards the large man in uniform at the entrance, but Nightingale muttered his thanks and decided to leave before she nodded him over.

Another name mentally ticked off on his list, though, once again, no real evidence.

CHAPTER 66

Until ten minutes previously, Captain Derek Price had always thought he led a charmed life. At fifty, he was married to his high school sweetheart, they had two beautiful, healthy daughters, and his military career had been one success after another, leading up to his current position as commander of the Naval Air Station, Joint Reserve Base, New Orleans. He had responsibility, amongst other things, for a Strike Fighter Squadron of FA18 Hornet fighters and Marine and Coast Guard Helicopter squadrons. He'd done well, his reports were good, and he was hoping for a new promotion soon. His reddish-brown hair was beginning to thin, his waistline to thicken just a little but a man couldn't have everything.

He sat in his office, running his eyes over an unimportant report, then felt a twinge of pain behind his eyes. Damned headache again. He shook a tablet out of an aspirin bottle from his desk drawer and washed it down with a glass of water. Probably stress, but the MO would let him know for sure.

There was a tap on his office door, he grunted, and in walked Commander Willard Sneed, the base medical officer. He was holding a brown manilla envelope. One look at his set, serious face sent a wave of fear through his commanding officer.

'Will, sit down. What can I do you for?'

His tone was forced rather than casual. 'The tests we ran, Derek. I have the results.'

'Hah, how long have I got?'

'Derek, this is serious. I don't know how to tell you.'

'Just tell me, Will.'

The older man took a scan picture from the envelope and placed it on the desk. Captain Price looked at it, but it conveyed nothing. He shrugged. 'You're going to have to spell it out for me.'

The MO sighed. 'You have a glioblastoma. A brain tumour. An aggressive one. It's growing.'

'There's no possibility of a mistake?'

'I'm sorry.'

The younger man nodded. 'So, what do we do?'

'Initially surgery, to remove as much of it as possible. Then radiotherapy. We'll do everything we can. But...'

'Give me the numbers, Will.'

'Okay, without treatment, you've probably got three months. With all the treatment we can offer, the average survival time is twelve months.'

Price put his head in his hands and sat motionless for nearly a minute. He straightened up and looked at the doctor. 'I'm going to fight this, Will. For me, but mostly for Lisa, Lucy and Nicky. I'm going to beat it.'

The doctor blinked his eyes and nodded.

'I think I'd like to be alone for a while now, Will, then I'm going to go home and talk to Lisa. Tomorrow we can talk and get started on that treatment.'

'Sooner the better, Derek. I'm so sor...'

'I know, Will. I know.'

CHAPTER 67

Derek Price was no drinker, but tonight he needed a beer. He knew his wife and children were out at a birthday party, so he changed into jeans and a sweater and drove off-base. He stopped at a bar he'd never been in before, where he hoped not to meet anyone he knew. It was called the Yardarm, which seemed rather appropriate. The garish purple lighting at the bar didn't appeal, so he took his bourbon to a booth at the back. He raised the glass and toasted himself. 'Here's to you, Derek.'

'Good health, sailor.' He spun round. The blonde looked around thirty-five. The electric blue dress was expensive and fitted her perfectly. She stared at him with dancing green eyes. 'Mind if I join you?'

He held up his left hand, waggled his ring finger and shook his head. 'Very kind of you, ma'am, but I'm a married man. Happily, so far, and I'd like to keep it that way.'

She smiled, and sidled into the seat opposite him. 'At ease, sailor. I'm not selling anything. And I'm not giving it away either.'

Captain Price raised his eyebrows in a question. He was in fair shape, but his babe-magnet days were far behind him, what could this woman want? 'So what can I do for you, Ma'am?'

'So polite, Captain. I'm here to help you, that's all.'

'Hah, that's quite a tall order, Ms...'

'Call me Gabriella, Derek.'

'How do you know...'

'I know many things which might surprise you.'

She focused her eyes on his, and a chill ran over him. 'Who are you?'

'You could call me a Guardian Angel, if you like. I am here to save you.'

'Why do you think I need saving?'

'One word. Glioblastoma.'

'How the hell…'

He started to stand up, but she leaned across the table, put her hand 1 his arm, and gently, but firmly, pushed him down. 'Don't worry out how. And I can help. I can take it away.'

'That's ridiculous.'

'Look at me, Derek. Look into my eyes.'

He held her gaze, and felt himself drawn deep into the green pools at flickered before him. She was saying something, but he couldn't ake out the words. It was soothing, filled him with confidence. He 1ew now that she was speaking the truth. His eyes widened. 'My od, you can. I believe it.'

'Good, but forget the idea of God. You will pledge your allegiance • quite another power. Listen carefully to me.' She leaned towards m and began to explain what was going to happen.

CHAPTER 68

Nightingale lay down on the hotel bed to try to think, but tiredness caught up with him, and his eyelids closed, He jerked them open to find that he was running down a narrow lane, lit only by moonlight. Ahead of him, he saw the figure of the woman Brigid, her red hair and green dress flowing in a breeze that he couldn't feel. She was facing him, her hands beckoning him towards her, but, no matter how fast he ran, she receded before him, and never came any closer. Her mouth was opening and closing, but the breeze carried her words away before they could reach him.

'Where are you?' shouted Nightingale. 'Stop, let me help you!'

'Tea. Bordeaux. Come to me, save me.'

'Stop moving away from me, what do you want? I can't hear you!'

'Save me, come to me. I need you, Jack Nightingale. Tea. Bordeaux. Myrtle. Come to me.'

'I can't hear you!'

Mist closed in between the woman and Nightingale, and he lost sight of her. He closed his eyes, opened them again, and found himself awake on his hotel bed.

He rolled over, grabbed his phone, and called Mrs Devereaux. 'I need your help again,' he said.

'I'll try.'

'I've had a message, some kind of summons maybe.'

'Who from?'

'That's the trouble, I don't really know, a woman I've been seeing in a dream.'

'Do you know her?'

'No, I've never seen her outside a dream.'

'What does she want?'

'Wants me to come to her, to save her from something, but I don't know what. Or where.'

'So what's the message?'

'It makes no sense. Three words. Myrtle, Bordeaux and Tea.'

'It doesn't suggest anything to me, Were they her exact words?'

'Well, yes. But in a different order. Tea. Bordeaux. Myrtle. It was hard to hear exactly what she was saying.'

'Could it be Thibodaux?''

'Yes, maybe, but what is that?'

'It's not a what, it's a where. It's a small town, about fifty miles from here along the Bayou Lafouche. Not the best of reputations historically.'

'Why not?'

'You never heard of the Thibodaux Massacre?'

'My school wasn't big on American History. Some Civil War battle?'

There was a short pause. 'No, maybe even worse than that. I guess you could Google it, but I might as well tell you, better that than you bringing it up in the town. People probably wouldn't appreciate being reminded.'

'I'm all ears.'

'It was actually about twenty years after the War. Slavery had been abolished, in theory, but black plantation workers had precious few rights. They were worked almost to death, housed in horrible little shacks and usually paid in *scrip.*'

'What's that, scrip?'

'They were paid in pasteboard tickets, not money, and the tickets could only be redeemed at the company stores, where all the prices were kept sky-high. The planters kept the books, most of the workers couldn't read, and they ended up in heavy debt. They weren't allowed to leave unless the debt was paid, so they ended up pretty much back in slavery.'

'I'm guessing they didn't have unions back then?'

'That's when things started to get really nasty. The sugarcane pickers joined a local branch of the *Knights Of Labor* which organised a strike, right at the height of the picking season.'

'And the plantation owners weren't happy?'

'Something like that. The governor sent in the military, and the planters employed their own paramilitaries. Long story short, the strike was smashed and something like fifty black workers murdered in Thibodaux. Nobody's sure of the exact number, bodies kept turning up for weeks. It put a stop to organised black labour until after World War Two. Not something to be proud of.'

'Not for most people, but maybe the members of the Nine Angles would see things differently. Someone's obviously trying to get me down there. Could it be that the mysterious plantation is there?'

'There are probably dozens of abandoned plantations down there, along with a few still operating.'

'I suppose conditions have improved?'

'The working ones rely on mechanisation. Some of the others were made into hotels and wedding venues, but there's a growing backlash against people using them, because of their history. A plantation wedding isn't exactly woke.'

'I suppose not. Any ideas about myrtle? Could it be a name?'

'It's a tree as well as a pretty old-fashioned girl's name, could be the name of somewhere, I guess.'

'Only one way to find out,' said Nightingale. 'It looks like I'm due a visit to Thibodaux.'

'Be careful, Mr Nightingale. It's a town with a high crime rate, and it seems someone will be expecting you.'

'Seems that way, there's that trail of breadcrumbs again. I'll watch my step.'

CHAPTER 69

The *Rounwytha* answered the ring of the phone then immediately pressed the red button to cancel the call. The phone rang again ten seconds later, and the process was repeated. The *Rounwytha* then redialled the caller's number, which was answered immediately. 'On whose behalf are you calling?' asked the *Rounwytha*.

'The Congressman.'

'An emergency?'

'It seems so. He has been advised that one of his medical team was seen talking to an Englishman who has been making enquiries in certain areas.'

'I understand,' said the *Rounwytha*. 'None of his medical team could offer any information which might lead anyone to us, but the Englishman is becoming a nuisance. A little discouragement may be called for. Who is the person?'

The caller named her.

'Ah, a Chinese woman, so much the more deserving. Thank you.'

The *Rounwytha* pressed a button on the desk and spoke into the intercom. 'Gabriella?'

The door swung open, and the blonde woman walked in. The blue dress from the night before had been replaced by a plain white shirt and black pants. She took the seat opposite the *Rounwytha*. 'Your report?'

'I think the Sailor will take our offer,' said Gabrielle. 'I am sure I was able to convince him that it is genuine. We were fortunate that our informant contacted us so quickly, his mind was still rather confused.'

'Your powers as an Adept are most useful to our order. I doubt that any normal person could be as convincing.'

Gabriella acknowledged the compliment with a modest nod of her head and a small smile.

'We will need him to join us at the plantation to make his pact on the second. Will he be prepared to do so?'

'I am sure he will. The news was unexpected, he has had no time to make plans, and he is desperate.'

'Does he truly believe?'

'Perhaps not fully, but he was raised in the Episcopalian heresy, so his mind is open to beliefs that are not of this world. I shall meet with him again soon, and bring him to full belief before the pact is made.'

The *Rounwytha* nodded. 'He will be a very useful addition, In his present position, he commands great destructive power, and he may rise still higher.'

Do we have a sacrifice?'

'Not as yet. Without the late doctor, we have had no suitable candidates. But the Loa has promised to provide one for us at the appropriate time.'

'And what of...the other creature?'

'It presents no threat to us, the girl will endure for another four days, by which time what is done will be permanent.'

'There is no danger?'

'None, everything has been considered.'

CHAPTER 70

In another life, Jack Nightingale had been a firearms officer in the Metropolitan Police in London, though he rarely thought about those years. Despite the United States being far more gun-friendly, he very much preferred to remain unarmed, but maybe this would be a good time to change his mind. He called Joshua and brought him up to date.

'Sounds like they're inviting you into their parlour, Jack. They must reckon you'd never pass up a chance to save a damsel in distress.'

'If she really needs saving. More likely she's bait.'

'Good point. But anyway, what might they want with you?'

'Beats me. If they wanted me dead, they could just send someone to shoot me. Listen, Joshua, can you fix me up with a gun?'

Wainwright laughed. 'Why ask me? Your new friend Mr Jefferson must have hundreds.'

'I thought your system might be a little more legal.'

Wainwright laughed again. 'Just yanking your chain, Jack. Look, you're in Louisiana. Anyone over eighteen has the right to carry a gun openly. Just take yourself to a gun store, show some American ID that says you're an adult, and take your pick. Buy yourself a nice holster and it's no problem.'

'What if I don't want people to know I have a gun?'

'Now that's a different matter. You need a concealed carry permit, for which you need to be a state resident, take some tests and wait ten days.'

'So in a holster on my belt is fine, but in my pocket or in an underarm holster...'

'Is a serious offence.'

'If I get caught.'

'Best stay away from cops then.'

'Good advice, in general.'

An hour later, three hundred and fifty dollars poorer, Nightingale was the owner of a Glock pistol and two boxes of shells. He wore it openly in its holster on his trouser belt for the fifty yards it took him to walk back to his car in the parking lot of the strip mall, then he put it into his right raincoat pocket, carefully checking the safety catch was on, and that there wasn't a round in the chamber. He turned Google Maps on, and let the calm voice on his smartphone guide him to Thibodaux.

CHAPTER 71

It was a quiet family dinner in the Price household, and Lisa Price was a little puzzled. Normally Derek was very appreciative of her cooking, and tonight was her Texas chilli, one of his favourites. The two girls picked up on his mood as usually they would all have been discussing what had happened at school or at work, maybe plans for the weekend.

Derek Price looked across the table at the three women in his life. His wife, Lisa, had kept herself in good shape with yoga and tennis, and looked five years younger than her real age. Her shoulder-length hair was still a uniform chestnut, though only she knew how much help she got from the colourist at her hairdresser. Lucy had inherited her mother's colouring and, at seventeen, was nearly as tall as her father. The younger girl, Nicky was blonde and wore her hair short, so it wouldn't fly into her face when she was playing soccer.

He'd planned to spend decades more with them all. To see the girls through college, happily settled with loving partners, rocking his grandchildren to sleep, maybe finally taking Lisa on that European tour. Now none of that was going to happen. Unless that woman could be believed.

'Earth to Dad,' said Nicky. 'Come in please.'

Derek forced a smile. 'Sorry sweetheart, I was miles away.'

'Hard day at the office? Did the Russians invade?'

'Ha, not this week. Just one of those days.'

'Problems?' asked Lisa.

'I've told you before, honey, the US Navy doesn't have problems. Just…'

'…moments of extra interest,' chorused the three females.

He laughed. 'Guess I use that one a lot. Time I left work behind me and concentrated on this chilli.' He took another mouthful and smiled approval. He looked at the three smiling faces again, his stomach lurching at the thought that if he died, he'd never see them again.

CHAPTER 72

Doctor Li-Chen Yang parked her white BMW in the underground garage of her apartment building. She had just completed her final shift of the week at the Medical Centre, and was looking forward to two days of relaxation. Byron would be coming round later on for dinner, and maybe they'd go out dancing afterwards, or maybe a quiet night in with a bottle of wine, depending on how tired he was.

She took her medical bag out of the trunk and headed for the elevator. Behind her, a tall black girl stepped out from behind a grey SUV. Dr Yang never saw her, just felt the agonising tug of the wire round her throat, cutting through windpipe and arteries, before she fell dead on the floor. The black girl walked back to the SUV and climbed into one of the back seats.

The driver looked round and smiled at her. 'Well done, *ma soeur*, exactly as instructed.'

The black girl stared straight ahead, but made no sound.

Thirty minutes later, the grey SUV stopped by the side of the bayou. The driver got out, opened the back door and held it, while the black girl got out, walked straight over to the waterside, then kept right on going. She sank without a movement or a struggle.

'*Adieu, ma soeur.*'

CHAPTER 73

Derek Price's phone started to ring and he fished it out of his pocket, trying to keep his eyes on the road. He glanced at the screen. It was Will Sneed. He thought about rejecting the call but realised that the MO would probably only ring back so he took it. 'Hi, Will.'

'Derek, where the hell are you?'

'I'm taking a few days off, Will. I want you to give me sick leave.'

'Of course, you shouldn't be at work anyway, but I thought you'd have shown up to arrange things. Listen, Derek, we need to get started on your treatment straight away. At this stage, every day could be vital.'

'That's just going to have to wait a while, Will. I need to take a little time.'

'That's just ridiculous, you don't have time to waste. We need to start your treatment now.'

'Just a few days or so, Will. There's something I need to try. If it comes to nothing, you can start the dicing and slicing then.'

'Derek, look, I gave it to you straight, there's nothing you can try. The treatment is your only option.'

'Soon, I promise. And one more thing, Will…'

'What?'

'I've told Lisa that I'm on a training course for a few days. Just in case she calls in.'

'Derek, for pity's sake, what are you doing? Get yourself back here, I'll check you into the hospital right away.'

'Can't be done, Will. Maybe I'll tell you all about it some day, but for the moment, please just do as I ask. As one last favour to me.'

CHAPTER 74

Nightingale was lucky enough to find a room at the first hotel he saw, right in the centre of Thibodaux. The Danserau House had been built in 1845, in the Italianate style, with a Second Empire roof. At least that was what the brochure in his bedroom told him. Nightingale just thought it was big, white and had lots of arches and verandas. The room was comfortable, the furniture old-fashioned rather than modern hotel flatpack. As far as Nightingale was concerned, its main attractions were its central location and ease of parking.

A short walk took him to Norm's Louisiana Grille, where a chicken sandwich and fries took care of his nutritional requirements. The place wasn't too full, one reason why Nightingale had chosen it. So Cindy had chance to chat between bringing out orders.

'New in town, mister?' she asked. She was in her twenties with dyed blonde hair and red lipstick that was several shades too bright for daytime use. He knew her name was Cindy because that's what it said on the name badge on her left breast.

He smiled. 'Does it show?'

'It's a small town new arrivals are easy to spot. Love the accent, you're Australian.'

Nightingale nodded. 'I sure am. So what's to see and do round here?'

'Pretty much everything, you're in what they call the gateway to Bayou country. What kind of thing you interested in?'

'Nothing special, just doing the tourist thing.'

'Why don't you stop off at the Chamber of Commerce Visitor Centre just along the road. They have all the brochures, maps and advice you might need.'

'I'll do that,' said Nightingale.

The woman at the Chamber of Commerce was also called Cindy, but this one was brunette, not blonde, and about twenty years older than the waitress. She was equally friendly, and Nightingale tried to look interested, as she pressed brochures on him and ran through a list of Thibodaux's cultural attractions. The Wetlands Cultural Centre and the Bayou Children's Museum didn't sound too exciting, and the Mudbug Brewery might have to wait for his next visit. He tossed a question to her, as nonchalantly as he could. 'I heard about a place called Myrtle something,' he said.

She frowned, thought for a while, then it came to her. 'Maybe they meant the old Myrtle Valley Plantation out on Highway 308, but it's not exactly a visitor attraction.'

'No?'

'It's an old sugar plantation, pretty much abandoned now. Back in the nineteenth century it was a huge concern, hundreds of workers, owned by the Lafayettes.'

'But they don't own it now?'

'No, the last member of the Lafayette family died just after the war. I heard some people from New Orleans bought it, were thinking of opening it up to visitors, maybe as a hotel or wedding venue, but it never happened. Plantations aren't too politically correct these days. The old house is still there, and the slave...er... workers' cabins, but I wouldn't recommend a visit. Once a place on the bayou gets neglected, it goes downhill pretty quickly.'

'Thanks. Looks like my friend got it wrong, or maybe he was here a long time ago.'

She smiled at him, but was already looking over his shoulder at the next visitor in line.

CHAPTER 75

Nightingale headed out on the 308. Myrtle Valley Plantation was abandoned, but it still featured on Google Maps, so he found the turnoff easily enough. About half a mile away from the plantation, he pulled off the narrow lane and changed into the boots and camouflage clothing he'd never got round to returning to the late Duane. He was no woodsman, but was hoping it would attract less attention than his suit, Hush Puppies and raincoat. He slipped the Glock and a box of shells into the jacket pocket. There was nowhere much to hide the car, but he pulled it a few yards off the path, and started walking.

After about ten minutes, the path opened up into a clearing. To his left he could see the waters of the bayou, and, perched along the bank rows of dilapidated wooden shacks, some with the roofs fallen in, doors hanging off. Some had been damaged by fire, and probably Louisiana's occasionally unfriendly climate.

Nightingale looked inside one or two, through window frames which had long been devoid of glass. There was no furniture left, usually just one room, with a masonry fireplace and dirt floors. Nightingale shuddered at the thought of the poor creatures who'd tried to find rest here in between their back-breaking unremitting toil in the fields. He wondered how many of the black workers had met their deaths here at the hands of the white militias. And how many more had simply been worked and starved to death.

Nightingale's experiences since leaving the Met had left him very sensitive to the presence of evil, and his skin prickled here. This was a dark and sinister place.

He walked away from the slave huts, across the clearing, to where the old plantation house still stood. It was a two-storey white building, with wide verandahs with steep roofs made of dark green slate. It was in much better repair than the shacks. It seemed to have been used recently but it didn't look as if there was anyone home.

Nightingale climbed the three steps onto the wooden verandah and knocked on the door. He waited a good three minutes, but there was no sign of life. He walked round the house, trying to find an open window, but they were all tightly shuttered. He thought briefly about breaking in, but couldn't think of any way to do it without leaving obvious traces.

At the back of the house were fields which had probably once grown sugar beet. In the distance, he saw the ruin of a large red brick building, which he assumed was the old sugar mill.

He shuddered again, then headed back to his car, where he lit a cigarette and called Mrs Devereaux.

After five minutes of listening to the phone ring, he gave up. He tried Joshua instead and told him what he had found, which admittedly wasn't much. 'Sounds as if it could be the place, Jack. I get the feeling the Nine Angles would enjoy working from a place where so many blacks suffered. All those tortured souls would create just the kind of atmosphere they'd enjoy.'

'No doubt, but they're not here now. And I can't run a one-man stakeout.'

'No, and could be they've finished with whatever they were doing. Killing Docteur Amede might have been a final house clearance. Voodoo's not my speciality.'

'I'm not sure the Voodoo connection was ever much more than a convenient cover for something a lot more evil. I tried to call Mrs Devereaux, but no answer. That worries me because they have servants so there should always be someone there to answer the phone. It's a pain in the backside, but I'll have to drive back up there to see if she's okay. I don't know anyone else I could ask.'

Nightingale hung up, but hadn't had chance to start the car before the phone rang again. 'Nightingale? It's Detective Matt Johnson. You still in town?'

'You told me not to leave.'

'People don't always do what I tell them. I need you to come over to the Devereaux mansion right now. You know where that is, don't you?'

'But what...' The police officer had already ended the call.

All the way back to New Orleans, Nightingale had a sinking feeling in the pit of his stomach. Hannah Devereaux had told him that

247

she and her husband rarely left home these days, and none of their staff had answered the phone. He had thought of calling the police at the time, but decided not to bother with the endless explanation that would have been necessary,

There was nobody on duty at the gatehouse when he drove up, and the gate was open. He drove up to the house, checked the Glock in his pocket and walked over to the main door. He had to walk around three Police cruisers, a half dozen other anonymous sedans, and an SUV. The doorway was covered with yellow police tape, but Nightingale ducked under it. One step inside, a uniformed patrolman stopped him.

'Jack Nightingale. Detective Johnson sent for me.'

The officer waved him inside. At the foot of the stairs a team were working over the body of the butler, which lay in a pool of blood. Nightingale guessed he'd been attacked as soon as he opened the door. Being as careful as he could be not to touch anything, Nightingale stepped round the group and made his way down to the library.

The first thing he saw inside the library was the body of a complete stranger, a large, shaven-headed white man in black shirt and jeans and heavy black work boots. The General's ceremonial sword protruded from his heart. Three paces past him lay the body of another man, identically dressed, but with dark hair and a few days growth of black stubble. There was a neat hole where his left eye had been. Both corpses were surrounded by CSI personnel, working calmly and methodically.

Matt Johnson was sitting in one of the armchairs and turned his head as Nightingale entered. A woman, who Nightingale assumed to be another detective, sat in the chair next to him on the right, taking notes. Opposite them, sitting bolt upright on the sofa, was General Samuel Devereaux, his face flushed and his eyes bright. His wife's wheelchair was next to the sofa, and they were holding hands, the General giving her regular reassuring squeezes.

Johnson gestured to an empty chair to his left. 'Glad you could stop by, Mr Nightingale. You took your sweet time getting here. The Devereauxs suggested you might be able to offer some help here.'

'So what happened here?'

General Devereaux opened his mouth to speak, but Johnson held up a hand to stop him. 'To save the General and Mrs Devereaux repeating their statements, I'll give you the gist. About an hour ago, these two unidentified gentlemen, armed with machetes, arrived at the gatehouse, killed the guard then drove up to the main door. They rang the bell, which worried the Devereauxs, since there'd been no message from the guard. Seems these guys opened the door, by force, and killed the butler who was on his way to investigate.'

Hannah Devereaux sobbed, and her husband took a handkerchief from his breast pocket and passed it to her.

Johnson continued. 'Next, they barged into the library here, still waving the machetes. That's where things went a little wrong for them.'

'Looks like they underestimated their victims.'

'They did at that. You might think the General would have slowed down over the years, but those guys would disagree. He grabbed his old ceremonial sword from over the fireplace and stuck the first guy right through the heart. Doc says he was dead before he hit the floor.'

The General flushed a little more, and nodded.

'And number two?' asked Nightingale.

'Well now,' said Johnson. 'For reasons I haven't gone into yet, it appears Mrs Devereaux was in the habit of keeping a .38 in the side pocket of her wheelchair. Apparently she was quite a good shot in her younger days. Hasn't lost much, it seems.'

Mrs Devereaux smiled but didn't say anything.

'Well good for you both,' said Nightingale.

'That's pretty much what I told them,' said Johnson. 'I'm surely glad it's those two that are headed for the morgue. Now, I still have a few questions. The Devereauxs have never seen either of these two men before, and they say they have no idea what they were after. They happened to mention your name, said you'd been round a few times, so wondered if you could shed any light on things.'

The door opened and a uniformed policewoman nodded at the detective. 'The ambulance is here, Sir.'

The General and his wife opened their mouths to protest, but once again, Matt Johnson stopped them with his upraised hand. 'We've been through this. Doc says you've had quite a shock, even if you're not showing any signs of it. I want you both in the hospital to be checked over. Chances are, they'll send you back pretty soon.'

Paramedics arrived, and the Devereauxs, still protesting, were taken out to the ambulance.

Matt Johnson sat back down on the sofa, facing Nightingale. 'Now, Mr Nightingale, it's time for our little chat. What have you got to tell me?'

'What makes you think I have anything useful to say?' He shrugged. 'Maybe it was a robbery gone wrong.'

'And maybe they were tooth fairies who got the wrong address. Look, there's no money kept in the house, the lady's jewels have plenty of sentimental value, but they're nothing special. This was a hit, and it happened after you'd been here asking questions about God knows what.'

Nightingale decided to tell the truth. Most but not all of it, and not all at once. The first item Johnson would find out for himself soon enough anyway. 'Okay, maybe I know some things, and some I can guess. I take it there was no ID on the two dead guys?'

'Not a trace. And the SUV they arrived in was reported stolen this morning.'

'I'll bet when you run their prints and DNA, you'll come up empty. Check their shoulder-blades. I'll give you ten to one you'll find a tattoo of a ram's head and a nine-pointed star.'

Johnson left the room, and returned inside a minute. 'Well now, looks like you win your bet. Which makes me even more interested in what you're going to tell me next.' He nodded at the woman detective. 'You getting all this, Sandy?'

'Shorthand and voice recorder, Sir.'

'Good, I wouldn't want to miss a thing. Keep talking, Nightingale.'

'That tattoo is the mark of a very nasty organisation, called the Order Of The Nine Angles.That's Angles, not Angels.'

Johnson gave a low whistle. 'Now that name rings a bell. Give me a minute.' He pulled out his smartphone and typed into it. 'Thought I'd heard of them. A neo-Nazi, racist, terrorist organisation. Three arrests of US military personnel in the last two years for passing them military secrets, and plotting attacks on fellow servicemen. Guy in Toronto, Canada, charged with the murder of a Muslim caretaker. Some guy in Cornwall, England, charged with stockpiling weapons to use against antifa activists. List goes on, but I get the idea - not friendly people.'

'And what's on the record just scratches the surface.'

'So what's their connection here, and with you?'

'You know a man called Jefferson?'

'Several. Which one might you mean?'

'You pick one. The one I'm talking about seems to have lost quite a few of his business associates to these people.'

'That's too bad. Not sure I'd care to pick a side there.'

The detective flashed him a tight smile. 'So, the big question, who's pulling their strings, and where do I find them?'

'See now, that's a problem area. The Order tends to work in small separate sections, all unaware of the members of other sections, usually not knowing more than a few other members themselves. They call them 'nexions.'

'All of this you've learnt since getting to New Orleans?'

'No. I've had run-ins with them before, in the UK. They don't wish me well.'

'Imagine that. Well, I can't say it's much help, I've got nobody alive to ask questions of, and from what you say, they wouldn't have much information to offer anyway. Sounds like you might be next on their target list. Might be better if you left town.'

'They might still find me.'

'So, you got a plan?'

'I wouldn't call it exactly a plan,' said Nightingale. 'I just keep making a nuisance of myself, and see what happens.'

'Nightingale, I can't arrest you for anything, but keep out of my way, and for pity's sake, stop turning up near dead people. By the sound of these people, you don't want to try to go after them alone. You find out anything concrete, you call me. At once.'

'Of course,' said Nightingale, trying his best innocent look.

'And drop by Royal Street tomorrow to sign a statement.'

'You can count on it, Detective.'

CHAPTER 76

Jack Nightingale had no intention of allowing Matt Johnson to find him for a while so he headed back to Thibodaux. He hadn't travelled more than two miles when his phone rang. He took the call on hands-free. 'Jack? Chris. I'm loose and I need to see you.'

'See now, I really don't think that's a great idea. I've involved you in this mess way too much, and there's no way I'm going to risk you getting hurt.'

'Getting hurt? They killed my sister.'

'I know, and I'm...'

'We talked about this yesterday. Skip it for now. I need to see you.'

'I said...'

'It's not your call, Nightingale. It's something I need to do. You talk to me, or I'm going to spill my guts to the cops. They'll be wanting to spend a lot of time talking to you.'

Nightingale knew when he was beaten. 'Same bar?'

'Not a chance, nowhere that anyone might expect. I have the feeling people will be looking for me.'

'You have a place in mind?'

'Yes, *The City Of New Orleans*. The 6pm departure.'

'What, is it a train?'

'No, the boat. Get yourself a ticket, sit in the upper deck bar. Make very sure you're not followed.'

She had gone before Nightingale had chance to ask any further questions, so, once again, Google had to provide the answers.

Day was turning to twilight as Nightingale walked up the boarding ramp of the *City Of New Orleans* steamship. He had never seen a traditional stern-wheeler, so took a moment to appreciate it. It was two hundred and fifty feet long, or so he'd read, with four decks. Its white paint looked as if it had been renewed that morning, and contrasted with the red of its deck trim and of the giant paddle wheel at the stern.

Nearer the bow, two tall, narrow funnels were already pushing out smoke. The steam calliope was pumping out the inevitable Dixieland jazz as Nightingale stood in the queue shuffling forward. There was no sign of Chris Dubois, nor any other faces he recognised. He was as sure as he could be that his car hadn't been followed, and nobody here was paying him any attention.

The trip wasn't too full at this time of year, so Nightingale had no trouble finding a vacant table in the upper lounge. He sat down. Nobody seemed to pay him the slightest interest. He had briefly thought that he might pass the time with a cigarette, but was unsurprised to see the notices forbidding it. There was no shortage of ventilation here on the open deck, so he just put it down to spite.

The five-piece jazz band at the far end of the bar started playing *St James Infirmary,* and Nightingale tapped his foot automatically. The ship's whistle blew a few times, and the great ship slowly got under way. Most of the passengers headed for the railings to watch the river slip past.

'What can I get you, sir?' asked the waitress.

Nightingale silently cursed himself for allowing his attention to wander. He hadn't noticed her approach. He looked up, saw a tall woman in black pants, a black shirt and a black peaked cap with the ship's name picked out in gold on the front. 'I'll have a Corona, please. Slice of lime.'

'Be right back.'

It took her less than a minute to return with two bottles of Corona, which she set on the table.

'Mind if I join you, Jack?' she whispered.

Nightingale laughed out loud. He'd just taken a casual glance at the uniform, rather than the woman. Might have been serious, if she hadn't been on his side. 'Changed career, Chris?'

'Not exactly. I have a friend or two here, they let me sneak aboard and lent me a cap. Now, why don't you lend me your coat to put over this, so we don't get interrupted by some guy wanting me to fetch him Daquiri.'

Nightingale passed across his raincoat with good grace, despite the fact that the New Orleans twilight was getting a little chilly.

'Thanks. You don't have to say anything about Frankie. I plan to do my grieving when this is all over. Right now I'm running on hate.'

Nightingale nodded. There were no words anyway.

'So, who did this Jack?'

'Some very nasty people called the Order of Nine Angles.'

'Who?'

'It's a Satanic, neo-Nazi organisation. Has branches everywhere.'

'Good to know, but I think I'd rather have the name of a person.'

'I don't have one for you.'

'No leads?'

Nightingale sighed. He wasn't a great liar, despite all the practice he got. 'I have some leads, but, like I said on the phone, I'm leaving you out of this. It's way too dangerous, and I work better alone.'

'Oh don't give me that old line. Two heads are better than one, no? I want in. These bastards killed my sister. They're going to pay for it.'

'Sorry, Chris. It's non-negotiable. I've got too many people's lives on my conscience already, I don't want to be looking over my shoulder trying to protect someone else. It's tough enough trying to protect myself.'

'Less of the macho man stuff, Jack, I'm not some chick who freezes at danger, screams then twists her ankle. I've got a brown belt in karate and a licensed .38, I can take care of myself.'

'I'm sure you can, but these people aren't just common crooks, they're plain evil. They don't care who they hurt, in fact it seems the more people they hurt, the happier they are.'

'My safety isn't your call.'

Nightingale held up his hand, the palm towards her. 'No. Just no. That's all.'

She blew the air out of her cheeks, then sighed. 'You're not going to move on this, are you?'

'Not an inch. I know how dangerous these people are. I had to kill myself to get away from them.'

She frowned. 'Say what now?'

'It's a long story. We don't have the time.'

'Alright, but get these bastards for me.'

'I'll do my best,' said Nightingale. 'You want another drink?'

'Not me. As long as we're here, you want to go down and take a look at the engine room?'

Nightingale would have looked at almost anything to get out of this conversation.

They walked down one of the staircases to the lowest deck on the port side, then headed through the door helpfully marked *Engine Room.*

The noise was deafening, but Nightingale stuck it out while they stared at the two giant pistons that drove the paddle wheel. There was a large multi-coloured poster, headed, *How A Steam Engine Works,* which Nightingale pretended to study for a few minutes, without learning much. Every minute spent down here was another minute he wouldn't have to spend deflecting Chris Dubois from trying to join up with him.

They walked back outside. 'Want to hear a fun fact?'

'Sure, why not?' said Nightingale.

'This is actually the ninth steamship with the same name, dates back to 1975.'

'That new?'

'Yeah. The first eight were all built in the 18th century, and owned by a guy called Captain Thomas Leathers. He used to like to race other steam ships. Now, guess what he used to do to increase the speed of his ship.'

'No idea,' said Nightingale.

'Get this, he used to throw fatty bacon or hog fat into the engines.'

'What? And that worked?'

'Apparently.'

'What a waste of good bacon.'

'Maybe. Now, let's take a look at the New Orleans skyline by night.'

For the rest of the trip, Chris Dubois was content to stay in tourist guide mode, which left Nightingale a little surprised. He'd expected a much longer argument, but he wouldn't have been surprised if she'd returned to the subject.

The ship docked on schedule, and they disembarked.

'Where are you parked, Jack?'

'I used the lot across the street. Another thirty dollars wisely invested.'

'I came by streetcar, can I get a ride with you?'

'Sure, where to?'

'I'll show you.'

Ten minutes later, in a part of town that Nightingale didn't know, she told him to pull over. 'This will do fine, Jack. I'm staying just round this corner with an old friend.'

'Take care. Chris. As soon as I have anything, I'll call you.''

'Oh, I will. I'll keep my head down for a while. Now you remember what I said, get those bastards for me."

'I'll do my best,' said Nightingale.

She closed the door, turned the corner and disappeared into the night. She didn't see the car that had been following them at a safe distance. And neither did Nightingale.

CHAPTER 77

Nightingale went back to his original plan of heading to Thibodaux. Twenty miles out of New Orleans he stopped at a strip mall to get a burger, and called Wainwright, breaking the news to him of the attempted Devereaux murders. 'Well, good luck to those old guys. Looks like you've got the Order rattled. Unless it was just a coincidence and some gang trying a break-in.'

'Not a chance, the dead men had the tattoo. It was the Nine Angles.'

'Two more of them down. You must be getting close, Jack.'

'Maybe, or perhaps they needed to make an example of someone. Hannah would have been just their kind of target. They're not big on racial equality. But I'll find them.'

'So come on, tell me, do you think you're getting close?'

'I am, but I can't put it down to my detective skills.'

It was time to tell him about the dream, the doll and the woman who had summoned him to Thibodaux. When he had finished, Wainwright was clearly unhappy. 'Now you tell me all this?' said Wainwright. 'Why did you wait this long?'

'It was just a dream, or that's the way it felt.'

'Jack, you should know by now not to keep things to yourself, even small things. I doubt it's just a dream, they seem to be leading you by the nose.'

'I doubt it too. But little do they know that I know that they know that I know.'

'There's that good old English sense of humour again. If you're not careful it'll be the death of you, Jack. These are not people to joke about.'

'I know, I know. The thing is, I'm not sure they've done a very good job of laying a trail. I may have found the place they've used, but there's no sign of anyone there now, and no indication of when they might be back. If ever.'

'Tell me about it.'

Nightingale described his visit to Myrtle Valley.

'It sounds as if it has just the sort of atmosphere that people working evil would enjoy. A place where black people were treated like animals.'

'But I have no idea when they might be there.'

'One moment, let me consult something.'

Nightingale waited patiently, He heard footsteps, the rustling of paper, then more footsteps.

'What did you say the name of this mysterious woman was? The woman in the dream?'

'Brigid.'

'Close enough. Did you know that tomorrow, February 2, is an important feast day in Voodoo. The feast day of Maman Brigitte.'

'And who's she when she's at home?'

'Apparently she is the consort of Baron Samedi. A very powerful Loa. Goddess of healing, and Queen of Death.'

'Terrific. Just what I needed to hear.'

CHAPTER 78

Captain Derek Price had checked into a two-star hotel a mile and a half from the French quarter, a neighbourhood where he knew nobody, and didn't expect to be recognised. The LA Rams baseball cap and aviator sunglasses helped his anonymity. As instructed, he sat in his room at two pm and waited for her knock. It came right on time, and he raced to open the door. She walked in and sat in the armchair facing him. Her blonde hair was hidden under a dark green trilby, and she wore a black raincoat over her white shirt and black pants. Her make-up was toned down from the previous night, it looked as if she was trying to avoid attention.

'You have come,' she said. 'I knew you would.'

Again he swam in her green eyes, and her voice came from far away. Soothing and inspiring confidence. He knew he would believe whatever she told him.

'Your head?' she asked.

'Aches a little, but only two aspirin so far today.'

'Soon the pain will be unendurable.'

He flashed her a tight smile. 'Are you here to cheer me up?'

'It's pointless to give false hope, you know what will happen to you if you do nothing. Your Commander Sneed was quite correct.'

'How...'

She laid a finger on his lips. 'It is not important how I know, it will be enough that I do. And I also know that, with or without the help of Mr Sneed and his team, you will not survive to next year.'

'There you go, cheering me up again.'

'This is not a joking matter, Captain. I, and my group, are your only hope of cheating death. Do you believe me?'

She stared into his eyes and projected the whole force of her will to him. He couldn't pull his gaze away. At last he nodded. 'I believe you.'

'Then this is what you must do.'

She explained what would be required of him.

'My soul?' he exclaimed when she had finished. 'Are you serious?'

She gave him no answer, just the same steady gaze that he found impossible to argue with.

'So how does this work?' he said eventually. 'Do I need to sign something in blood?'

'You have seen too many films. It will be sufficient to make the pact with words.'

'Okay, so what do I say?'

'Your pact will not be made with me, but with the Loa.'

'The what?'

'The demon, the representative of the darkness.'

'And when do I meet this Loa?'

'Very soon, at the appointed place.'

'Where?'

'You will be taken there at the right time. For now, you will come with me, and we will keep you in a place of safety until then.'

Derek Price stared at the floor. Twenty-four hours before, he would have laughed the woman out of the room for talking such nonsense. But that was before he'd heard his death sentence, and before he'd stared into the woman's eyes. He nodded. 'I accept.'

'Good. But know this. There will be no turning back now. We are committed to you, and you to us.'

'I accept.'

'Very well. Take off your right shoe. You must be marked as one of us.'

'What do you mean?'

'All of us bear the mark of the Order. Some have a large brand on the shoulder. For those of us who need to be more...discreet...we have another system.'

While he took off his right shoe, she rummaged in her handbag and brought out two small items. One was a cigarette lighter, the other was a small wooden-handled tool, with a square metal end, She held it up, and he saw the tiny star and horned head. He gave her a quizzical look but she said nothing, just clicked the lighter and held the tool in its steady flame. For a full two minutes, she held it there, then quickly pressed the hot metal into the pad of his big toe. He smelt the burning flesh, and winced, but didn't cry out. She took a tube of cream from her handbag, squeezed some onto her index finger, and rubbed it into the flesh, The pain subsided.

'Now, you are forever marked as a member of the Order Of The Nine Angles. Come with me.'

CHAPTER 79

Nightingale wasn't feeling particularly hungry, but who knew when he might have chance to eat again, so he walked out of the hotel, took a left and wandered into Norm's Louisiana Grille. He took a seat at a booth, ordered a sparkling water from Cindy and let his eyes wander down the menu. 'Number four, medium,' he said, and she told him he'd made a good choice.

It was too late in the evening for the place to be full, but even so, there were a few other diners. Nightingale paid them no attention, and they ignored him.

From across the street, cold eyes watched him enter the restaurant and sit down. The watcher ducked into a bar, chose a table at the window with a good view of Norm's, then ordered a tomato juice. Small sips made it last an hour and ten minutes, which was just as long as it took Nightingale to finish his meal, pay, then head back to his hotel.

A smile played over the watcher's lips.

'Soon now, Jack Nightingale. Very soon.'

CHAPTER 80

Nightingale lay on his bed in the hotel room, staring at the ceiling, willing his mind to go blank. If Wainwright's information was correct, he was likely to receive a summons tonight. If he was wrong, he had no idea what to do next or where to go. The Order of Nine Angles could only exist in a state of secrecy, and he didn't have a hope of penetrating it alone. Nightingale still lay on the bed, smoking another cigarette, in flagrant defiance of hotel regulations. If he was right, he probably wouldn't be coming back here to listen to the management's complaints. At eleven o'clock, he made a call.

'Mr Jefferson? It's Nightingale. I have an address for you. It's about seventy minutes away, I suggest you send some people. Might I also suggest you wait outside, and enter very carefully.'

It was eleven-fifteen when his eyes lost focus, the lids drooped and he was once again on a mist-shrouded road, but this time he recognised it. He could just see her in the distance, and her voice was only a whisper.

'The time is now, Jack Nightingale. Come to me, Save me. Be mine. And one more thing…'

CHAPTER 81

Nightingale opened his eyes, walked to the wardrobe, put on his Hush Puppies slipped into his raincoat. His hands went to his neck, and he unfastened Mrs Devereaux's locket and dropped it into the waste bin in the bathroom. His eyes stared into the distance, as he opened the door, walked down the stairs and headed out the front door, completely ignoring a cheerful 'Good Evening' from the lady manager. He walked to his car, climbed in, fastened the seat-belt and drove off.

Across the street, in the shadows between street lamps, a figure emerged from the doorway of a closed store and crossed the road.

Nightingale drove too fast through the warm Louisiana night in the direction of the Myrtle Valley Plantation. Even with the air conditioning on, the Escape felt like an oven and his clothes were soaked in sweat. He kept shaking his head to clear it, and spots danced sporadically before his eyes. He swallowed hard as bile rose up into his mouth, but his senses remained dulled. He was driving automatically, his conscious mind had no idea where he was going.

He was concentrating so hard to keep the car in a straight line that he nearly missed the turn-off and had to drive across the median to recover. Three miles down, he turned off onto the dirt road that led to the plantation. There was no sign of life, but a heavy mist hung over the place, forcing him to slow down to a crawl.

Five minutes later he pulled up, a hundred yards before the plantation house and shook his head, as if waking up.

'How the hell did I get here?' he asked himself.

He turned out the car lights, grabbed the flashlight from the glove box, and opened the door. He listened as carefully as he could, but heard nothing except an occasional rustling and splash from the direction of the bayou. There was no sign of any other vehicle, and no lights could be seen from the shuttered windows.

He turned on the flashlight, and started to walk to the plantation house.

He never heard the sound of the engine behind him that was turned off a hundred yards away, nor did he see the lights.

As he got nearer to the house, the mist thickened into a solid wall of fog, on which the flashlight made little impression. He broke off a thin branch from a tree and held it in front of him to probe for obstacles as he followed the track. The voice in his head was back, and growing louder.

'Come to me, Jack Nightingale. Save me.'

Was it his imagination, or were there now two voices, calling in unison? One low and persuasive, the other harsher, perhaps tinged with fear. They seemed to blend together, always calling insistently.

'Come to me, Jack Nightingale. Save me.'

He shook his head. He knew he wasn't asleep, couldn't be dreaming. Was he hypnotised? He closed his eyes, and the vision of Brigid swam into his consciousness, only to flicker away and be replaced by another figure, one he couldn't quite recognise. Then it was gone, and Brigid was calling him again.

'Come to me now, Jack Nightingale. Save me.'

Eventually he reached the house, which was completely dark, not a sound coming from its shuttered windows. As it came into view, the fog lifted completely. He stood there for nearly two minutes, trying to make sense of what he saw. Was it all just a false trail?

But still the voice in his head was calling, and he walked around the house. The windows and the massive door were shut, but fingers of light shone around their edges.

Nightingale reached out and pushed at the door. It swung open.

The place seemed somehow larger inside than outside, perhaps due to its almost complete lack of furniture. Most of the interior walls had been removed, leaving one room which ran the entire length and width of the ground floor. The walls were painted white, but almost completely covered in symbols and pictures, of animals, real and imaginary, words in languages Nightingale had never seen. At the far end of the cavernous room stood an altar, made of roughly carved wood. There were several robed figures standing there, but Nightingale's eyes were drawn to the woman who stood in front of the altar. Her green dress showing off her magnificent figure, contrasting with the flaming red of her hair.

'Brigid,' he said, though the word caught in his throat.

'So you have come at my command, Jack Nightingale,' she said. 'And what better place for us to meet than this place of death, despair and misery.'

'So you have come, Jack Nightingale,' echoed another voice in his head, a voice Nightingale now recognised. He turned his head to the left, and his jaw dropped. Nothing could have prepared him for what he saw.

A pentagram had been drawn on the floor, complete with the necessary candles, holy water and burning herbs. In the middle of it stood a young black girl, totally naked, completely motionless, her long hair hanging down her back. Opposite her, inside the top point of the star, stood another motionless figure, her jet-black hair cut in a spiky fringe. She wore inverted silver crosses in her ears, a matching silver pendant, a black plastic T-shirt, leather leggings and black knee boots. She gazed straight ahead, unmoving, her eyes black pools of emptiness. The black and white sheepdog by her side gazed upwards at her, but never moved a muscle.

'Proserpine?'

Brigid smiled 'It seems you are acquainted. She is our prisoner. Helpless.'

'A Princess of Hell, a prisoner?'

'Oh yes. The negro girl was summoned back from the Gates of Death and given a simple task. She was placed in the pentagram, and told to utter the words of summons. She cannot leave now until the words of dismissal are spoken, and they never will be.'

'You'll keep her here for ever?''

'I very much doubt that. The girl's body will deteriorate, and she will return to the Gates of Death. At that time, it may be that the power of the pentagram will dissolve. Or it may not, and Proserpine will stay there until this building collapses under the weight of years.'

'You'd better be a long way from her when that happens.'

'It will be of no consequence by then. Our purpose will have been served, she will be unable to prevent us.'

'Us?'

'Our order. My order. The Order of the Nine Angles.'

'But Proserpine is its leader. It is her order.'

'No longer. A younger, stronger leader is required to take the Order into the next Aeon. The power of this Nexon, this group, is growing daily, its members have been given the power to prolong their lives. And their Earthly leader will join with me, and be reincarnated here as Vindex, the Avenger.'

'You're mad.'

She laughed. 'Oh no, Nightingale. Not mad. Have you still not understood? I am Brigid, Maman Brigitte, Sekhmet the Huntress, I am Loa. I am all these things and I am your destruction.'

As she said the final word, the figure of the beautiful woman shimmered and dissolved. What stood there was indescribable, a creature of scales, teeth, claws, constantly changing shape and colour. Nightingale flinched backwards and fell to the ground.

Whatever it was stared down at Nightingale. 'My form does not please you? Try the other again then.'

Brigid returned, a mocking smile on her face. 'You prefer this form? The one that brought you here? You creatures set such store by appearance. Now your weakness shall destroy you.' She held out her left hand. 'Come Elizabeth.' Another woman emerged from the shadows behind her. Nightingale estimated she must be in her mid sixties. She had greying brown hair and large green, plastic-framed spectacles. She was dressed in a brown pants-suit and flat green shoes. She would have been inconspicuous in any crowd, a typical housewife, kindly grandmother. Nightingale was certain he had never seen her before.

'You have not met the earthly leader of our group,' said Brigid. 'This is Elizabeth, the *Rounwytha*, the one who will take the Order into the next aeon.'

Nightingale got to his feet and wiped his hands on his raincoat. 'She doesn't look as if she'll make it into next week,' said Nightingale.

'I hope your humour will be a consolation in your last few moments. Elizabeth's earthly frame may be growing weaker than it once was, but we shall alter that.'

Elizabeth lifted her head and spoke. Her voice was surprisingly strong. 'Yes, Nightingale. I shall be renewed and reincarnated as Vindex, the Avenger strong and immortal. And for this we need the body and energy of one who comes here willingly, and the soul of another.'

'You're mad,' said Nightingale. 'Stark, raving mad.'
'Mankind has always said that about its visionaries,' said Elizabeth. 'And about a lot of mad people too.'
The woman smiled. 'Perhaps it is comforting to you to try to be amusing in your final moments, though I doubt it will help in the eternity of agony that lies before you. You have lost, Nightingale. My order continues to grow, and its more powerful members have their lives extended far beyond the norm. They will be the next evolution of mankind.'
'Like the Governor, the Police Commissioner, newspaper editors, Senator…'
'I congratulate you on your detective skills, Nightingale,' said Elizabeth, 'though you only discovered what you were meant to. What we used to bring you here.'
'Breadcrumbs,' muttered Nightingale.
Nightingale glanced at his watch. Seventy minutes had elapsed since his call to Jefferson. The cavalry should be arriving at any moment.
'Expecting someone, Nightingale?' asked Brigid. 'If I were you, I wouldn't get my hopes up.'
The door behind Nightingale opened, and Harold Jefferson walked in and moved to the front of the room. He wore a black fedora and his hands were thrust deep into the pockets of his heavy, black overcoat. He nodded at Nightingale. 'Evening, Jack, you're not looking too good.'
'I think I might have just taken a turn for the worse,' said Nightingale. 'I was hoping you'd bring reinforcements.'
'Can't help you there, Jack. I don't need an audience for this. Just me and Percy tonight, and Percy's lying outside with a bullet through his spine.'
'Looks like you changed sides pretty permanently.'
'I changed sides a few weeks ago, after I had a couple of little talks. One with a doctor, who explained what pancreatic cancer was and how long I had left, and one with the *Rounwytha*, who explained why I didn't need to be afraid of it. Tonight's ceremony is going to see me back to A1 again.'
'You really think so? I thought you didn't believe in Voodoo.'

'I've seen it happen. You spoke to Dr Yang, she told you about her patient.'

Nightingale's hand came out of his raincoat pocket, holding the Glock steady at the centre of Jefferson's body. 'Okay, this has gone far enough. I'm leaving now, and you're coming with me.'

A smile played across Jefferson's face, and, behind him, Brigid dissolved into laughter.

'You really think your little toy will solve anything, Nightingale,' said Brigid. 'Very well, go ahead, shoot.'

Nightingale tightened his index figure on the trigger. Nothing happened. The trigger would not pull, the gun would not fire. Sweat stood out on his forehead, as he strained to move his finger. Nothing. He swore and threw the pistol on the ground in frustration.

Brigid laughed and clicked her fingers, and the gun flew from the floor into Elizabeth's left hand. 'There is nothing wrong with your toy, Nightingale. It will not fire because I willed it not to. It will work perfectly, if I decide it should.'

She smiled again, and Elizabeth shot Jefferson through the centre of his forehead. He crumpled to the ground without a sound.

'That's going to make him a lot more difficult to cure,' said Nightingale, staring at Jefferson's corpse. A halo of blood was spreading around his head.

'That was never our intention, Jefferson was always marked for death. His organisation will fall without his guidance, and we shall take over. To think, he genuinely believed that one of his inferior race could join our Order. Bringing him here was so much easier than sending some creature to try to kill him. He thought your health would be transferred to him, but we have quite another recipient in mind.'

'And who might that be?'

Brigid clicked her fingers, and a tall blonde woman in a long white dress walked in, leading a man by the hand.

'This is the Adept Gabriella,' said Brigid. 'And her guest. Our newest neophyte, soon to be an initiate, Derek. Captain Derek Price,'

'Captain of what?' said Nightingale. 'And what's an Adept?'

'Adepts are a high rank in our order, soon she too will attain the rank of *Rounwytha*, like myself, the most psychically advanced of our members, We live reclusively, apart from men, perfecting our abilities, preparing to reach the rank of immortals. Tonight I shall attain immortality, Vindex the avenger will be incarnate in me.'

'Captain of what, Mr Price?'

Gabriella looked at the man and nodded, giving him permission to speak.

'I'm not sure who you are, or why you're asking, Sir, but my name is Captain Derek Price, US Navy, and I'm the commanding officer of the New Orleans Naval Air Station.'

Nightingale shook his head slowly and let out a low whistle. 'You're keeping strange company here, Captain.'

'Perhaps I am, Sir, but I have my reasons.'

'Wild guess,' said Nightingale, 'you've been told you're dying, and these people have convinced you they can save you. In exchange for...'

'Enough,' shouted Brigid. 'He has made his choice. His pact will be sealed and the sacrifice made.'

'And I'm the donor?' said Nightingale.

'How little you know, Nightingale,' said Elizabeth. 'Something quite different is required of you. Maman Brigid will claim your soul, a doubly valued soul, since it is highly prized by two other demons. In exchange, she will bestow immortality on me, and I shall become Vindex. The Avenger.'

''A twice sold soul, yet never claimed,' said Nightingale. 'I didn't realise I was such a valuable commodity.'

'Oh yes,' said Brigid. 'Taking a soul such as yours will increase my power beyond measure. I shall be free of my duty of obedience.'

Nightingale stared at the older woman. 'Listen, Elizabeth, *Rounwytha*, you can't believe you're going to achieve immortality. It is forbidden, even for a Loa.'

It was Brigid who replied. 'What was forbidden will no longer be. A new order is being initiated. Your soul will bring it about, though you will not be here to see it. You will have died in despair. As for the second donor for our sacrifice, I believe she is here.'

She snapped her fingers and a door at the side of the room opened. Chris Dubois was standing there, a robed figure either side of her, gripping her arms.

'Chris? What the hell?' He looked over at Brigid. 'Why is she here? She's nothing to do with this.'

'She involved herself when she took you up in her plane. We were going to cull her, but this way she can be useful.'

Gabriella picked up a long bone-handled knife with a curved blade from the altar and took a step towards Chris. 'This time there will be no mistake, *Rounwytha.*'

The *Rounwytha,* Elizabeth, put a restraining hand on her arm.

'Not now, Gabriella. We have need of her as a sacrifice to take the place of our Captain.' She passed the Glock to Captain Price. Shoot her if she moves. But shoot to wound, not to kill.'

Chris Dubois ignored them all, and the gun, Her eyes were completely focused on Gabriella's face. 'You'll pay for what you did to my sister,' she hissed.

'Soon you will be joining her,' said Gabriella.

Elizabeth clicked her fingers. 'Enough from you two. We shall take the girl first. By the *Conjure de Dhalibu* she will sacrifice her health and life-force to the Captain. Normally she would die from his tumour inside a few months, but there seems no point to prolong her suffering, so the Captain will shoot her then. You shall watch this, Nightingale. Your suffering will amuse me greatly.'

'What have I ever done to you?' asked Nightingale.

'Your value is your soul, Nightingale. Your suffering will be some small repayment for the trouble you have caused the Order in the past. Now you shall see the powers of a *Rounwytha,* the powers I have honed over decades of study and devotion.'

Elizabeth turned her gaze towards Chris, widened her eyes and spoke in a low, commanding tone. 'Now, Miss Dubois, listen to me. Listen only to my voice, listen to me and walk towards the altar.'

Nightingale looked on in horror as Chris's eyes lost focus and she took the first step forwards. The robed men released their grip on her arms.

'She is an easy subject,' said Elizabeth. 'My powers of control are too strong for her to resist. It is a weakness with the inferior races.'

Nightingale desperately tried to move forward to stop her, but his legs refused to obey. The smile on Brigid's face widened.

'I hold you in my power, Jack Nightingale. Kneel before me.'

Nightingale fought with all his strength, but felt himself sinking to his knees. Chris took another step forward.

Nightingale looked pleadingly at the Captain.

'Are you just going to let this happen? What kind of man are you?'

The Captain shook his head, but his gun hand never wavered. 'I'm a dying man, without this ceremony.'

'You have children, Captain?'

'That is none of your business.'

'I'll take that as a yes. Would you sacrifice a daughter to give yourself a few more years of life?'

'I'm doing this for my daughters, so I'll be there for them.'

'This girl here is someone's daughter. What gives you the right to sacrifice her to save you?'

The captain's gaze lowered, he couldn't meet Nightingale's eyes.

'And her death will be just the first step, these people will have you in their power for the rest of your life.'

'Silence, Nightingale,' shouted Brigid. 'His choice is made, his pact will be completed tonight. He is one of us.'

'No!'

The single word seemed to echo round the room, filling it from all sides.

'No,' repeated Derek Price. 'I'm sorry about causing all this, but I can't watch it happen. I may not be one of the good guys, but maybe I'm a little better than you think. I'm not buying myself more years at the cost of this girl's life. Stop it. It's over. I don't want to go through with this.'

'Quiet!' shouted Brigid. 'You are committed. You have joined us.'

'I guess I quit then.' Too quickly for anyone to stop him, he placed the Glock in his mouth and pulled the trigger. Blood and brains splattered over the wall as his body slumped to the floor.

'Fool!' shouted Elizabeth kicking savagely at his corpse. 'You utter fool. And you have accomplished nothing. The girl will still die.'

'It is of little importance,' said Brigid. 'There will be others who will join us in due course. Now, Nightingale, I will have your soul. It is time.'

She fumbled inside her robe and held up a small figurine, carved in black wood. The raincoat, shoes and tiny cigarette were unmistakeable.

Chris's eyes regained their focus, as Elizabeth's attention was distracted by the captain's suicide. She stopped walking forward and shook her head, as if to clear it.

'Jack, it's you, that doll is you!' shouted Chris, but Nightingale was silent, staring in horror at the doll, sweat pouring down his face.

This time it was Brigid who spoke. 'The doll binds you to me, Nightingale, you cannot resist me now, The doll is you, you are the doll. *Li feu.*' She held up her left hand, and a long jet of flame shot from the index finger and burned brightly. She moved her hand towards the doll, and Nightingale could feel his insides heating up.

'Do you know what I am going to do, Nightingale? This is the flame of a Loa, and with it I shall burn out the centre of the doll which binds you to me. And as I do so, your soul will be burnt from within your body and sent to Hell. Your body will be burnt to ashes, while the girl watches, and you will die knowing that she will soon follow you into death, her strength and essence sacrificed to bring immortality to Elizabeth, to Vindex. Join with me, Elizabeth. Take my hand.'

Elizabeth took the Loa's right hand, and a red aura sprung up round the two of them.

Nightingale strained every muscle, but he couldn't rise from his knees or move away.

'Now, on your face before me, Jack Nightingale!'

He fought against her will, but it was no use, he lay full length on the floor. Chris knelt down beside him. 'Jack, what can we do?'

Nightingale tried to speak, but no words came. Inside his head, the voice of Lucifuge Rofocale rang. 'Summon me now, Nightingale, speak the words.'

The voice was so loud it sounded as if the demon was in the room. Nightingale looked around, but Lucifuge Rofocale wasn't there.

'Only I can save you,' said the voice in his head. 'Summon me, or face destruction. Summon me, now!'

But there was another voice, fainter, but clear. 'No, Mr Nightingale. You cannot triumph over evil with a greater evil.' Nightingale couldn't understand how or why Mrs Steadman was talking to him. How did she know what was happening?

And now a third voice. Proserpine. 'Free me from the pentagram, Nightingale. Speak the words to dismiss me. You know I have your interests at heart. Your soul is mine, not hers.'

Some choice, thought Nightingale. Either involved summoning a demon from Hell without the protection of a pentagram. That never worked out well. But if he did nothing, his soul would be lost. Could he trust them? Either of them?

He made a supreme effort and groped in his raincoat pocket, fighting against the unspeakable pain in his stomach. He found what he was looking for, and held it up in front of him. It was the doll from *Papa Dimanche.* 'Let me go, or I'll tear its head off!' he shouted. At least he tried to shout, but the words came out as a hoarse whisper.

Brigid looked over at him and laughed. 'Excellent, you return to me my doll. It was useful as bait, to establish the connection between us and bind you to my will, Nightingale. Now its usefulness is ended, give it to me.'

'I swear I'll pull its head off.'

'Do what you wish, you don't really think I would offer you a powerful weapon with which to destroy me? It's just a doll, Nightingale, designed to draw you to me. A mere harmless children's toy. You might as well just throw it away.'

'You know, that's not a bad idea,' said Nightingale. 'I think I will.'

Brigid's triumphant grin turned into a look of horror as she realised what he was about to do. 'No,' she screamed. 'Do not dare...'

Nightingale raised his arm and flung the doll away from him with what little strength he had left. Luck - or something darker - guided his aim, as the doll flew ten feet, knocking over the nearest vial of holy water at the apex of the pentagram, and destroying its integrity.

There was an appalling scream that seemed to come from all directions at once, a horrendous growling and snarling, and a blast of hurricane-force wind, as time seemed to bend in on itself. The room was filled with angry roars and terrified screams.

Nightingale dropped down and pressed his face to the floor until the ghastly noise stopped and the wind died down. He never actually lost consciousness, and was aware of movement in the room, but he probably lay sprawled on his face for ten minutes or more before the strength started to flow back into his body. Eventually he rolled over and sat up. Chris was lying on the floor, several feet away. She was starting to sit up, shaking her head in confusion. The black girl lay motionless inside the ruined pentagram. There was a pile of ash and bone where Elizabeth had stood.

Gabriella was getting to her feet, but there was no sign of the Loa Brigid. All the robed figures had been reduced to a bloody pulp.

Chris rose to her feet, hurried over to the altar and snatched up the curved knife. She moved across to Gabriella, landed a vicious kick to her stomach, and, as the blonde girl started to crumple back to the floor, she grabbed her long hair with her left hand, and held the knife to her throat. 'This is for my sister!' she screamed.

'No!' shouted Nightingale. 'If you do that you'll be as bad as they are. Leave it to the cops, Put that knife down.!

Gabriella twisted her face in contempt. 'Don't plead with this halfbreed on my account, Nightingale. I welcome the chance to walk into Hell and be reunited with my *Rounwytha.*'

'You're not helping, love,' said Nightingale. 'Come on, Chris, put it down, let's call the police.'

'And tell them what? What evidence are you going to produce against these people. Sorry, Nightingale, but I'm the judge and jury here. Sentence has been pronounced.' The knife flashed across the throat and Gabriella's blood spurted across the floor.

Nightingale buried his head in his hands. He didn't look up as Chris left.

CHAPTER 82

A week later and a thousand miles away, Nightingale walked out
of a bar where he'd drunk the best part of four bottles of Corona. He
stopped as he heard an all too familiar voice behind him.

'Got a cigarette, mister?'

He turned slowly. There she was, dressed pretty much as before,
but this time with the collie dog by her side, affectionately rubbing its
head against her knee. He took out his pack of Marlboro and threw one
to her, and it was lit by the time she caught it.

'So you live to fight another day, Nightingale?' she said, with a sly
grin. 'Body, heart and soul intact, it seems.'

'No thanks to the efforts of your little gang.'

'I told you before, Nightingale, some of them pledge allegiance to
me, it doesn't make me responsible for everything they do. Trying the
immortality thing is off limits. Maman Brigitte should have known
that full well. Maybe she was just amusing herself . Nasty sense of
humour some of those Voodoo Loa.'

'Yes, so I realised. Eventually.'

'She played you for a fool, Nightingale, had you charging straight
into the lion's den. It's a very powerful help to all kinds of charms
having a victim who shows up willingly. Though incarnating Vindex
within that woman was never going to happen.'

'So what's likely to happen to her?'

'Brigid? Well, that's not my department, Nightingale, but one thing
Hell isn't short of is punishment systems. It'll be a long time, even by
my standards, before Brigid causes any more trouble.'

'And what about the Nine Angles?'

'Well, that *nexion* is currently leaderless. The woman was
connected to Brigid when you pulled your little conjuring trick, and w
sent her back to Hell, so they won't be troubling anyone any further.
As for Ms Dubois, I like her style, no mercy in that one. You going to
be seeing her again?'

'I doubt it, she was very insistent that I wasn't her type.'

'No, But perhaps she's my type. Maybe I'll offer her a deal some day.'

Nightingale shuddered and changed the subject. 'And what about those old people who should have died by now?'

'Oh, I doubt they'll last much longer, Nightingale. Things have a way of getting back to where they should be. Cancer often recurs, for example. What doesn't kill you, comes back and gets you next time.'

'The Balance,' muttered Nightingale.

'Maybe. You came very close to destruction this time, Nightingale. And you very nearly lost your soul.'

'Close, but no cigar.'

'True enough. Odd, I don't remember reading anything in the papers about the slaughter at Myrtle Plantation.'

'Maybe somebody came and cleared up,' said Nightingale.

'Wonder who that might have been?'

'Friend of mine,' said Nightingale. 'He just loves feeding alligators.' He smiled and lit a cigarette of his own.

'I was wondering why you didn't just speak the words to summon Lucifuge Rofocale,' said Proserpine. 'He'd have taken them down to Hell in a second.'

'Yes, he would have. But there's always the outside chance that he might have taken me as a bonus prize once he'd been summoned. I don't trust him. Him taking me would have left you cheated, and that would never do. And he might not have bothered releasing you, I seem to recall you didn't part on the best of terms in New York. He might still owe you a grudge.'

'Who knows? Certainly not you. But now you've cheated Lucifuge Rofocale again, he won't be pleased with you either.'

'Oh, he wasn't,' said Nightingale. He tried and failed to blow a smoke ring. 'We've already spoken, but unfortunately he disobeyed his own advice, and didn't read the small print. Our little deal was for me to stop them, not necessarily to summon him to stop them.'

'So you still get your reward?'

Nightingale shrugged. 'He's not happy, but a deal's a deal.'

'Oh it is. So, the deal was that he resets time for you. So why aren't you back in your grotty flat in Bayswater, trying to keep your old MG running and failing miserably to summon up the courage to do something exciting with the lovely Jenny?'

Nightingale smiled, but didn't rise to the bait. 'Not happening. Tried that once. Didn't work out too well.'

'So?'

'So, he reset time, but not for me.''

She focused her huge black eyes on his, and he shivered as she seemed to look right into his soul. Finally she tutted and pulled her gaze away.

'You know, Nightingale, if you were any softer, you'd melt. Well, good luck, it may work out. More likely not, things usually come out the way they're written.'

'Then I just hope for the best.'

'Hope is the worst thing of all, Nightingale.'

'Maybe. Anyway, it's good to have you back. I guess you owe me one.'

'Guess again, Nightingale And I wouldn't be so sure that it's good to have me around. I don't always have your best interests at heart. You should remember that.'

She turned and walked away, the dog trotting by her side. Thirty yards away, she turned a corner, and was gone.

CHAPTER 83

The clock on the mantelpiece chimed twelve times to mark the start of the New Year and a new day in Paloma's life.

She was sitting in her favourite armchair in the sitting room of *Casa del ruiseñor* reading a detective novel in Spanish, when she felt the sudden pain in her jaw. She turned her head and opened her mouth to ease it, and it faded away as suddenly as it had come.

'Just cramp,' she said to nobody at all. 'My own fault for sitting here so long in the cold.'

She got up and made herself a cup of hot chocolate, before settling down on the sofa again, and resuming her book.

It was an hour later that Sooty pushed through the bars outside the open kitchen window, padded across to her chair and rubbed against her ankles. She leant down and rubbed his head, and he purred contentedly, before walking over to his food bowl and taking a few mouthfuls. He walked back over to the sofa, and jumped up to lie on Paloma's lap. She scratched his ears, and he started purring all over again.

'Happy New Year, handsome,' she said. 'Let's hope it's another good one for us.'

She gave a sudden shiver, and pulled her cardigan round her more tightly.

'Brrr. Must be time for bed. Felt like someone just walked over my grave. Come on, Sooty, you can keep me warm.'

The little black cat nodded and purred.

THE END

MORE JACK NIGHTINGALE STORIES

If you enjoyed New Orleans Night, you might also enjoy these two Jack Nightingale stories. They are novellas, each about 35,000 words long, which is about half the length of a novel. They are both set back when Nightingale was working as a private detective in London, before he was forced to start a new life in the United States.

THE WHISPER MAN

He's charming and good looking, he makes you laugh and he has a twinkle in his eyes. He's the sort of guy you'd be happy to spend time with. Until the moment when he asks you if you want to know a secret. You say yes, of course, and you lean towards him. That's when he whispers in your ear and everything changes. Within hours you are dead and your soul is gone forever. You've just met The Whisper Man.

When supernatural detective Jack Nightingale hears about a rash of suicides across London, he realises that it's more than a coincidence. Something has come from the bowels of Hell to wreak havoc in the world, and only he can stop it. But to do that he'll have to put his own soul on the line. And to make his life even more complicated, the police have found a book full of names of people who have been marked for death. And Nightingale's name is in it.

The Whisper Man is set between Nightshade and Lastnight, back when Jack Nightingale was in London working with his long-suffering assistant Jenny McLean and his nemesis Superintendent Chalmers was always on his case.

You can buy The Whisper Man for the Kindle here - https://amzn.to/3wrLCVe

WITCH HUNT

Supernatural detective Jack Nightingale has always dealt with unusual - and dangerous - cases. So when a serial killer starts killing victims using Witchfinder methods of execution, Nightingale is asked to help. As the body count mounts, Nightingale realises that the killer is on a mission of revenge for acts committed four hundred years ago. And he and his long-suffering assistant Jenny McLean are both on the killer's hit list.

You can buy Witch Hunt for the Kindle by clicking here -

https://amzn.to/3gvUxhH

Printed in Great Britain
by Amazon